AN IMPERFECT GENTLEMAN
THE NOTORIOUS NIGHTINGALES

WENDY VELLA

This is a work of fiction. Any resemblance to actual persons, living or dead, business establishments, events or locales is entirely coincidental. All rights reserved. Except for use in a review, the reproduction or use of this work in any part is forbidden without the express written permission of the author.

An Imperfect Gentleman is published by Vella Ink

Copyright © 2024 Wendy Vella

Sign up to Wendy's newsletter: wendyvella.com/subscribe

WENDY'S BOOKS

The Notorious Nightingales
The Disgraced Debutante
An Imperfect Gentleman
The Fallen Viscount

The Raven & Sinclair Series
Sensing Danger
Seeing Danger
Touched By Danger
Scent Of Danger
Vision Of Danger
Tempting Danger
Seductive Danger
Guarding Danger
Courting Danger
Defending Danger
Detecting Danger

The Deville Brothers Series
Seduced By A Devil

Rescued By A Devil
Protected By A Devil
Surrender To A Devil
Unmasked By A Devil
The Devil's Deception

The Langley Sisters Series
Lady In Disguise
Lady In Demand
Lady In Distress
The Lady Plays Her Ace
The Lady Seals Her Fate
The Lady's Dangerous Love
The Lady's Forbidden Love

Regency Rakes Series
Duchess By Chance
Rescued By A Viscount
Tempting Miss Allender

The Lords Of Night Street Series
Lord Gallant
Lord Valiant
Lord Valorous
Lord Noble

Stand-Alone Titles
The Reluctant Countess
Christmas Wishes
Mistletoe And The Marquess
Rescued By A Rake

To Blake
Happy fortieth wedding anniversary.
There is no one in the world I would love to have snoring next to me.
Love you lots.

Wendy xx

CHAPTER ONE

"Why is the scent of lemons so strong?" Alexander Nightingale muttered as he walked down the street. Looking around him, he couldn't find the reason. No trees planted nearby. No vendors selling citrus fruits anywhere in his vicinity.

Burrowing deeper in his overcoat, he kept walking; it was that or turn into an icicle.

London in late November was experiencing a cold blast of weather. Wind sliced through Alex's clothing, and he now wished he'd stayed home to toast crumpets with his family. Instead, he'd uttered something about meeting someone vaguely to his uncle when he enquired as to his destination. He then pulled on his outer clothing and left the house.

He wasn't himself today. Not quite true—he was Alexander Nightingale, family member of the Notorious Nightingales. Devil-may-care man with a love of many things, but top of the list was his family, food, and then women.

Lately the last on that list had not held the appeal they normally did. Alex was a shocking flirt and loved every minute of being the Nightingale male women adored. But flirting, chatting, and enjoying all the wonderful little things about women had recently started annoying him.

Take Miss Simpkin, who sold him éclairs from her mother's bakery. Just yesterday her pouty lips had irritated him, when up until then he'd often wondered what kissing her would feel like. Then there was the considerable bosom of the widowed Ms. Hayden, which had not once drawn his eye yesterday when he'd chanced upon her.

"Maybe I'm ailing for something?"

Walking at a pace fast enough to warm him, he took the route down Leaker Lane and crossed to Beaky Road, where he knew there was an excellent tea shop. Should nothing else come of this excursion, there would at least be a warm beverage in his future.

He'd woken to a barrage of words filling his head, which was not unusual, and yet most often happened when he was close to someone who wanted him to pass on their thoughts to a loved one.

Communicating with the dead was no easy feat, and whoever this... Frank? Francis? was. He or she, they were bloody persistent. Alex had not had a spirit like this in some time... if ever if he was honest. He wondered if he or she was as annoyingly insistent before passing.

"Good day to you, sir," a man said with cheerful determination that Alex was in no way feeling. He nodded and managed a smile, then stalked on.

The buildings to his left and right were a mismatch of sizes and widths. Some had windows he could peer in; others just doors that walked right out to the street. A hanging chime in the window told Alex he should investigate further when his mood was not quite so sour, as his little sister Matilda loved those.

"I'm moving," he muttered as the voice in his head

continued with the barrage of words, none of which made any sense but told him he needed to keep walking.

Apparently, his destination was directly in front, but as yet he was unsure where that was going to take him, or why. Alex had been plagued with a sleepless night. He'd risen with the need to get out of the house at the earliest opportunity and breathe some fresh air in the hopes of finding some calm from the noise inside his head. The words had been coupled with several visions of a large house he'd never seen before and a necklace.

Alex was constantly bombarded with thoughts, both dark and light. Thoughts he usually kept hidden from everyone he loved. His family had suffered enough; they did not need to know about the chaos inside his head that he sometimes thought would eventually turn him mad.

So here he was walking on a bitterly cold day with others who were doing the same by necessity or a need for fresh air.

"Mr. Nightingale. What has you out and about on a day like today?"

"Just needing the exercise," Alex lied to the man that lived in his street. Short, old, as many were in his neighborhood, Mr. Alvin wore a brown knitted cap pulled low to his brows and a matching scarf wrapped to his nose that made him look like a ferret. Two dark, intent eyes stared at him.

"If you don't mind me saying, you look in a bit of a miff, sir," Mr. Alvin said.

That was another thing about the residents of Crabbett Close—most of them were more than happy to make their opinions known freely.

"I am quite well, I assure you, Mr. Alvin."

"Well now, it's many a storm I've seen, Mr. Nightingale, but when it's one brewing inside a body, then action is needed."

Mr. Alvin was the Crabbett Close resident who had a

quote or poem for most situations, and because the words were far too close to the truth, Alex simply nodded.

"I'll be on my way then. It's a mite cold out here for these old bones. But you'll remember Lord Byron's words, sir," Mr. Alvin added.

"I will?"

"Be thou the rainbow in the storms of life. The evening beam that smiles the clouds away, and tints tomorrow with prophetic ray," he said before he wandered away with a raised hand.

Alex shook his head. The man was quoting Lord Byron to him. Of course, he also knew the words had meant search for the light in the dark. How had Mr. Alvin known he was feeling dark? Deciding he would never know the answer to that, as the workings of the elderly residents in Crabbett Close were a mystery, he walked on.

"It's lucky I like lemons," he muttered, still looking for the source of the scent. *Why am I being bombarded by the smell of them?*

"Beg your pardon?"

"Sorry, just talking to myself," he said to the lady he was passing. She gave him a look suggesting he wasn't right in the head before hurrying away.

She wasn't wrong; Alex hadn't been right in the head for quite some time, but it was a family thing and not entirely his fault.

The sound of raised voices had him moving to look down the street.

"Bloody women! They've no right to vote!" These words were uttered by a portly gentleman, moustache quivering as he glared at something.

"What appears to be the problem, sir?" Alex asked, taking in the crowds that were forming on both sides of the street.

"Women!" he spat out with a plume of white air. "All this

rubbish about equality. Good Lord, do they not understand men are simply superior!" His bushy brows drew together in a line.

The letter *F* slid into his head again. *Frank?* Alex thought, and then an *H*. He was used to this type of thing happening. For years he fought to shut away the dead people who had chosen him as their connection with the living. Drinking had helped and behaving badly. But when that had not been an option due to his family's disgrace and removal from society, he'd embraced it along with his other siblings who had similar abilities.

"Are we superior?" Alex asked the man in a mocking tone, which he failed to hear.

"They are considered legally incompetent and irresponsible," the man said and then continued to rant and rave about the women marching down the street toward them. "Vote," he scoffed. "The country will be driven to ruin the day that happens."

Had any of the ladies in his family been present, the man would have had his ears blistered for speaking those words.

"Not all of us see women that way, sir," Alex said coolly. He wasn't fiery like his siblings, who would have yelled their response. He was the one who brought humor into a situation. He'd found it could mask many things and deflect when deflection was needed. However, today he had no patience for ignorant fools. "Some men think women are intelligent and articulate, and more than capable of matching us in many ways."

The man barked out a laugh. "Good jest, sir."

Alex was about to explain it was no jest when the sound of a drum had him searching the street again. A large group of placard-carrying women were coming toward them.

"This is ridiculous!"

"What is ridiculous?" a lady asked the man at his side. She

had stopped before them. In her hand was clutched a sheaf of papers. At a guess, Alex thought she was part of the marching party. Squinting to focus on the signs, he saw the words, *equality for women* and *women's suffrage movement.*

"This nonsense about women wanting to vote or have equality!" the man roared at her. "Utter rot!"

"There is no need to yell, sir. She is standing directly before you," Alex said with more force.

"Him and his sort do not see change necessary," the woman said. Her cheeks were red from the wind, but her eyes were shooting fire. "They feel threatened because he fears being faced with what women can really do, and I assure you it will be a great deal better than men. Read this and attend, as you may learn something." She slapped a piece of paper into the man's chest and placed one into Alex's outstretched hand before walking on.

"There will be no change!" the man bellowed to her retreating back.

Alex read the pamphlet.

Women have rights too. Public meeting 5:00 p.m. Thursday, number 4 Saddling Lane. Men & women invited.

There must be change.

Only law-abiding citizens to attend.

"Stuff and nonsense." The man balled his pamphlet and then reached for Alex's. He raised it out of his way.

"This is mine, and unlike the more narrow-minded men in our society, who see women as a threat, I support them." He then tucked it into his pocket.

The man's face flamed red, but before he could speak, the drumbeat got louder, and suddenly the street before him was filled with women.

Studying them, he found Mrs. Creedy and Mavis Johns from Crabbett Close, both carrying placards. He wasn't sure how the elderly Mrs. Creedy was keeping pace with the others, as, to his estimation, she must be close to eighty, but Mavis Johns was holding her arm, so perhaps she was aiding her. Seeing him, they waved. Alex made a show of waving back so the fuming man at his side could see.

The name Harry popped into his head clearly this time as his eyes scanned the first row of marchers. The one closest caught and held his attention. She was looking his way, having witnessed the lady arguing with the idiot at his side. The placard in her hand was raised, but it was the shadow behind her that had his focus.

H, Frank. Lemons and necklace. Words were tumbling one over the other and sent his way from the young deceased woman who was the shadow.

Murder.

CHAPTER TWO

She wore a black bonnet with a large brim almost obscuring her face. Alex caught a glimpse of pale skin and large eyes but was not close enough to see the color, and a mouth forming a hard line. Her cloak was black and fastened at the neck. But it was the person from her past standing behind her that drew his eyes.

Friend. They'd been friends when this woman was living, and she now wanted him to communicate with the lady marching, which presented more than one problem for Alex.

If he was honest, he'd wondered a time or two if someone wouldn't have him committed. However, he'd worked on his delivery a lot since the first time he'd finally, and reluctantly, embraced who he was, as had his siblings.

The voices that slid in and out of his head wanted to be heard, and clearly, they'd selected him, whether he liked it or not. Alexander, one of the disgraced and Notorious Nightingale siblings, was to be their conduit.

"Go home! You are all making fools of yourselves!" the idiot at his side roared. "A woman's place is at her husband's side doing his bidding! And you, sir, are a disgrace to your fellow man!" He glared at Alex.

"Have a care, sir," Alex growled back to the man as he yelled in his face. His breath was as foul as his demeanor. "I do not tolerate anyone speaking to me as you are. Especially as clearly you are not worthy of my respect."

The man's mouth opened and closed like a codfish.

"Now, if this is too offensive to you, then leave, as these women are bothering no one, but you, however, are."

"They are bothering me! How dare you, a man, take their side!"

Before Alex could speak, the woman he'd been studying was suddenly standing before him. Her placard was raised as if she would bring it down on the man's head.

"You, sir, are an idiot!" she snapped, and her accent told him she was American, not British.

"I am a man, and therefore superior!"

"Superior?" the woman scoffed. "I see nothing to suggest that—only that you like to roar and posture and have not an iota of understanding to the plight of others! To me that suggests you are indeed inferior!"

"Nicely put," Alex said, studying her. She was turned slightly, so he could only see one eye, but it was deep blue, almost indigo. Color rode high on the ridges of her cheekbones.

"I will not be spoken to by the likes of you!" the man continued to yell, jowls wobbling, face the color of a ripe strawberry. "Especially as you are not even British but American!" The words came out laced with disgust, as though being born beyond their shores was a crime. "I am an Englishman, and therefore a great deal more important than a Yankee!"

"You, sir, are a fool!" the woman snapped. "Like so many of your kind!"

"Yankee!" the man spat at the woman.

"English imbecile," she replied.

"I'll take that," Alex said as she raised her placard in a threatening motion. "No need to get arrested. That would hardly help your cause." He wrestled if from her grasp. "Plus, he is really not worthy of your time." Alex smiled; she did not respond. "The man's clearly a fool who is intimidated by change."

"Fool is it!" The man spun to face him again.

The woman tried to grab the sign back, but as Alex held it aloft, she couldn't reach it. He placed a hand on her shoulder and nudged her back into the line and followed.

"Calm down," he said, urging her closer to the large lady in a spectacular blue hat to her right, which effectively wedged the irate woman between them.

"How? You have my sign and stopped me from giving that man a piece of my mind!" She shot him a look that should drop him to his knees. Alex was made of sterner stuff. His siblings harassed him constantly.

"Even if you gave him a piece of your mind, it would still not aid the man. He has no wits to add them to. I took the sign from you, as it was about to become a weapon," he added. "And I'm sure you had no wish to end up incarcerated."

"He would have deserved it. His type is who we are fighting against."

"Undoubtedly." Before she could speak, he added, "Now who is Francis, Frank, or Frankie?" He spoke the names as they slid into his head. "And why do they like lemons?"

Her gasp was loud, even with the noise of the drum and the yelling.

"Why did you ask me about Frankie?"

She was small, he thought. *Delicate*, he added in his head.

"Was she a friend of yours? Does your name start with

H?" Alex asked. He did not have time to ease into the details like he usually would. They were marching, and he would soon lose her. He needed answers now. Especially as the woman called Frankie was throwing visions and words into his head.

"Who are you? Why are you speaking to me like this?"

She tried to move away from him, but as the only way was forward, it wasn't easy, as they were marching at quite a clip.

"Who sent you?"

"No one sent me, but your friend is attempting to make contact with you—"

"No." She shook her head furiously. "You lie. Frankie is dead. What do you want from me?"

"I want nothing from you. I am just attempting to give you information, as this Frankie is most persistent." And those words just made him sound like a fool, but before he could clarify, she spoke.

"I did not harm my friend, and never would, but no one listened. Now leave me alone, sir. I will not speak of that time again."

He wasn't sure what any of that meant, which was usually the case. Sometimes Alex felt like he was walking through thick fog with no hope of finding his way out.

"Raise that sign, sir, if you are in our line!" These words were accompanied by a nudge in his spine to keep him moving. Alex raised the sign.

"I am not trying to upset you. I am attempting to communicate with you on behalf of your friend." She tried to move away from him again. "Look, I just want to talk to you, not accuse you of anything. She is most insistent, and I fear will not leave me alone until I say what needs to be said."

Usually, Alex started conversing about loved ones, or someone who had passed. If they were receptive, he continued; if not, he walked away. However, he'd terrified this woman in his haste to speak, and now she wanted to flee.

"She loved you," he said. "Her death—"

"Stop!" the woman cried. "I don't understand why you're speaking to me like this. It is cruel to do so. How do you know Frankie? Who put you up to this?"

Alex looked forward again, searching for the right words. His eyes studied the people lining the street, and it was as he reached the end, he found Gray his brother-in-law still some distance away. But Alex had excellent eyesight.

Damn.

"Frankie is showing me a necklace with an angel on it."

Her gasp told him she knew exactly what necklace he spoke of.

"Get out of that line, you idiot!" another man called to him. "What are you thinking supporting this ridiculous cause?"

"He is not a small-minded bigot like you!" someone yelled back.

"Tell me why you mentioned Frankie's necklace and know so much about her?" The woman's accent was stronger now. "Why are you speaking to me like this so many years after she passed?"

Alex blew out a breath. He was making a mess of this but plowed on. "Look, it's confusing, and you won't believe me, but it's her wish that I discuss some matters with you. I fear she will not leave me alone unless I do."

His brother-in-law was drawing closer now, and with him was that idiot Constable Plummy. The man was supposed to keep the community he lived in safe, but it was fair to say he was hopeless at that. He was also in love with Alex's family's housekeeper, so he spent most of his time there.

"I'm not discussing this further with you. Now leave me

alone." Her voice was shrill. "Someone sent you to speak with me, but I do not understand why or who would do that."

A vision of a scone topped with honey slid into his head. "Are scones with honey one of your favorite things?"

He turned, and her eyes were locked on his. One blue eye, and one green. He'd never seen eyes like that before. They were wide and fringed with black lashes. Her eyebrows had risen too, and her mouth was now open. An interesting face, Alex thought. Even with all her hair tucked up in that ugly bonnet, there was something intriguing about her. Leaning in, he tried to get a closer look at those amazing eyes, but she lowered her head so her bonnet obscured them.

Had he imagined the different colors?

"How do you know I like scones with honey?" She sounded panicked now, and who could blame her. "I did nothing wrong. It was not me who pushed her or had a hand in her death." The words came out high-pitched. "Frankie was dead when I found her."

Alex saw a set of men's hands then, and they were wrapped around a neck. Frankie was showing him her death.

Something hard hit Alex in the stomach as he looked at the devastation in her eyes. It felt like the ground he stood on shifted two feet to the right. He was off-balance and did not care for the feeling one bit.

"I didn't harm my friend, and never would. I don't know who sent you, but I did nothing wrong and—"

"No one sent me," Alex assured her. "I just—"

He saw the two men running toward them from the left, both yelling abuse, but Alex could do nothing to stop them pushing another of the suffragettes. The effect was like dominos, and the women all staggered. Harry, or whoever she was, tumbled into him hard. Alex stumbled but could not keep upright. Closing an arm around her, he listed to the right out of the line and then fell. The weight of the woman landed on top of him, and the breath left his lungs with a loud whoosh.

"A-are you all right?" Alex wheezed out the words.

"Unhand me!"

"I was saving you," he said, now sitting upright with the woman kneeling before him. The brim of her bonnet had bent to cover her eyes. She was attempting to get away from him and raise it all at once.

"Hold still," Alex ordered. She ignored him, so he gripped her wrists to stop her hands from moving against his thighs and perilously close to his groin. "Desist. Let me lift you."

He used his free hand to push up her bonnet and got a good look at her face.

"Your eyes are two completely different colors."

"As they are my eyes, I have known that since birth, sir. Now release my wrists!" she snapped.

"You're ungrateful is what you are. I just stopped you from hitting the road and cushioned your fall," Alex said. He then set her back on her feet. "Perhaps what you should be saying is thank you."

"Thank you?" She had her hands on her hips and was glaring at him.

Alex rose; he was at a distinct disadvantage down here with her sending dark looks his way.

"Thank you for tormenting me with the memory of my dead friend? For speaking of her love for lemons and mine for scones? I have no idea what smokey game it is you are playing, sir, but you will not play it with me!"

Alex could see the tears in her eyes and was sorry he'd put them there, but this Frankie was a determined sort and continuing to fill his head.

"Leave me alone. I have said all I will about that time, and as no one believed me, I do not know what your purpose in discussing it is!"

Her words finished on a shriek that had him wincing. Alex watched as she picked up the placard he'd dropped. She then stomped off up the road before he could stop her.

"Well done for standing up for women, sir," a lady said.

"Thank you." Alex wasn't sure what to do now. He could follow her, but then she'd just continue to yell at him. Frankie was still filling his head with words and visions, which suggested he would indeed have to speak to that woman again if he wanted peace in his life.

Murder. Justice for two.

"Well hell," Alex muttered as he watched her walk away from him.

CHAPTER THREE

Harriet Shaw shot a look over her shoulder, but the man had not followed. He was still standing where she'd left him, watching her. Strangely, she'd not thought him mad, but then she also knew that many seemed sane but in fact were not. But then the words he'd spoken had all been true. Frankie loved the scent of lemons; she had owned a necklace with an angel on it. How had he known about her friend? How had he known she loved scones topped with honey and cream?

"Get back into the line, Harriet!"

She ran, catching up to the group.

"What was that about?" Milly, another of the suffragettes, asked her. "One minute you were there marching with that man, and then you both disappeared."

"He was, ah, he was interested in our cause, and we both tripped," she lied.

No way was Harriet going to mention what she'd talked with that man about. Why now, after five years, was someone discussing Frankie?

"He was a right handsome one," Milly said, nudging her as they walked.

He had been handsome. Tall, well-dressed, and well-spoken. She'd seen men like him before. Too good-looking. They thought that every woman that came near them would start twittering and acting the fool. Harriet was not one of those.

How had he known so much?

The noise from those watching grew louder as they reached a large group of spectators. Some cheered their support; others, mainly men, raised their fists.

"They see us as a threat," Milly said. "We are the future!" She yelled the words, raising her placard.

"Go home to your family where you should be!"

Miss Alvin, who carried a sign, shook it at the man. "You'd be nothing without us women!" she cried in a remarkably strong voice that carried a great distance, considering she looked about ninety years old and walked with stooped shoulders.

They marched on down the street, and the next, and then drew to a halt on a narrow strip of grass between two buildings when the crowds had thinned.

The temperature had dropped significantly, and Harriet wished she'd chosen to wear a scarf. But as she'd been in a hurry to leave the house before any of her family came home, she'd forgotten.

"I saw you fall on that man, Harriet, and I said to Amelia, who was marching at my side, that if I'd taken a tumble onto someone like that, I would have stayed there."

The women around her ranged from her age—Harriet and Milly were the youngest—to a great deal older. Mrs. Alden, who had just spoken, fell in the middle grouping. Tall, thin, with cheekbones that could slice bread, the woman had a voice like an angel and often sang when they marched.

"Yes, well, it was simply an accident, and I'm sure he'll be bruised tomorrow after me landing on top of him." Harriet was not very humorous like some. She tried and usually failed; however, that got her a laugh that she was quite proud of.

"Right then. We'll all be at the meeting. Bring as many folks as you can. Our job is only just starting!" Mrs. Lucas, the leader of their suffragette group, called from somewhere up ahead. "Actions over subjugation!" She had a voice that carried a great distance. "You're dismissed!" she added.

The women all scurried off in different directions, eager to get out of the cold.

"Harriet, dear, we have some knitting for you. Would you like to call by for a cup of tea and collect the items?"

"I'll come by soon, Miss Alvin."

"Lovely. I'll have some treacle cake ready." Harriet loved Miss Alvin's treacle cake. It was sweet, and the syrup ran down the sides. She usually ate two pieces when she visited.

"Harriet, dear. Will you walk me home?"

"I'm not marrying your son, Mrs. Hand." Harriet ignored Milly's snort.

"He's quite taken with you, dear, and asked if you would call this evening."

Mrs. Hand lived with her son who was nearing fifty. She'd been trying to marry him off for years, and her focus was Harriet at the moment. She hoped soon that moved to some other poor woman. At first she'd been flattered, but the persistence had made her blunt. If she gave this woman one flicker of interest, she'd be walking down the aisle to wed her son.

"Norman is a lovely man, but I have no wish to marry him or any man, Mrs. Hand. Now I must leave, or I shall be late to meet my sister at the lending library. Good day."

Milly fell in beside her as she walked away quickly.

"When you arrived, she stopped asking me to visit. The way I see it, we need to find someone else for Norman."

She had met Milly at her first rally six months ago. Unlike Harriet, she came from a working-class family, with four brothers and two sisters—all who had no problem with their sibling marching through London streets waving placards. Unlike Harriet's family, who would lock her in her room and hurl the key into the Thames if they ever realized what she got up to when she left the house.

"I agree, but who?" Harriet asked.

"I was thinking about that. What about Miss Tilly?"

Harriet stopped at Milly's words and stared at her. "That's a brilliant idea, and I wonder why Mrs. Hand has not thought of her before."

"Likely because Miss Tilly is shy and keeps to the rear of our gatherings. We'll plant the seeds at the meeting tomorrow night. I'll see you there."

"See you there," Harriet said.

After Milly left her, Harriet made her way toward the lending library. It hadn't been a lie that she wanted to go there; the lie was that her sister Catherine would not be meeting her. Catherine would be out with their mother doing something young ladies of society should do.

"But not me," Harriet muttered. Her family gave up on her long ago.

Dashing down the street leading to the building that housed the library, Harriet came to a halt as she saw the two men coming toward her. A shiver of unease traveled through her as she looked at their faces. One was Tapper from the Gail Lane orphanage where she visited weekly; the other was a face from her past. A past she'd never wanted to relive, and yet twice today she was doing just that.

Harriet wasn't sure why she didn't want them to see her, but she felt the urge to seek cover. Tapper and Mr. Sydney could be acquaintances, and there was no reason at all why they shouldn't be. Why then did something about seeing them together feel off? Looking for a place to hide, she saw a shop. Opening the door, Harriet hurried inside.

"It's going to be a cold winter, you mark my words," a male voice called to her from beyond a tall row of shelves.

"It is," Harriet called back.

"You have a look around, and I'm here to assist should you need it!"

"Thank you." She moved to the window where a display of books and... looking around her, she saw a wand and a black top hat. Beside it was a cape. Harriet had hidden in a magic shop.

"That small red book to the right of the window display is an excellent choice if you are just starting your magic journey," the voice called.

"Thank you. It does look an excellent resource." Harriet looked out the window. She could see Tapper and Mr. Sydney. Seeing them together was no business of hers. She was simply unsettled after the conversation she'd had with that man today. That was all this was, she told herself.

Mr. Sydney had worked at the Templar Academy for girls that both Harriet and Frankie attended. He'd helped bring her friend's body out of the water the night she'd drowned. The night Harriet had been accused of involvement in her best friend's death.

The men started moving, and it was then she noticed the two young boys they had with them. Billy and Tommy from the orphanage. What were they doing with Tapper and Mr. Sydney? The children rarely, if ever, left the orphanage, and then only as a group, or so she believed.

Don't you think it's odd that those children are always calling at the kitchen door at all hours, and they leave with sacks filled with things, Harriet? The conversation she'd had with Frankie the day before she died replayed in her head. Why was she thinking about that now?

"It's about learning one thing and perfecting it before moving on to the next. Folks today, they are always in a hurry. You mark my words, if you buy that book, you'll be creating magic in no time," the voice said from behind her.

"It is my fondest wish to do so," Harriet lied.

She noted the sack Tapper carried and wondered what was inside. As if sensing her, he turned. Harriet stepped back quickly. Pressing herself to the wall, she counted slowly to ten and then looked again. He was gone.

Had Tapper seen her?

"Stop this, Harriet, you're being nonsensical," she whispered. Picking up the book, she hurried to the counter.

"You won't be disappointed," the man standing behind it said.

He was the tallest person Harriet had ever seen. She had to tilt her head to meet his eyes. He wore a top hat that made him taller, and around it, several brightly colored ribbons.

"I am Mr. Brown."

Harriet had thought a man who looked as this one did, with his bright red waistcoat and matching necktie, would be called something far more flamboyant.

"You won't regret that choice either, especially if you have already started hearing voices."

Looking at the book she'd picked up in haste simply because she thought she owed the man after hiding out in his shop, she noted it was titled *The Voices Within.*

Harriet felt another shiver traverse her spine. She was a practical type who dealt in reality; this book was far from that, and yet she wanted to read it.

Perhaps I am ailing for something. That would be a reason for all this odd behavior she was exhibiting.

"It's my hope that I begin to understand them," she said

when he looked at her, clearly waiting for her to say something.

"Most don't believe," Mr. Brown said, taking her money. "But we're fools if we do not see what is possible inside us. That some who walk among us can see and hear a great deal more than others."

"Yes, well, thank you for the book. I shall enjoy reading it," Harriet said, clutching it to her chest for no other reason than she felt a need to.

Stepping outside, she looked up and down the street but saw no sign of the men she'd been hiding from. Hurrying back the way she'd come, Harriet decided to forgo the lending library and hail a hackney. Turning the corner, she ran into someone.

"Apologies." Harriet stepped back.

"Quite all right," the man said, turning. The smile fell from his face as he looked at her. "You!" he said loudly.

Harriet backed away from Mr. Sydney. The last time she'd seen this man he'd been carrying the body of her dead friend and blaming Harriet for her death.

She hurried back down the street she'd just walked, away from him. Reaching another main road, she searched desperately for a hackney and saw one rolling toward her. Turning, she looked over her shoulder and saw Mr. Sydney watching her.

Raising her hand, the hackney stopped. After giving her address, Harriet climbed inside but did not glance out the window again.

"Breathe, Harriet." She inhaled and exhaled several times.

Why was she worried? Mr. Sydney had recognized her but what did that matter? Tapper was not with him, and even if he was, why would they be concerned about seeing her? *Why was she concerned about seeing them together?*

She lowered the book to her lap and stared at it.

Mr. Brown had said, "Most don't believe." Her thoughts went to the man who had marched with her today. The man who knew she liked scones with honey and Frankie liked lemons.

"Surely not?" Looking at the book again, she ran her hand over the cover.

Had Frankie's spirit been talking to her through that man? It was almost too unbelievable, and yet here she was looking at a book about the voices within, and he'd known all those things about both her and Frankie.

She'd woken up today believing she knew for the most part how her day would unfold, and yet it hadn't gone at all to plan, and now she wasn't sure what to think.

"I need to lie down," Harriet muttered. *Lock the door to my room and never leave again.*

She doubted lying down was in her future, however, as she had reading to do.

CHAPTER FOUR

His brother-in-law had not yet questioned Alex why he was marching with the suffragettes because he'd seen some boys causing trouble, and as he was a Scotland Yard detective, he'd felt compelled to investigate.

After Gray had finished lecturing them, which had terrified the two boys who were about to steal from the woman selling fruit buns, Alex had purchased four and handed the boys two.

"That did not help, Alex," Gray said as they walked on.

"Of course it did. It showed them that if you pay for food, then you receive it without the weight of the law coming down hard on you."

Gray sighed and took the bun Alex held out to him.

"I say, aren't you the idiot who marched with those women?"

Alex had received many comments on his marching thus far. Some women congratulated him on his forward thinking; the men, like this one, glared at or insulted him.

"I am not an idiot but a man who happens to believe

women should not be treated as beneath men," he said loudly.

"Good day," Gray said, grabbing Alex's arm and walking. "What the hell are you about?" his brother-in-law then asked. "And why are you scowling? You are the brother who smiles not scowls."

Gray was married to Ellen, the oldest of the Nightingale sisters. Once a society darling, like the rest of the siblings, she'd been ruined in their eyes and no longer worthy of their company.

"What do you mean, 'what am I about'?" Alex hedged. He then took a large bite of bun so he couldn't speak again.

What was the name of the woman he'd marched with? Frankie had put the initial *H* in his head, and the name Harry. But he could have that wrong and perhaps it was Henrietta or Heather? When her soft weight had fallen on him, Alex had the urge to hold her there in his arms, even as she'd glared at him.

He didn't react like that to women. He enjoyed their company but never felt a connection of souls with any. Or at least that's what his aunt Ivy called it.

"You'll know when it's right, Alex, as you will react differently when the woman who is meant for you is close."

He'd muttered something about the fact he could hardly wait, when inside he thought it utter rot. For all Alex was the happy, easygoing Nightingale, he kept those he didn't know at a distance. He enjoyed the company of women and loved to flirt, but any physical connection was purely a mutual slaking of lust.

He was not an ever after type like Ellen and Gray or his aunt and uncle. Besides, he doubted any woman would understand what went on inside his head.

"Why were you protesting with those women, Alex?"

"It was an accident actually."

"How does one march with women in a suffrage rally by accident?"

The scent of lemons had eased, but it was still there lurking inside his nostrils. Alex thought that until he got this woman—Hazel? Or perhaps Hortense? No, that didn't suit her—to understand she had things he needed to tell her, he was going to be plagued by the spirit of Frankie.

Who had murdered her? Hester? had said she didn't do it; that she was not to blame. Had she been accused of playing a hand in her friend's death? His head hurt trying to sort it all out.

"Talk to me, Alex. I can tell something is troubling you. In fact, it has been for some time."

Gray was tall, always immaculately dressed, and his blood was bluer than the Nightingales'. The middle son of an earl, he'd decided when his aunt and uncle died and left him all their money that society was no longer for him. Unlike the Nightingales, who had no choice in the hand they were dealt, Gray had walked his own path. It had led him directly to Scotland Yard.

"I could not believe my eyes, sir. You protesting with those women." Constable Plummy appeared.

"I thought you were heading off to do your duty?" Alex asked the man.

Dressed in his customary uniform of blue tailcoat with his armlets, white gloves, and top hat, he was the silliest man Alex knew, and he'd known a great deal in his lifetime.

"I am doing my duty by walking this street and keeping people safe. I could not believe my eyes when I saw you marching, Mr. Nightingale."

"Is that not allowed then?" Alex demanded. "A man marching in support of women?"

"No indeed," Plummy spluttered. "It is not done at all."

"And yet if I believe the women protesting may have a

point, then surely it is something I must back up with action so there is change in the future," Alex said.

In fact, until that moment, he'd not thought much about the plight of women. He knew what being a man allowed him to do and what his sisters couldn't, but he'd taken no steps to change that. Which simply said he was as bigoted as that fool with the moustache.

"Well... I... well," Plummy said, clearly not sure how to answer that.

The American woman had intrigued him; there was no getting around that fact. Those eyes were stunning. He'd hoped speaking with her would rid him of Frankie, but he now had more questions than answers, which meant he had to see her again.

"I think you should go and make sure those women have disbanded and are not being insulted, Plummy," Gray said. "You may not share their beliefs, but your position should be unbiased, and everyone is under your protection."

Plummy's shoulders, already ramrod straight, drew back further. "At once, Detective Fletcher."

Gray had that authoritative way about him that had people running to do his bidding. Well, if you weren't a Nightingale, they did. They were a fickle, unruly bunch if Alex was honest, with a distinct lack of respect for authority, which annoyed his brother-in-law.

"I will see to it at once!" Plummy saluted and then hurried away.

"His heart is always in the right place," Alex added.

"At least some part of him is," Gray muttered. "Now tell the truth of why you were marching with a women's suffrage group, Alex, and why you have seemed off lately."

"I felt it was the right thing to do," Alex said, not meeting his brother-in-law's eyes or answering his other question.

"No, you didn't, and you've already told me it was an accident, and clearly, due to your sour demeanor, you did not enjoy it."

"Just because I'm a man does not mean I do not support—"

"You cannot bamboozle me with righteous indignation to throw me off the scent, Alex. I am onto you and your family now."

Alex sighed.

"I'm your friend, and I'm now family. Tell me what is bothering you if you won't discuss why you were marching."

"There really is nothing wrong but a dose of lethargy that happens to us all at some time or other."

"It doesn't happen to me," Gray said.

"But you are not normal."

"Hello, why is Alex looking annoyed? It's usually Leo who wears that expression." Ellen, his sister, had arrived.

Like all his siblings, Alex loved her deeply, and she could annoy him just by walking into the room. When society turned from them, they had tightened their circle. Hardened and found a way to survive. It wasn't until Ellen met the man at her side, they let a stranger into their ranks. Now she'd started to change again. She smiled and laughed more. A carefree laugh that he hadn't even realized she'd lost until he'd heard it.

"Hello, my love." Gray kissed her on the cheek. He then placed a hand on Ellen's back in that way people in love did. Always touching and looking at each other in nauseating ways. "Alex is trying hard not to tell me something."

"I protest," Alex said. "It is not hard at all."

"What are you trying hard not to tell Gray, brother?" Ellen demanded.

Blond, pretty, some said, and dressed today for the cold in a thick deep ruby jacket with a matching bonnet. She looked happy, and for that, they owed a debt of gratitude to Detective Fletcher.

"Nothing," Alex said, looking at the toes of his boots.

"Is it to do with your odd moods?" Ellen asked.

"I did ask him about that, but as yet, he has not answered," Gray added.

What had that *H* stood for? She really didn't look like a Hypatia? The scent of lemons grew stronger again. Leaning closer, he sniffed his sister.

"Why are you sniffing me?"

"Are you wearing some kind of lemon scent?"

"No."

It was definitely Frankie again then.

"I found him marching with a women's suffrage group, carrying a sign," Gray added. "He told me it was an accident. I'm trying to get to the bottom of it."

"And the problem with him marching is what?"

Alex felt his dark mood lighten, and he smirked as his sister turned to glare at her husband.

"I have no problems at all, if his motives are pure." This time it was Gray who smirked as his sister spun back to face him.

"Tell me there is not a young lady marching who you thought pretty enough to walk beside her and pretend to champion the cause?" Ellen's brows now met in the middle.

"I am wounded, sister." Alex placed a hand on his chest and looked pathetic. "As if I would do such a thing."

Gray snorted. "He was angry and annoyed when he reached me. And as you say, that is not Alex."

"I wonder if we can move out of this frigid wind and find a cup of tea and perhaps a slice of cake. Teeter's Tea Shop is near, and I am quite frozen through from my marching, but as the cause was dear to my heart, I had to participate. The women were most complimentary, and as you can imagine, being the only man, I was heckled mercilessly by those watching," Alex said.

"Who heckled you?" Ellen looked outraged at the bystanders. "How dare anyone heckle my brother when he is marching for such a wonderful reason. I would have joined you had I arrived in time."

"Nightingales." Gray sighed. "You're all bloody exhausting. One minute arguing and then defending each other. And for your information, my sweet, I don't believe him. Your brother is up to something."

Ellen turned back to look at him. Eyes narrowed, she studied Alex. "Did a voice tell you to do what you did, brother?"

Alex had never been able to lie worth a damn, especially not to someone who experienced visions inside her own head.

Ellen smiled, then patted his cheek with a gloved hand. "Come along then, and we shall have the whole story, but for whatever reason, I am proud of you for marching."

He sent Gray another smirk and then followed his sister as she stalked off down the street, leaving them in her wake. Sticking his hands in his pockets, he felt the pamphlet. Alex knew where he'd find the woman with the *H* initial now. *Hannah?*

5:00 p.m. Thursday evening, number 4 Saddling Lane. Men & women invited.

Only law-abiding citizens to attend.

As he was definitely, mostly, a law-abiding citizen he could attend. Alex wondered why he was so intent about this. After all, the dead had been visiting him for years, and he'd not gone out of his way to make contact with the living they wished to communicate with.

There was something that didn't feel right about the entire situation, and then there was the woman with the lovely eyes and... he couldn't actually work out why she intrigued him, but she did.

"I fear I will never thaw out." Alex raised the collar on his overcoat.

"Be grateful you are not begging on a street corner. Then you'd have reason to moan," his sister said.

"I thought I was the victim here?"

"Clearly she's moved on," Gray said, opening the door to the small tea shop that had a large sign in the window stating that no one baked finer cakes than Teeter's Tea Shop, which he could attest to.

"Oh, Mr. Nightingale, how lovely to see you!"

"Mrs. Heckle." Alex bowed at the woman approaching him. He hoped she was leaving, as the shop was full, and her departure would mean a table was free. "I hope your son has secured the position."

The wrinkled face creased as she smiled. "He's started this very day, and right happy he is thanks to you."

Alex waved his hand about. "It was a small matter to help him."

She smiled and patted his hand. "It meant a great deal to my Liam, Mr. Nightingale, and I'll forever be grateful."

"What was that about?" Ellen demanded after Mrs. Heckle had left.

"Nothing. Her son was having trouble with something. I had a chat with him."

"There is more to this." Ellen stepped in front of him when he tried to move. "Just as there is more to your mood."

"Let your brother have his secrets, love. You don't need to know everything," Gray said.

"I thought you asked him for the reason he was marching?" Ellen snapped at her husband.

"Oh, don't worry, I'll have that out of him by day's end.

But the business with that woman's son is not something he needs to share, Ellen."

His sister huffed, sounding like a disgruntled puppy. Before she could continue questioning him, a voice called to them.

"Hello, Nightingale and Fletchers!"

Alex found Gray's cousin Ramsey waving at them. He sat alone with what seemed to be an excessive amount of food for a single person. Relieved that *A*, food was in his imminent future, and *B*, it would throw his sister off the scent, he hurried to the table.

"Move it, Ellen. Ramsey has food."

"Are you expecting company, cousin?" Gray asked as he pulled out a chair for Ellen.

"No. I am hungry," Ramsey said. "Come, we shall eat all this, then order more."

Alex did not need a second invitation.

"What has you all out here in the cold," Ramsey asked as Alex took his first bite of a currant scone slathered in jam.

"Alex was marching with the suffrage movement," Gray said.

"Which I am incredibly proud of," Ellen added loyally.

Nightingales might argue and debate fiercely with each other. They might call the other on their untruths, but no one else was allowed to do that.

"I say, Alex. Good on you," Ramsey said. "I've rarely thought about the plight of women, as I'm normally too preoccupied with myself, but it is a worthy cause."

Alex snorted. He would go to the next suffrage meeting if the infuriating, lemon-loving Frankie didn't let up and continued to hound him, but right now he would warm up with food, tea, and good company. Family, Alex thought. He would not have survived without them.

CHAPTER FIVE

"Actions over subjugation!" someone chanted.

Harriet was standing in the small room in Mrs. Haven's home with the members of their branch of the women's suffrage movement four days after the march. They did not usually meet as frequently as they had of late, but as the rally, which they had placed flyers all around London advertising, was tomorrow night, it was important they were ready to gain support for their cause.

"We must hand out as many pamphlets as we can," one of the women who stood with Harriet said. "Get as many people to attend as possible."

She felt a stab of guilt that she could house the meeting in her family's home and still all these women would not fill even a single room, such was the size of the Shaw town house.

"Men and women. We need more people if we really wish for change," another said.

She didn't feel precisely comfortable among them but understood them, as their cause matched her own, and they accepted her. Harriet straddled two worlds and felt at ease in neither.

She kept her family life separate from the other activities she got up to. No one knew any personal details about her, even Milly, who she was closest to.

The marching was a concern, and yet she doubted her family would see her, as they'd not expect her to be there.

Covering her mouth as she yawned, Harriet thought it would be home to bed early for her tonight. She'd stayed up the last two nights reading *The Voices Within*; it had been surprisingly well written and informative. She wasn't sure why she needed to, but her thoughts kept circling back to the man who had marched with her. The one who spoke about Frankie. He hadn't been far from her thoughts since the day she'd fallen on him right there in the street.

"It was pleasing to see a man walking among us beside our Miss Short," Mrs. Shonda Lucas said, using the fake name Harriet had chosen when she'd joined the suffragettes. She'd had no wish for them to connect her to the wealthy Shaw family. "I have hopes for many more!" Mrs. Lucas continued. Big of personality and stature, the woman was one of the national leaders for the women's suffrage movement.

The man had shocked and angered her over what he'd known about both her and Frankie, but given time and reading *The Voices Within*, she now wondered if her late friend was speaking through him from the grave.

"Make your husbands join us!" Mrs. Catherine roared, jarring Harriet from her thoughts.

"My Charlie says if I want change, then I need to see to it myself," Mrs. Craddle said. "Said he would rather have a boil lanced than be seen marching."

There was a chorus of agreement from the other married women at that.

"Change is afoot. We must seize the day!" Mrs. Lucas said with a rallying cry. She always wore dark gray, with a short half cape around her shoulders, and a wide black bonnet.

"She's got the voice for it," Milly said from beside Harriet.

"It does carry a great distance," Harriet agreed. She didn't have the heart to tell the other women that she was sure the man had simply been marching to speak with her about Frankie.

"You may all leave now, ladies, and I will see you tomorrow night at our rally. Harriet, if you will speak on the number of supporters we have through England, as I know you are corresponding with other leaders."

She nodded, feeling her heart sink to her toes. Harriet loathed public speaking.

"Our cause has only just begun," Mrs. Lucas said. "Stand strong in the face of those that would deter us from our goals."

"Have you enjoyed the meeting, Miss Haven?" Harriet said as they reached Mrs. Haven's daughter, who had made the tea tonight. Pretty with golden hair and dimples, Harriet was sure she caught the eye of many young men.

"I have indeed. It was most informative."

Harriet saw the necklace then. It sat above the neckline of her dress. A gold heart with an angel on it; there were two rubies for eyes. Everything inside her stilled as she studied it.

"Miss?" the girl prompted her. "Are you all right?"

"S-sorry," she managed to stammer. "Th-that necklace, where did you get it?"

Pretty color flushed the girl's cheeks. "Albert got it for me. We're engaged, you see, and he had it made specially, as he calls me his angel."

Surely it was not Frankie's? "I, ah, had a friend who wore similar," Harriet said quickly as the girl lifted it to show her. "She loved it a great deal but is no longer with us."

Miss Haven's smile softened. "I'm sorry about that."

"I—ah, do you know where your fiancé got it?"

"She doesn't," a man's voice said from behind her. "It was a surprise."

She turned to see who had spoken, and saw the young man standing there. His eyes widened briefly, almost as if he recognized her.

"Do I know you?" Harriet asked.

"We've never met," he said quickly.

"Will you tell me where you got this necklace made?" Harriet demanded.

His eyes narrowed at her sharp tone. "Why?"

"I-ah, I want to get one made for my mother. She would love it."

"I can't remember the name. You got a cup of tea for me, love?" he said, looking over Harriet's shoulder at Miss Haven.

"Of course," she replied.

Harriet mentally shook herself, she was staring at the man because he seemed familiar to her, and that was clearly making him uncomfortable. "Congratulations on your engagement," she said in a voice that sounded stilted.

Why would that have been Frankie's necklace? Surely there could be two exactly the same?

"Good evening," Miss Haven's fiancé said.

"Good evening." Harriet managed to get her legs moving and walked from the house behind the other women.

"It's bloody freezing out here, Harriet. Me ma will have a nice hot meal ready if you'd like to join us?" Milly said as they followed the other women down the street, oblivious to the thoughts swirling around in Harriet's head.

"Thank you, but no. My family will also be awaiting me," Harriet lied. She then looked over her shoulder and saw that Miss Haven's fiancé was watching her. A chill chased through her.

Did she know that man? There had been something about him that niggled at her memory.

"Next time then. Now you get on home. It's freezing out here, Harriet. I will see you at the meeting," Milly said. She raised a hand, then headed off down the road with the other women.

"I'll drop by soon, Miss Alvin," Harriet called to the elderly lady leaving. "I've been a bit busy."

"The knitting will be ready when you arrive, Harriet. Don't fuss!" Miss Alvin called as she walked away with her friend Mavis Johns.

Waiting a few minutes, Harriet then followed. It wasn't that she didn't want to go to Milly's house. It sounded wonderful that she would be walking in the door to the scents of a home-cooked meal with her family. The problem was she loathed lying, and as she was living just that, she avoided close connections with people so they didn't ask her personal questions.

Frankie had been an outcast like Harriet. Was that the necklace that had gone missing the night before her dear friend died, and if it was, how did it end up around Miss Haven's neck? And why was Miss Haven's fiancé familiar to her? She always remembered eventually, as her brain rarely discarded anything.

Walking down the long, narrow street, Harriet turned right when she reached the end.

"Think, Harriet." Then the memory hit her. He'd been a gardener at the Templar Academy for Young Ladies both she and Frankie attended. She was sure of it. He was older now, but she never forgot a face. *Had he stolen the necklace?*

Why was all this happening now when her friend had been dead for years?

First that man had talked to her about Frankie and said things no one but she knew, and then there was seeing

Tapper and Mr. Sydney together, and now this. What did it all mean?

Pressing her temples, she tried to find clarity. This was done with; she did not want to go back to that dark time in her past when her friend died.

A tingle of awareness had her looking up and then down the street. Something felt off, as if she was being watched. *Was Miss Haven's fiancé following her?*

"And now you're imagining things." Which annoyed her. Harriet was solid and grounded in reality. She left imaginings and unrealistic expectations to others.

Raising her hand as a hackney approached, she gave the driver the address, then climbed inside.

Pushing the myriad of confusing thoughts aside, she focused on what needed to be done now. Getting inside her house without anyone seeing her. Later, she would think about Frankie and the necklace.

Her family was entertaining tonight, so she would have to enter the house from the servant's entrance. Out the windows, lamplight showed her people walking the streets, and as the carriage rolled on, their dress changed from working folk to those wearing expensive clothing, and the houses grew larger. When the hackney stopped down the street, Harriet got out and paid the driver.

"Good night, miss."

"Good night," Harriet said. She then struck out along the street to her family's home. A place she had learned to loathe because only one person inside it believed in her; the others thought she'd played a hand in her friend's death, and she would never forgive them for that.

CHAPTER SIX

The Shaws had arrived in London six years ago and stayed. Her father's business had kept him here and his wife, who loved London society with all its nuances, intrigue, and gossip. Three years ago, they had moved to this street, which her mother thought was in a better area.

Harriet could recount all the names of those who lived in the homes she passed, as her mother spoke of them constantly. Reaching the end of a row of five with impressive three-story facades and fencing, she found the Shaw residence. It fronted the street with the others, but a private lane at the end showed whoever was looking that the Shaw house was larger than most and had two entrances. At the rear was a building that housed horses and servants. Knowing that carriages would be arriving soon for her mother's "little gathering," she walked down the cobbled mews to the stables and would enter through the rear; then no one would see her.

"Evening, Miss Harry."

"Hello, Percy," she said to the man standing outside the

large double doors that led to the horses and other things needed to transport the Shaw family hither and yon.

Short, fit, with boundless energy, he was one of her father's staff, and she was never sure of his title. Footman come driver, she thought. From the day she returned home from the Templar Academy, he had often been her companion whenever she left the house. Correction, when he saw her leave the house. Harriet had become excellent at subterfuge.

She liked Percy very much, even if he never hesitated to voice his disapproval over her actions, which he did often.

"You sneaked out to one of those meetings, didn't you?" He glared at her.

"Not sneaking precisely. I had a meeting, yes, and it ran late. There was no need for you to come, as I was quite safe, I assure you. I am now attempting to slip inside and up to my room before the guests arrive."

"They'll find out what you're up to one day, Miss Harry, you mark my words. You can only have so many headaches and weak chests before they grow suspicious." His busy gray brows drew together. "You should be attending that soiree."

"Do you dislike me that much you would wish that for me, Percy?"

He slapped his tattered cap against his thigh as he studied her.

"'Tain't right is all I'm saying. You're a lovely young lady. You should be doing what the others are, not skulking in and out of the house so no one sees you've been lying to them for years."

"Three years," she added.

"It's a touch more than that, but three here in this house."

"And it's not lying precisely, more stretching the truth. Besides, I often ask my parents' permission to leave the house."

"But you don't go to where you tell them you are. A lie is a lie, and I'm calling it straight."

She sighed because he was right; she did lie to her family constantly, but it was that or go mad.

"How is Maryanne?"

His face creased in a wide smile, and the diversion worked.

"She's well, and my first grandchild due any day now."

"Excellent. I should have another payment for you shortly."

"It's a right difference you've made for us all, Miss Harry. The staff are tucking money aside for retirement because of canny investments."

"Now, Percy, I will tell you again that there is no need to worry about me. I am quite happy with my life and take no risks." Harriet crossed her fingers behind her back at yet another lie. "And I enjoy helping you all with your finances. Now I must go in."

She had a good head for numbers, and investing was something of a hobby for her. She read the newspapers whenever she could and had also talked with Mrs. Leander, who was one of the suffragettes. Widowed young, she had decided her lot in life was not to live off her relatives but achieve financial security for herself and her children. She'd taught Harriet and some of the other women much about investing.

"No more going out at night without me," Percy cautioned.

"Of course." Harriet raised a hand as she walked away. They both knew she was lying.

Opening the gate that led to the small gardens, she entered. Hurrying through, she took the path to the servant's door and inside. Scents and noise bombarded her.

"Good evening, Miss Harriet."

"Good evening, Cuthbert," she said to the family butler who was standing in the kitchens supervising, which he often was. He looked like a butler should, especially an English one. His hair had silver wings he swept back. His bearing regal. Most importantly, he had a voice that carried a great distance without actually yelling. Her mother had interviewed nearly twenty men before Cuthbert to ensure just the right person who suited her exacting standards was hired.

"Will you be joining the family this evening, Miss Harriet? They are to entertain Lord and Lady Richard and Mr. and Mrs. Shubert."

Like the rest of the Shaw staff, he was not surprised to see her in the kitchens, as she always left and returned this way, so her family did not realize she wasn't locked in her room.

"I will not." This was a conversation they had often. "If it is not too much of an imposition, I would like a tray in my room." The scents of roasted meats were mingled with the spice of the fruit that would fill tiny pies, which were her father's favorite. Harriet's tummy rumbled.

He nodded his regal head and silently managed to portray his disapproval, and Mrs. Dickens, the Shaw cook, tsked.

The staff were all in on her deception. Harriet had soon learned that they knew everything that went on in the household; therefore, she had to find a way to ensure their silence. She'd done that by learning all she could about them and their families and helping them invest their money so they could retire comfortably. It had been working well for three years. She had great hope it would continue to do so.

There had been a few moments when she'd thought her family would catch on to what she was really up to, but as they didn't care, it had proved remarkably easy. They only saw what they wanted to when it came to the disgraced eldest Shaw daughter.

"Good evening," Harriet said. She then hurried up the back steps to her room.

The Shaw town house was decorated by one Mr. Flatterblatt, who was a renowned interior designer. He had been recommended to her mother by someone in society, who no doubt was titled. To Harriet's eye, it was a mismatch of styles, but Heloise Shaw called it flamboyant elegance with touches of Egyptian influences.

Climbing the rear stairs, Harriet reached the third floor, which was her domain. She was the only Shaw up here.

Realizing soon after her return from the academy that her mother did not really want her to enter society with her mismatched eyes and damaged reputation, Harriet thought it was time to live her life as she chose. To do that she needed to come up with a way that her family would leave her alone. Harriet had started complaining of headaches and sore chests. A few weeks later, she asked her mother if she could sleep on the third floor, as it was quiet. Her mother had acquiesced, happy to have the child she had no idea what to do with out of sight.

It had worked well, Harriet thought, reaching the top step. Her heart dropped when she saw her brother.

"What are you doing up here?" Her family never came to the third floor.

Oscar was tall with red hair like their younger sister, Catherine. He was dressed as a gentleman and had fitted into London life with ease, unlike Harriet. As yet, no woman had stolen his heart, but she thought that would happen given time, even considering he was a brash American as some of the English called them.

"Where have you been?" he demanded.

"Out."

"Where?"

"Nowhere important. Just taking some air, as my head

was sore today. Shouldn't you be downstairs getting ready for the guests?"

"I've seen you sneaking out of the house, you know."

His words shocked Harriet, but she kept her expression calm.

"I don't sneak, and Mother or Father know where I go if I do leave the house."

"I am not a fool like the others in this family who believe you are taking a walk, visiting a bookstore or library. I know you are also not locked in your room faking illnesses. Until now, I didn't care what you got up to, Harry, as long as you brought no further shame down on our family."

"I have brought no shame on you," Harriet snapped, as the old, raw wound stung.

"What is this?" He held out a piece of paper, and she knew exactly what it was.

"How would I know what it is?"

"Don't lie to me, Harry. You've never been very good at it. I found this piece of filth lying about in the gardens outside."

Drat. It must have fallen out of her pocket. She bit back the need to yell at him that it was not filth.

"I forbid you to meet with those rebellious suffragette women." His tone was sanctimonious and had her wanting to slap him. "You need to stay away from them. Imagine if it came out what you were doing. The family would be mortified in the eyes of society."

"You have no right to forbid me from doing anything, and I will not stand here and listen to your deluded lies about what I am doing. Now go away and annoy someone else, Oscar," she said, her voice no longer calm. "I am the sibling no one knows about, so there is little chance if someone saw me, not that I'm admitting to anything, they would know who I was."

Guilt flashed across his face. "Harry, maybe it's time you entered—"

"Do not finish that sentence." Harriet raised her hand. "I will not walk among people who believe I was there and watched my friend drown that night. That I then made up a story to cover what happened." Her words were cold. "If my own family does not believe me, I doubt society will, and I know they have long memories."

"Harry—"

She never spoke of that night and had locked the memory away inside her head. Yet since that man spoke of lemons and Frankie and she'd seen that necklace, the helpless rage, sadness, and hurt had returned.

"I doubt you can begin to understand what it's like, even five years after her death, to know that those who share my blood don't believe me. When, in fact, it's possible someone ended Frankie's life and still walks free."

"Don't be silly. We know it was likely an accident. It's just unfortunate others believed differently," Oscar said in that condescending way only an older sibling could have. "Because it was you who found her—"

"And I'm lying about the details?"

"Perhaps you didn't remember them clearly. There is no point in rehashing this again. It's done with, Harry, and I'm sure if you want to enter—"

"I never want to enter society and all its fake horridness," she cut him off again. "Go and enjoy some silly young ladies simpering and smiling and leave me alone, Oscar. Don't bother yourself with me, as you haven't for years. Let me live my life, and I'll let you live yours."

"Harry, it's not like that."

"It's exactly like that." She jabbed a finger at him. "Do not speak about anything we have discussed with Mother and Father, Oscar. You owe me that much at least."

"Harry, let's talk—"

Ignoring him, she stomped around him and to her room. Unlocking her door, she opened it and slammed it shut behind her. She then turned the key in the lock. Not that anyone would enter, but still, she would take no risks.

When she'd moved up here, her mother had allowed her to decorate how she wished, as no one but Harriet would see it. She'd chosen a large, comfortable bed and two wide, old, and soft chairs that had been tucked away in a corner up here. She had rugs on the floor, a long cabinet she stacked books on, and a thick blanket for when she wanted to sit and read.

One of the chairs sat under the window, and beside it, a small table piled with yet more books. It was a place to think and plan.

For the most part, she was alone—except for Catherine, the youngest Shaw. The sisters loved each other and, when allowed, spent time up here together. She shared some meals with her family, and occasionally guilt had a parent or her brother seeking her out, but mostly it was just Harriet living her life as she wanted.

At twenty-six, Harriet was doomed to be a spinster. If she hadn't blackened her name, through no fault of her own, she would likely be downstairs with her siblings socializing or married by now.

Turning up the lamps, she began taking off her bonnet and coat and then hung them up. Then, after peeling off her gloves, she unlaced her sensible black boots. A tap on the door had her answering it.

"Thank you, Sadie." Harriet took the tray from her maid. "I have no further need of anything. Good night." Closing the door, she locked it again and then took the tray to the table beside the chair. Opening the small chest she kept locked under her bed, Harriet found the book she hadn't read since the day she'd finished writing in it.

Today the memory of her friend was strong. Taking a deep breath, she exhaled slowly and opened the first page of the diary she'd kept at the Templar Academy for Young Ladies. Her parents had sent her there to obtain the skills she would need to secure the hand of a titled and wealthy young man.

She let the memories come and go as she skimmed over the pages, but it was near the end that she stopped and made herself read the entire last entry. It began with:

Tonight, I found my friend dead in the river, but not by my hand. Never that. Frankie was the only person who understood me.

CHAPTER SEVEN

"I brought lemon drops to sustain us," Alex said, sucking on the sweet. The bite of citrus filled his mouth, waking up every one of his senses. "Ah, here we are," he said, reading the piece of paper in his hand. "This is the place."

Number 4 Saddling Lane was a long, narrow brick building with two large doors that made it appear barnlike. One was open, and he dragged his eldest brother, Leo, inside.

"You will owe me a great deal after this, Alex," Leo said under his breath.

"It's not like you haven't made me do many things I didn't want to. Think of it as repayment." Alex looked at the chairs set up on either side of a narrow aisle. They were half full, and most were women. It was nearing 5:00 p.m., but the place was lit with lamps every few feet, as dark had already fallen.

"It's frigid," Leo moaned, burrowing deeper into his overcoat. "I could be at home in front of the fire eating fudge that Bud made. It's her new recipe. And give me an example of anything I've made you do you haven't wanted to?" Leo demanded. "You may appear malleable, but we all know that's a facade."

Leo was the eldest Nightingale sibling. Tall, with the family coloring, he was the largest of the family and had the surliest attitude. Now a viscount after their father's untimely death, he cared nothing for the title. As they no longer walked in society, it offered very little except ridicule. Alex sometimes felt Leo was the one among them that had not adjusted to their change in circumstance yet, no matter how much he protested otherwise.

Sometimes, when he thought no one was looking, he wore an odd expression. A combination of sadness and despair, but when questioned, he would not speak on the matter.

"You made me go with you to the pickled-food-eating competition. It took me days to get the stench out of my nostrils and mouth."

"Did I?" Leo said, his voice all innocence when, in fact, he knew very well just what he'd done.

"Yes."

"You said the pickled walnuts were superb."

"The pickled eggs were not," Alex snapped. "Besides, it's not like you have to do anything this evening. Just sit before the fire brooding—"

"I am not a nesting hen, Alex."

"I brought you because women appear to find your sullen attitude and appearance tolerable. I'm hoping that means they will talk to you."

"Is this your way of telling me you need my help, brother? If it is, you need lessons in your delivery," Leo snapped.

"I'm looking for the lady from the march, Leo," Alex said. "This Frankie is excessively annoying and persistent, and I fear if I do not tell this *H*-initial woman everything she wishes, I will be plagued with her until I die."

"I am not sullen," Leo added, sounding exactly that. "But I can understand that would be frustrating."

If Alex was honest, if only to himself, the lady he'd marched next to that day along the street had been inside his head too. Especially her pale face, and those spectacularly odd eyes.

Leave me alone. I did not harm my friend, and never would. She'd said those words to him, and they'd made him curious. Who thought she'd hurt her friend?

"What?" Leo said as he slid into an empty bench seat at the rear of the assembled women. Alex followed.

"What?"

"You grunted."

"The lemons are back stronger than ever, and also an older relative of someone with the initial *C*." Looking about him, Alex wondered who they belonged to.

"Is it hell?" Leo asked, nodding to a lady two rows ahead who turned to look at them, as clearly there were not many men present.

"Sometimes, but I can shut them out. Like locking a door. It's taken a while to perfect that skill, but I'm better at it now."

"Has Father's spirit—"

"No, and I really have no wish for him to." Alex looked at the backs of heads, wondering which one had a name with an *H* initial. He'd settled on Hannah, as she looked like a Hannah to him. Not that he knew any, but still, it suited her. He needed to get her to listen and understand he meant her no harm. *What did he mean?* Alex wasn't sure how to answer that, but he knew the sadness and fear inside the woman he'd marched with had been real, and it had touched him. That and the desperation he felt in spirit Frankie.

"True. Besides, there is little Father could say that we'd want to hear." Leo's tone was bitter.

"Exactly, although perhaps I would have a few words to say to him." Alex held out a lemon drop, and Leo took it, popping it into his mouth.

Leo grunted.

"And you, brother? Are you still denying your abilities?" Alex asked.

"I have no ability," Leo gritted out.

In fact, the eldest Nightingale did have a gift. He could find things that were lost. However, he refused to acknowledge it.

"I've found a place that I wish to take a lease on, Alex."

He turned in his seat to look at his brother at his softly spoken words. Their previous conversation was forgotten.

"There is room for us both," Leo added.

"I know we've discussed this, Leo. Know that we should have done this before now and likely would have had our world not imploded, but it's still a shock to hear that you have found us a place to live."

"An excellent word for what happened."

"To leave them, our siblings, Leo. Is it the right thing to do?" Alex gave voice to the one thing that would stop him. Had stopped both the elder Nightingales from leaving Uncle Bram and Aunt Ivy's home—the first real one they'd had.

"I thought you would feel that way, as do I," Leo said. "So, the town house is a five-minute walk from the house."

"Tell me you haven't secured a property in Simpkett Lane, Leo?"

His brother smiled. "A gentleman by the name of Mr. Laurie leased it to me. Uncle Bram was the one to tell me about it. There are four bedrooms, so we can have the others to stay."

"Well, I never" was all Alex could come up with. Simpkett

Lane was an easy walk from the rear of their property in Crabbett Close.

"I shall take you to inspect it soon."

"Yes, I would like that, Leo, very much." He felt a stirring of excitement at the prospect.

"So this person called Frankie who likes lemons is the reason I am sitting here in this drafty building surrounded by a group of militant women? That, plus you need me here so they will take one look at me and sigh over my handsomeness."

Ignoring the handsome comment, Alex said, "Are they militant because they choose to want better rights than they currently have? That they wish to vote and have a say in the way the world—"

"All right, you can stop now, and militant was perhaps not the best word to use."

"Possibly not, and while theirs is not a plight I have thought of before, I have begun to since that march, Leo. It's not right, you know, that their lives are so restricted by men."

Leo grunted.

"Is that an agreement grunt?"

"As opposed to a denial grunt?" Leo asked.

"If you are here to heckle, I suggest you leave!"

Looking to the row closest, Alex and Leo found a large lady dressed in gray. She wore a short half cape, and her lips were in a hard line as she studied the Nightingale brothers with a disapproving look.

"No indeed, ma'am. I marched with you holding a placard just days ago," Alex said, smiling. Leo continued to scowl, which was his usual expression.

Her eyes narrowed as she studied him, but then she smiled, and her face changed completely, looking softer.

"Indeed, you did, sir, and you saved one of ours from

hurting herself. It is good to see you once again, and you've brought a friend, I see."

"My brother. He is shy and does not leave the house often. We make him occasionally," he said. "Speaking is not easy for him, you understand." The breath wheezed from Alex as Leo jabbed him in the ribs with a very pointy elbow.

"Well now, that's kind of you. Hello," she said loudly, as if Leo was hard of hearing.

"Hello," Leo said and then jabbed Alex again. "There are only three men in this room, and two of them are us. You don't think they will turn on us, do you?"

"Unlikely," Alex said. "They'll just try and convince us their plight is a worthy cause... which it is."

"Hello, my lord and Mr. Nightingale."

"Dear Lord, tell me it isn't so," Alex moaned, sinking lower in his seat beside Leo.

"Hello to you, Miss Alvin and Mavis," Leo said. "And to you also, Miss Varney. I did not attend the march, but of course my brother Alex did. He did not mention seeing you there however."

The women all lived in Crabbett Close, where the Nightingales had moved to upon returning to London. It was fair to say the street was not normal in any way. Its inhabitants were noisy, and the kindest people Alex had ever met. They'd welcomed the Nightingales when they moved into their Uncle Bram and Aunt Ivy's home with open arms.

"Oooh, Mr. Nightingale, how wonderful it is to see you," Tabitha Varney said, giving Alex her most flirtatious smile. "Had I known you would be attending the march I would have of course joined the other suffragettes!"

Tabitha was a woman who wanted a husband. Alex wasn't sure of her age but thought perhaps in her late twenties. Her long blue jacket was open exposing her dress, which was low in the bodice, and on her face was a flirtatious smile. Lately she'd transferred her attentions to Alex, when before she'd been intent on securing Leo as a husband.

"How wonderful that Tabitha Varney is here," Leo said out the side of his mouth. Alex could hear his laughter.

"Shut up," Alex hissed.

Leo then made kissy noises, which had Alex growling.

CHAPTER EIGHT

"Now, Tabitha Varney, we are not here for you to flirt and solicit the attentions of men," Mavis Johns said. Large, with a build that rivaled several men Alex knew, the woman was an Amazon, especially at the Crabbett Close games. "We've a purpose, and that's supporting our sisters. You'll leave Mr. Nightingale alone and follow me. Tonight is not a night to find yourself a husband, and as I've already told you, have some self-respect for pity's sake."

Leo muffled his snort behind his gloved hand as Tabitha batted her eyelashes at Alex, completely ignoring Mavis's words.

Clucking her tongue, Mavis said, "Good evening to you both." She then dragged Tabitha Varney with her as she walked away. Alex exhaled loudly.

"It's both your faults, you know," Miss Alvin said before following. "'Tain't right or in anyone's favor to be such beautiful steppers." She then winked and followed the others.

"Did Miss Alvin just call us fine pieces of horseflesh?" Leo asked.

"I've been called worse."

"True. Thank God for Mavis Johns," Leo added as they watched her march Tabitha Varney to a seat. She waggled her fingers at Leo; he ignored her.

"Amen."

"If I could have your attention, please."

Their eyes were drawn to the front where the lady who had greeted them was talking. Alex had not seen the woman he'd called Hannah, but he was sure she was here.

"My name is Mrs. Lucas, and I'm determined along with many in England to see change for women!"

He listened as she rallied the women with a stirring speech. Alex searched for Hannah, but it wasn't easy, as bonnets made things a bit more difficult. He'd have to wait to search the faces of the women present.

"We must not weaken but stay strong!" Mrs. Lucas roared, drawing Alex's eyes back to her. "Our path is clear, and to waver is to weaken. No matter the danger ahead, we will persevere as long as there is breath left in our bodies."

"That's a rallying speech," Leo said.

"We will no longer simply accept what men have told us we must. Where they fight for their rights and freedoms, we women are expected to watch and do what is proper in their eyes. I say no to that! I say we have as much right as they to be heard."

"And that." Leo pulled off his gloves and started clapping loudly. "It sent chills down my spine."

"Don't tell me you're actually enjoying yourself?" Alex asked.

"I'm not sure enjoyment is the word I would use. It's made me uncomfortably aware of the plight of women when before I ignored it, which is not something that sits well now, along with all the other things I chose to ignore."

"What things?" Alex asked.

"While you were away fighting for your country, I was being a self-indulgent fool bent on pursuing a lavish, indolent lifestyle. I was a man of little substance, Alex."

"Leo, you were the heir. It was not expected that you would join the Army. It was expected you do exactly as you did," Alex said. Like it always did when he thought back to those painful days when he'd wondered if the injury would kill him, his hand went to his shoulder.

"You always do that." Leo's words were low and angry as he looked at the hand. "Always rub where you were shot and don't even realize it. I should have been with you. Should have cared for you when you fell."

"But you were not because Father would not allow it." Alex did not think about his time in the Army often. Not all of it was bad, but as he'd only been there five months before he was shot, he did not truly suffer as others had. He'd been shipped home, and there he'd stayed because his family had needed him, and his arm, while strong now, had taken some time to heal.

His one regret was that he'd never know what happened to those he served with. Their time together had not been long but because of what they'd endured, he'd grown close to a handful of men.

"I should have gone with you anyway, and to hell with him," Leo snarled. "It wasn't like he ever made any sense, but we simply took his word as law."

"And now we don't have to," Alex said. "And you were there when I arrived home and helped me heal."

His family had all supported and loved him, and he would be forever grateful for that.

"Now, Miss Short, if you will come up here and talk on what is happening with your sisters around the country," Mrs. Lucas said. "Come along, Harriet, don't be shy."

"She's got a wonderful voice. It carries a great distance," Leo said.

The tension gripped Alex so fast he'd dug his fingers into his brother's arm without realizing it.

"What's wrong?"

"Nothing. Sorry," Alex said, looking at the woman now walking up to stand beside Mrs. Lucas.

"Is that her, Alex?" He nodded to Leo's whispered words. "What is Frankie saying?"

To anyone else, it would be an odd question, but not to a Nightingale.

"She's up there beside her—a gray shadow to the right. Murder, water, jewelry. The words are tumbling through my head."

"Then you must speak to her, Alex. If she is persistent, then perhaps there is a great deal more to this."

"I know. I can't remember ever having a spirit like this."

Harriet. Alex had not thought of that name, but it suited her too. She was pale and clearly nervous being up there. In fact, he'd say she was terrified. Alex watched her inhale and exhale slowly. She then nodded to Mrs. Lucas who took a step back to allow Harriet to speak.

"Good evening," she said and then cleared her throat. "I would like to discuss what our organization is achieving across England, and the women, like us, who are protesting for change."

"She's American," Leo whispered. Alex nodded, not wanting to miss a word of what she said.

She talked about the different chapters of the women's suffrage movement that had formed all over England and then discussed rallies and attendance numbers.

"Clearly, unlike the other woman, she doesn't like public speaking," Leo said.

"Who does?"

Harriet Short wore the same large black bonnet covering her hair, so Alex was still no wiser as to its color. The black cloak was the same also.

"Strength will win out. Determination will succeed. Persistence will make our voices heard," she said. "Good evening to you all."

After a rousing round of applause, Mrs. Lucas spoke again.

"Tea will be served now."

"We get tea. You didn't tell me that. I would never have refused," Leo mocked him.

"Amusing, I'm sure."

"Now be nice, Alex, or I won't protect you from Tabitha Varney if you don't behave."

Alex shuddered. "I know the transferring of her affections from you to me is in some way contributed to you and Ellen. I just haven't worked out how you did it yet."

"As if we would do something so underhanded to you, Alex," Leo said with a straight face.

"I will make you both pay in some way. That sister of ours is now protected by her law-abiding husband. You, however, I can get at easily. So, watch your back, big brother."

"You don't scare me," Leo scoffed.

They both rose and moved into the aisle now the talking had finished. It was good to stand, as his toes were turning numb.

"Now, brother, your Miss Short is up ahead speaking with another woman. As luck would have it, Miss Alvin and Mavis are there also, which gives you the perfect opportunity to approach."

Miss Alvin wore her frilly gray, once white cap beneath her bonnet, an old gray-and-black-checked cloak, and at least three scarves to Alex's count. The woman was nearly eighty; he was sure of it. Mavis Johns was no-nonsense in complete mouse-brown clothing, and Tabitha wore a multitude of color. None of them matched.

"Ah, now here they come, our handsome Crabbett Close residents," Miss Alvin said, holding out a hand to wave Alex and Leo closer.

"It takes a lot to make me blush, but that woman can always achieve it," Leo whispered, his eyes on Tabitha who was now pouting.

"Gentlemen, let me introduce you to Miss Short," Miss Alvin said.

Harriet looked ready to run from the barn when she saw it was him who approached.

"Clearly she recognizes you from the mad man who accosted her at the march," Leo said softly. "Mind you, that is a typical reaction of women when they see you. After all, I am the handsome Nightingale."

"You'll keep," Alex replied.

"Miss Short and Miss Brown, allow me to introduce you to Lord Seddon and Mr. Alexander Nightingale."

The mismatched eyes grew wider. She was pretty, Alex thought, but perhaps interesting was a better term.

"Good evening." Leo bowed, and Alex followed suit. The woman curtsied.

"That's a lofty title to find at such a gathering," Miss Brown said. Tall and dressed in subdued colors like the other women, this one looked about Harriet Short's age.

"Not all noblemen are unaware of what goes on around them," Leo said with a smile that had broken a few hearts when he walked in society.

As Alex had kept his eyes on Miss Short, he saw her flinch at the word "nobleman." Did she dislike them? It was not an uncommon emotion for those in the lower classes. They had so little while a few had so much, and the people he'd once walked among cared little for the plight of anyone but themselves.

His father had ruined his family with that kind of thinking.

CHAPTER NINE

"Perhaps we could have a cup of tea, ladies. The night is fiercely cold, and something to warm us before the trip home would be most welcome," Alex heard Leo say.

"Indeed, come along then, my lord." Miss Alvin led the way to the tea with the other women, leaving Alex alone with Miss Short. She began to follow, but he wrapped his fingers around her small wrist, holding her at his side.

"Unhand me," she said, her voice a low growl. "Why are you here? Have you come to harass me again?"

"I did not harass you and will not harm you. I wish only for a few minutes of your time," he said. "I completely understand how my words must have upset you, but I would ask that you listen to what I have to say. Just give me a few minutes of your time. It's all I'm asking for."

Alex had decided that he needed to approach her differently this evening. He must stay calm and rational if he was to get her to listen to what he had to say.

"Go away," she whispered, her eyes shooting to where the others had congregated around the tea table.

Her skin was soft, the pallor tinged with a flush of pink along the ridges of her cheekbones. A small nose and an upper lip shaped like a cupid's bow. The eyes, however, were what drew a person in. One a deep blue, and the other the color of oak tree leaves. Her lashes were straight and dark, and her brows a deep brown, which suggested her hair was dark also.

"What do you want from me?"

He'd met a few Americans in his life, and unlike some of the upper-class British, he liked the accent. It was interesting, especially when spoken by this woman. Her voice was a bit gruff—almost a growl.

"My story is not an easy one to tell, but I shall try," Alex said. Honesty was really the only way forward here. If she ran screaming from him, so be it; at least he'd tried for the lemon-scented Frankie. Alex just hoped that didn't mean she'd haunt his thoughts forever.

"I cannot harm you here surrounded by your fellow suffragettes, and really do wish you no ill. I want only to talk. Will you allow me that?"

Her eyes studied him for several seconds, and then she gave a jerky nod.

"What was your relationship with Frankie?"

She studied him through those lovely eyes filled with suspicion and sadness. Clearly, whoever this Frankie was, she'd been important to Miss Short.

"She was my friend. I don't understand why you are asking me about her now, many years after her death. Why you know so much," she added. "Are you investigating her death?"

"No, I am not." *Yet,* he added silently and wasn't sure why that word had slipped into his head.

Alex usually didn't tell people what he could do. Some knew, but those he trusted. To tell a total stranger wasn't exactly a risk; after all, he could simply deny it. But something told him nothing but the truth would do in this moment.

"This is going to be hard to believe, Miss Short, but I will ask you to bear with me."

"I am quite intelligent. If you speak slowly, I shall grasp it."

"I am not doubting your intelligence. It is simply a matter of believability," he added. "Sometimes those that have passed want to communicate to those they knew in life, and they do that through me."

He watched for her reaction. The horror or running away screaming. It did not come. Instead, she kept her eyes on his.

"Spiritualism do you mean?"

"I do, yes. What do you know of it?" Alex asked, intrigued. There were two different groups of people when it came to such things: those who thought anyone believing or suggesting they could communicate with the dead were blithering idiots, and those that didn't. The Nightingale family were firmly in the second group.

"Not a great deal until five days ago, but I have been reading a book, which has opened my mind to the possibility that some people could communicate with the dead."

"It is hard for those with sturdy souls to see things differently, Miss Short."

"And why is it you believe I have a sturdy soul when you don't know me?"

"Do you?" Why had this woman piqued his interest? Was it the Frankie connection?

"Frankie believed in the ability of some spirits to communicate and tried to convince me. She also told me often that my late grandfather was hanging about."

"*L* name, had a fondness for cake?"

Her eyes widened as she nodded.

"He is here with Frankie," Alex said softly. "She wants me to communicate with you."

She changed before his eyes and seemed to crumple. Her eyes filled with tears, and her shoulders hunched. "Oh, Frankie," she whispered. "My dear friend. I miss her so."

"Are you all right, Miss Short?" He touched the hand she had clenched at her side.

She rallied, sniffing loudly, and then pressed her other hand to her mouth. "S-sorry."

"Quite all right. It's not every day someone tells you they speak to the dead. Neither is it every day that person is believed," Alex said, watching as she wiped her eyes and nose on her sleeve. She looked like a small child.

"I'm not sure what I believe," she whispered. "You were right. I do have a sturdy soul and like facts, and yet…"

"If I may ask, what is the book you are reading?"

"*The Voices Within.*"

"Yes, that would start you thinking, and then with what I've told you, I'm sure your beliefs are being challenged." Digging in his pocket, Alex found the handkerchief he kept there and handed it to her.

"Thank you." She dabbed at her eyes. "But it is not just you, sir. There have been a few other things connected to Frankie that cropped up lately, when I'd thought that time was behind me." She wiped her eyes again and blew her nose loudly. Most young ladies would never do such a thing in his presence. He found he liked it.

"I want to believe you." Her eyes were damp with unshed tears as she looked at him. Alex felt that look to his toes. "I know what it's like not to be believed," she said softly.

"Who didn't believe you?"

She waved his words away. "What does Frankie want to tell me?"

"We don't actually converse like you and I are. The information comes to me in different ways, like the scent of the lemons, images, or words."

Her only answer to that was a nod.

"Her shadow was with you when you marched. That's how I knew it was you I needed to speak with."

"She's really here?" The whispered words were full of hope. "Does she know who... I don't know how to ask this."

"How about I tell you what I know?" He touched the hand she had clenched in a fist around his handkerchief. "Then you can ask me questions?"

"Yes, please. I would be most grateful."

That she was willing to listen and possibly believe him made some of the tension inside Alex ease.

"Tea, Mr. Nightingale?" Mavis Johns called.

"I'll be right there, Mavis," he replied. "If you would pour two cups, please."

She raised a hand in acknowledgement, and he refocused on the interesting woman with the amazing eyes.

"I saw a necklace that had a gold locket with an angel. I believe the eyes were rubies. She also showed me a red cross."

"The necklace was the one Frankie lost. It had been her mother's," Miss Short said, sniffing as she fought back tears. "But I'm not sure about the cross."

"I believe it's the symbol for the Knights Templar."

Her cheeks lost what little color they had as a look of understanding crossed her face.

"Do you know what this is alluding to, Miss Short?"

She nodded. "I-I believe so."

"As Frankie seems to want me to connect with you, clearly you and she were close," he said. Digging in his pocket, he pulled out the twist of paper the remaining lemon drops were in. Opening it, he held it out. "It's a lemon drop," he said when she looked at them suspiciously. "It may make you feel better." Which was possibly the most stupid thing he'd ever said, but the woman was clearly upset, and lemon drops helped with many things after all.

"Th-thank you," she whispered, taking one. He watched as her mouth opened and she popped the sweet in.

She had a lovely mouth, Alex thought. Soft lips, the top almost a bow shape.

"Yes," she said, snapping him out of his thoughts. "We were the best of friends. I have been closer to no one else since." She sucked on the lemon drop.

"Will you tell me how she died?"

"She drowned."

Which would explain why, when Frankie first slipped into his head, he was short of breath. Alex bet his new horse there was a great deal more to this story; he just wasn't sure why he wanted to know all of it. What was driving him to seek the details.

"Drowned. So no one else was involved?"

"Wh-why are you asking that?" If possible, she was even paler now.

"Because you told me when we were marching that you were not involved."

"Did I?"

He nodded.

"Wh-what else is she showing you, sir?"

"Your tea is ready!" Mavis called.

"I don't think here is the place to continue this, but I will ask you one more question, Miss Short, before we take tea. And it may shock you, but I want your honesty."

She nodded solemnly.

"Do you believe your friend was murdered?"

Her eyes, if possible, grew bigger. "I most definitely believe that there were nefarious circumstances surrounding Frankie's death, but as no one would listen to what I had to say, it was not investigated. Th-they thought I was involved and lied to cover it up."

"I'm sorry," Alex said. The words sounded inadequate in the face of her obvious distress.

"I want to find out who, if anyone, had a hand in my friend's death, sir. I don't believe I can find peace until I do, but the endeavor has been fruitless, as I am one person and have no idea where to turn for help, so I was forced to give up hope of finding answers."

"I may have someone you could speak with about what happened, Miss Short." Of course, he would need to convince Gray first. "But I will caution that, as time has passed, it will be harder to identify a killer if indeed there is one, and I can make no assurances." Alex pulled a card out of his pocket and handed it to her. "Can you call here on Friday at 2:00 p.m.?"

"You live in Crabbett Close?" She studied the small white rectangle.

"I do, yes."

"I-I am due to call there to see Miss Alvin."

"Perfect. Then you know where it is."

"Very well, I will see you then."

Alex knew she had many questions, but unlike his sisters, she did not ask them and simply walked away from him. Back straight in that shapeless cloak and overlarge bonnet. Alex was intuitive; it went with what he was. His hunch was the story regarding the death of her friend Frankie was one with many twists and turns, and on Friday, with his brother-in-law's help, he would find out more.

"Lord Seddon was just telling us that the woman's suffrage movement is dear to your heart, Mr. Nightingale." The woman standing with Leo and Mavis Johns said.

"He's too kind, but of course I have taken my lead from him, my eldest brother, in most things, and this is another.

Lord Seddon is a man with a need to right wrongs. He seeks justice daily for those who struggle to secure it for themselves," Alex said. "If I can be half the man he is, I will be happy. He, too, will march alongside you."

Alex heard Leo's hiss of angry breath but did not look his way.

"And now, if you will excuse us, we will leave you to your tea," Leo said. "Thank you for allowing us to be part of your meeting this evening."

"We have a march tomorrow and next week on Wednesday. We will meet outside here at midday should you wish to join either one," the woman said.

"Thank you," Alex said, looking around for Miss Short. She was nowhere to be seen, which made him feel a stab of regret. He'd wanted to see her again before he left, which was reason enough to leave.

When they were outside on the street, walking away from the women, Alex said, "I will remind you that you started that. I just finished it."

"Yes, but now we will have to march. Nightingales never give their word and not follow through." Leo looked disgruntled.

"It's not like we are not disgraced in the eyes of society anyway. What's something else to add to that."

"True. Did you clear things up with Miss Short, and now hopefully you will have peace from the lemon woman?"

"Yes, and no."

"Elaborate," Leo said in that lord of the manor way he had that annoyed his siblings excessively.

"Yes, I managed to convince her I was not a madman—"

"Not strictly speaking true but continue."

"But now I have more questions than answers, and she is calling at Crabbett Close to discuss them. I hope to convince Gray to speak with her also."

"Why?" Leo looked at him.

"Her friend was murdered, Leo, but she was implicated. She attempted to clear her name and failed. I know no more than that."

"Alex, is it wise to get involved? You know nothing about what happened, or that woman. How many years ago did it happen? The trail could be long dead by now."

"Quite some time, I believe, and I understand your concern, Leo, but I don't think Frankie is going to leave me alone until I do something."

"Has that happened before?"

"A spirit haranguing me?"

Leo nodded.

"No. They can be insistent, but nothing like this one."

"Odd then, but we are the Notorious Nightingales, so it's hardly unexpected. But I will add that you do not get involved with this alone."

"I doubt that woman, Miss Short, has murderous intentions toward me, Leo, considering I approached her."

"I understand that, but who knows where any of this could lead. You need to show caution," his brother gritted out.

"I am not a child, Leo, and I have told you we are going to speak only, and with my big, strong brother-in-law who is a detective to keep me safe."

Leo stopped suddenly and turned to face him.

"What?" Alex looked around for the reason.

"That woman intrigues you."

"Who?"

"You know very well who. Miss Harriet Short with the lemon-loving deceased friend."

"No, she doesn't," Alex scoffed. "I've spoken no more than a handful of words with her."

"I watched you speaking with her. You were leaning closer; I saw your interest, brother."

Alex punched Leo hard in the arm and continued walking because the truth was Harriet Short did interest him, and he didn't like that one bit.

CHAPTER TEN

Harriet left the meeting with yet more questions swirling about in her head.

"Come on, a few of the others are going to a tea shop nearby to warm them up," Milly said, grabbing Harriet's arm. "I promise you they have spiced cake that you will not want to miss."

"At this hour?" Harriet protested.

"It's not that late, just dark, and you never come out, so you must."

"Very well," Harriet said, as tonight her parents thought she was at the library listening to a lecture with other gardening enthusiasts about Philip Miller's *The Gardeners Dictionary*. She'd not asked her mother, as she would have said a woman's place is to learn things that her future husband would wish her to be proficient at. Her father had waved her away and told her to have fun.

"Come along. It's colder than my aunt Fanny's heart. She was a right tarter," Milly said, urging her out the door.

She and Milly fell in behind the other women who were going to the tea shop.

Since Oscar had told Harriet he'd seen her leaving the house, she'd decided to ask her parents' permission, where possible, if she had something she wanted to attend. It was another lie on top of many, but at least George and Heloise Shaw knew she was not in her room.

Perhaps she could get Oscar some of those lemon drops to sweeten him up, as clearly he was now suspicious. She'd enjoyed them after all, and her brother did have a sweet tooth.

"I saw the man with you again. The one from the march. Miss Alvin told me they were toffs," Milly said. "Don't get your hopes up there, Harry. Their sort is just amusing themselves by coming to that meeting tonight."

"Which means what? That we are not worthy of their time?"

"I've had experience that tells me we're not," Milly said, and something in her tone suggested that experience had hurt.

"We are worthy, Milly. Never forget that," Harriet said. She'd spent the last few years believing the opposite, but she had no wish for her friend to feel that way about herself.

"Their sort doesn't usually take time with the likes of us, Harry. Mind you, I have no idea what your lot in life is, as you are very tight-lipped about it. You could be bleeding royalty for all I know."

"Yes indeed. I'm the American line of the British royal family. Princess Harry from New York."

Milly dipped into a curtsy. "It's pleased I am to meet you, Princess Harry."

Harriet laughed, and it felt good. She didn't have much to laugh about in her life, which made her sound pathetic. She had a great deal more than most. Food, shelter, and money to buy books. But sometimes the loneliness crept inside her, and that was why she did the things she did.

"Clearly you and the handsome Mr. Nightingale talked about lots of things when you stood alone."

"We weren't alone," Harriet said. "He was enquiring about the suffragette movement and wanted more details about what he could do to aid us." She wasn't about to tell Milly the real reason she'd conversed with the man.

"Really? That does surprise me."

"He may be a good man, Milly." Why she felt the need to defend Mr. Nightingale, she was unsure, but it definitely had something to do with Frankie. If that man had indeed spoken to her friend, which she now believed after reading *The Voices Within*, then he'd taken the time to track her down. She could not be angry with him for that. Especially if he could help her find a resolution for Frankie's death. *Had she been murdered?*

"It's over there, just around the corner. Betsy's Tea Shop is the best place for spiced cake," Milly said, pointing across the road.

Harriet looked left before they crossed, and it was then she saw the man. A shiver of awareness traveled through her because it felt like he was staring at her. *Was that Miss Haven's fiancé?* His cap was pulled low, but he was about the same size.

"Hurry it along, Harry, a horse is coming."

She was tugged across the road, and when she looked back, the man had disappeared. *Had she imagined that he was watching her?* Was she just unsettled after everything that had been happening?

Harriet had never thought of herself as an unsteady person.

"In you go," Milly said, opening the door to the shop they now stood before. The building was gray, and the only thing alerting her to this being a tea shop was a small sign hanging above her head with the words "Betsy's Tea Shop." The word "shop" had faded so it was hard to read. The only indication there may be something going on inside was the small window, through which she could see Mrs. Winter, who was a member of the suffragettes.

"How does anyone know this is here?" Harriet asked.

"Everybody does." Milly looked at her. "But clearly not you. Where do you live, Harriet?"

And this was the reason she never spent time with these people away from the suffrage marches or meetings. People asked questions that she did not want to answer.

"I live about fifteen minutes from here." Which wasn't a lie, but that was a carriage ride, not walking.

"Do you have family, or do you live alone?" Milly asked.

"I have family. Shall we sit with Mrs. Letiker and her daughter?" Harriet said, heading their way.

"Stop, Harry," Milly hissed, but it was too late; she'd already started that way.

"Hello!" Mrs. Letiker waved, as did the two other tables of ladies from the meeting. "Come and sit with us."

"God's blood, you could have picked anyone but them," Milly whispered.

"But it is not Miss Letiker's fault her mother cannot stop talking. Surely we cannot punish her by sitting with the others and leaving those seats free at their table?"

Milly sighed loudly. "Fine, and you're right, damn you."

"Excellent."

The exterior of the tea shop continued inside. Dull walls, and a mismatch of tables and chairs were dotted about the place. All were full of people her mother would say were beneath her. Harriet thought them good folk. No paintings hung on the walls or rugs were on the floors; in fact, it did not inspire her with confidence that the food would be anything but bland.

"How many siblings do you have?" Milly asked.

"Two. Hello, do you mind if we join you?"

Mrs. Letiker, unlike her daughter, liked to talk, and it did not matter which subject. Taking a seat beside the woman, Harriet asked her if she enjoyed the meeting, then sat back and listened, as Mrs. Letiker would not draw a breath until they left the tea shop.

The tea and spiced fruitcake arrived just as Mrs. Letiker launched into a detailed description about her neighbor Mr. Clancy's third cousin who lived in Scotland. Harriet took her first bite and managed to stifle the moan.

"I told you it was good," Milly said, giving her a wink. "Do you have any brothers that I should meet?"

Milly would be a lovely sister-in-law. Funny, pretty, and intelligent. However, she lacked the one quality her mother wished for above all others in a future daughter-in-law. She wasn't of noble birth.

"I would not wish my brother on any woman I respect. He has terrible habits and is excessively annoying," Harriet said.

"I have a brother like that," Milly added.

They sat and drank tea, and when Mrs. Letiker paused to sip hers, which surely went cold more often than not, they drew her daughter into the conversation.

Sitting in this little shop, Harriet thought that perhaps she'd been wrong not to come here with the other women, especially Milly, before. It was nice, even if Mrs. Letiker had moved on to her sister's husband's bunions.

Her eyes went to the window, and she saw the back of a man's head. Was it him? Had he been looking in the window at her? Harriet was not impulsive, but when he was no longer visible, anger that someone appeared to be following her had her rising.

"I really must go, as my mother will start worrying if I am

not home soon. Thank you for the tea." Patting Milly on the shoulder, she hurried out the door and stopped, her eyes searching the lane before her. He wasn't in sight.

How was that possible when he'd been here just seconds ago? Walking in the direction she was sure he'd taken, Harriet searched but did not find him. An opening no bigger than her arm span could explain why he had disappeared. She entered cautiously, but only far enough that she could leave with haste or scream.

"If the man following me is in here, I demand you show yourself!" Her voice seemed to bounce off the narrow walls on either side of where she stood a few feet inside. "I'm not moving until you do and have friends nearby." Still nothing. She waited a few more seconds, but there was no sound, not even a shuffle of feet. Clearly, he had fled the scene. Now her anger had cooled, she thought it was time to leave. Harriet had always believed she could be brave when required but not foolish. Had she been thinking clearly, which she now was, chasing that man had not been a terribly smart move.

She was sure it was him she'd seen earlier, but Harriet couldn't be certain in this light. Many men wore dark clothes and hats pulled low. In truth it may be Miss Haven's fiancé, but then again it may not.

"Am I losing my mind?" she whispered.

Turning, she started the few feet back to the opening. Before she could reach it, something collided with her from behind. Stumbling several steps, she struggled to stay upright but tripped and fell onto her knees. The impact forced her to the ground, and her cheek landed on the sharp edge of a stone.

Harriet then heard retreating footsteps. Struggling to her feet, she picked up her skirts and ran out the opening and back the way she'd come with Milly. Heart pounding, she didn't think about anything but getting to safety, and to do that, she had to reach a busy road and more light. Chest heaving, she pushed herself on until she heard the clop of hooves; only then did she slow to a walk.

Dear God what had just happened?

Desperate now to get to safety, Harriet looked for a hackney but saw none. She walked fast, dodging around any people she encountered, until finally she saw what she wanted. Raising a hand, the driver pulled his horses to a halt before her.

"Are you all right, miss? Your cheek is bleeding."

"Oh, y-yes, I fell. Could you take me home please?"

"Course I can. You give me your address and get inside now in the warm, miss." The man smiled, and it was gentle, and Harriet felt the sting of tears. Sniffing, she gave him what he needed and then climbed inside.

Now she was safe, the tremors started. Tears leaked from her eyes, and a loud sob slipped from her lips.

Someone just pushed me over. Harriet clasped her hands to stop them shaking. Now she'd stopped running, the pain in her body was making itself known to her. Her knees burned and her cheek stung. Fumbling about in her pocket, she found the large white handkerchief Mr. Nightingale had given her and pressed it to her face.

Now she could think, Harriet allowed herself to admit that going into that narrow opening had been the actions of a naïve fool, and she tried never to be one of those. When she was not shaking and terrified, she would remind herself of that.

Why was someone following her? Harry had done nothing to make anyone think she was trying to bring up the past. In fact, the opposite was true. She'd avoided it for years until that day at the rally when Mr. Nightingale had approached her. However, something told her this was related to Frankie's death.

Tomorrow, when she was herself again, she would think things through from every angle, but for now, she just wanted to go home and be safe.

CHAPTER ELEVEN

"I wonder what Miss Short's story is?" Leo said as he and Alex continued their walk home after an ale and pie at the Speckled Hen, which just happened to be a short hackney ride from the suffragette meeting.

"And I would care why?" Alex said calmly. Snapping would simply be a sign of his guilt. He'd been saying things like this to annoy Alex since they'd left the meeting. His brother had somehow become aware that Alex thought Miss Short interesting, and as much as he'd denied it, his brother would not be swayed.

"Because you like her. Therefore, we need to know more about her."

"You have no idea what you are talking about, Leo. Shut up," Alex said. "And I'm not sure if you are aware, but we are about to walk past Henry's fencing salon."

"I miss fencing," Leo said. "Correction. I miss fencing with others that I can beat with ease."

"You can't beat me with ease," Alex scoffed, eyeing the tall wooden building warily. He'd spent many happy hours in there once.

"You're predictable. I say let's go in and you can see how much your fencing has deteriorated since last we were there."

"We've not been there since—"

"Then perhaps it's past time. Uncle Bram goes and said we should join him. Yes, there will be talk, but what do we care for that?" Leo said. "Come, brother, we do not need anyone's approval."

"So, you believe it is finally time to face at least one of our demons?"

Leo nodded.

"Very well."

They entered, and Alex felt every muscle in his body tense but kept his expression blank. Once he'd loved this place. The camaraderie. The competition of pitting himself and his skills against another. Here he'd spent hours with his friends. Friends he no longer had, which in some cases, was as much his fault as theirs.

"Well now, who knew you were both still alive."

"Lord Sutton." Leo bowed, and Alex did the same to the man coming their way. He had been an acquaintance of their father's, but a good man for that.

"My hope is your absence has made you slow and ungraceful, Lord Seddon. You also, Mr. Nightingale." The man had a genuine smile on his face, so Alex relaxed.

"By God, Alex?"

The words drew his eyes. A tall man with a head full of blond curls he'd always loathed was approaching. Stephen Blackthorne was his second cousin on his mother's side and he and Alex had always been close.

"I hadn't realized you were back, Stephen."

"Six months," his friend said, grabbing Alex and hugging him hard enough to crack his ribs. "I've tried to find you for months, Alex. I'm so sorry for your loss and that I was not here for your father's funeral or the following fallout. All I can say to that is society is an ass."

"Well said," Leo added. "It's good to see you again, Stephen."

Seeing his cousin made Alex realize just how much he'd missed him. How much he'd locked away the life he'd once lived, both the good and the bad.

"And you fared well, Stephen? No injuries from the war?" Alex asked.

"None. How is your shoulder?"

"Healed well," Alex added.

"I'll put my name forward to take you on, Nightingale." Baron Ellington now stood beside Stephen. They'd been acquaintances once. Close enough that they'd gone away on hunting trips together and spent nights doing the things young men did. However, the man had turned on him, along with other members of society, after his father shot himself because he'd lost a fortune gambling, thereby sending his family to hell.

"Well now, Ellington, it will be my pleasure." Alex bowed. "How wonderful to see you again, as it has been overlong. I can't remember how long exactly, as you disappeared so quickly I was never quite sure where you went."

"You're not fencing against him," Leo said.

"Yes, I can see how that would worry you considering..."

"Considering what, Ellington? And be very careful what you say because, unlike you, I care nothing for what anyone outside my family think of me," Alex said softly. "I am loyal to those who stood with me, not the gutless cowards who turned their backs."

"Alex," Leo cautioned.

"How dare you call me a gutless coward!"

"Did I? Well if it fits, then I suppose I did," Alex drawled.

"Go away, Ellington." Stephen's words came out a growl.

"Surely you are not still friends, Blackthorne?" Ellington scoffed.

"They are my cousins," Stephen snapped. "Not just friends, Ellington."

"Their father owed a lot of money when he took the coward's way out—"

Alex was inches from the man before he could finish the sentence. "My father," he said. "Not me or my siblings, Ellington. Be very careful what you say next, as I am no longer governed by the rules and society you still covet. I will not hesitate to retaliate in an ungentlemanly manner."

"Ellington, you are a bigoted, small-minded fool, and anyone with all their wits would know that," Stephen said. "Alex has always been worth two of you."

"Yes, he has." Leo's tone was menacing.

Ellington bared his teeth, and Alex clenched his fists, ready to strike. He felt it again, the shame and anger that had once been his constant companion.

"Back away, Alex." The words came from behind him and were not loud, but he heard them. "At once, nephew."

Bramstone Nightingale was one of only a few men who could make Alex stand down in that moment. He retreated two steps with Leo, who had been at his side.

"Stay," his uncle said moving to his other side. "Blackthorne, good to see you again," he acknowledged Stephen before focusing on Ellington.

Tall like them, Uncle Bram was their late father's brother, and a man loved and respected by the Nightingale children. Uncle Bram and Aunty Ivy, his wife, had stepped in to take care of them when they'd been unsure what to do next and how to survive in the world they'd suddenly been plunged into. Alex and his siblings would never forget that day he had arrived at their London town house. A place that had become their sanctuary from the abuse and vendors demanding money.

"Yes, do stay like your uncle says, Nightingale," Ellington snarled. "I want to take you apart."

"You had better watch your mouth, Ellington, or I will be closing it for you, and there will be several teeth missing when I do," Alex snapped back.

"That will do, Alex," Uncle Bram added. "Now who is fighting me out of you two?" He looked at Leo and Alex.

"I'm fighting him." Alex jabbed a finger at Ellington. "Now." He was consumed with rage as he remembered the snubs and slights he and his family had received from people like the man before him.

"Ellington?" Uncle Bram wrinkled his nose. "Very well, if you must, but it will be an unfair match. You will have to go easy on him, Alex, as he has not improved since last you were here. You are no longer a soft nobleman like him, and you will take him apart in no time."

"How dare you!" Ellington was red-faced now, and his fists were clenched.

Uncle Bram stepped in front of Alex before he could move.

"Be warned that if you continue with this, Ellington, you will not win. I will let them both have you and be damned with the consequences. Then I will finish what is left. No one, and hear me well when I repeat this, no one insults or harms my family ever again, or they will answer to me."

Uncle Bram was, for the most, even-tempered—unless you went after his family. Then he was a lion protecting his young.

"My advice at this point, Ellington, is leave," Leo said. "If you are not game to take us on."

"I speak for everyone when I say we don't need the likes of you here!" Ellington said.

"You don't speak for me." Another voice entered the fray. "In fact, you speak for no one but your small-minded gaggle of friends. Be gone, you fool, and welcome, Seddon and Nightingale. It's about time you returned. Your uncle has been wishing it for some time now."

The man who had spoken was tall with gray hair at his temples. A man Alex knew well, as his twin sisters were friends with Ellen.

"Lord Sinclair." Alex bowed.

"There is the door, Ellington. I suggest you scamper through it at once," another said.

"Duke." Alex bowed again to the Duke of Raven. And then suddenly they were surrounded by men.

"Good to see you again, Seddon, Nightingale," Mr. Zachariel Deville said. "What is that foul stench?" He wrinkled his nose as he looked at Ellington. "Ah, I see where it is emanating from now."

Those of Sinclair and Raven blood joined the Devilles as they stood united against Ellington. It was humbling, Alex thought. These were good men. It was wrong of him to have forgotten that the society he'd been banished from still had many people he respected in it. People who would never turn from his family.

"This is not done!" Ellington looked like he was about to explode as he glared at Alex.

"Oh, I think it is," Michael Deville said. "We all know the reason no respectable club will allow you to play a hand within their walls, Ellington. It seems your inability to count correctly has caught up with you."

Ellington was now so red he looked ready to burst. His mouth opened and closed, and then he stormed by them and out the door they'd just entered with his posse behind him.

"Be very wary of that fool, nephews," Uncle Bram said. "He is trouble for both of you."

As Alex was watching Ellington, he saw when he reached the door and turned to look at them. Black, angry rage poured from his eyes. He thought his uncle's advice was sound.

"So tell me if I'm correct, Alexander," Cambridge Sinclair said. "Did I or did I not see you walking in a suffragette march?"

"You did." He wouldn't lie.

"Excellent. I was there to write an article for the *Trumpeter*. My wife sent me, as clearly, she is now running the paper. I will want a statement from you to add to that."

Alex tried to remember the words spoken at the meeting he and Leo had just attended. "I think women no longer wish to simply—"

"Stop!" Cam raised a hand. He then closed his eyes.

"What's he doing?" Alex asked Lord Sinclair.

"Clearing his mind. Apparently he doesn't have much room in there, so he needs to clear it to hold more information."

"All true," Cam said, opening his eyes. "Proceed."

"You could always write it down. I'm sure someone here will have something," Leo said. "After all, every word Alex speaks must be remembered."

"Brothers." Cam sighed. "They're bloody annoying."

"Amen," Alex added.

"So, give me something for my story." Cam waved his hand at Alex.

"Women will no longer simply accept what men have told them they must. Where we fight for our rights and freedoms, women are expected to watch and do what is proper in a man's eyes. I think they are saying no to that now. They believe they have as much right as us to be heard."

Silence greeted Alex's words, and then Cam smiled. "Bloody brilliant. Em will love it."

"Strength will win out. Determination will succeed. Persistence will make our voice heard," Alex added. "They have plenty of things they say like that."

"Do they really? I must interview some of them," Cam said. He and the others then wandered off debating the matter of women's rights.

"You said that perfect. Well done, brother," Leo whispered in his ear.

"I knew there was a reason for my excellent memory."

Leo snorted and took the foil Uncle Bram threw at him. Shrugging out of his jacket, Alex did the same. He wondered what the sweet-faced Harriet—Miss Short—was doing right now.

CHAPTER TWELVE

Harriet knew her family was out for the evening and had managed to avoid anyone seeing her until she reached the servant's entrance of her home. Thankfully Percy was not lurking, awaiting her return; he would have had conniptions if he'd seen her cheek. She'd not been so lucky when she'd stepped inside the kitchens. Mrs. Dickens had squawked like a mother hen when she saw Harriet, which had brought Cuthbert and the rest of the staff rushing to see what was going on.

The butler had asked what happened, and after an explanation about how clumsy she was falling on a loose cobble, Harriet was then bundled off to her room. Water was brought for washing, and salve for healing. After Sadie had tended her cheek, she was then to rest and take tea with the nip of brandy that had been added to steady her nerves.

"What am I to do now?" Harriet paced around the room. Should she speak to her father? But what would she say? Sorry, I've been going out to all these places you don't know about, and now it seems someone from my past is following me due to Frankie's death. He'd never believe her, and she'd be locked in her room until she drew her last breath. Especially if her mother found out.

The life she'd carefully cultivated could come tumbling down.

The assault must have something to do with Frankie. So far there was Mr. Nightingale, Miss Haven's fiancé, Tapper, and Mr. Sydney who could be following her. But why? What had them worried enough to threaten her?

She was just contemplating changing into her nightdress when someone knocked on her door.

"Yes, what is it, Sadie?" she asked her maid.

"A young boy called Melvin has called at the servant's door, Miss Harry. He was most insistent he speak with you. Mrs. Dickens told him to leave, as you were unwell, but he got upset and said Anna from the orphanage is ill."

"Tell him I will be down in a matter of minutes please."

"I'm not sure you should do that, Miss Harry. Perhaps one of us could help him?"

"I appreciate your concern, but I will come and see Melvin, Sadie." The maid didn't look happy but left.

Harriet ran for her cloak. The thick, fur-lined one. Her gloves were the same, and then she stomped her feet back into her boots. Her body felt a great deal older than it had this morning. She had aches and pains that tomorrow would result in a great deal of stiffness, but right now she couldn't think about that. Stuffing her money and the twist of paper on her bedside table into the small bag she carried around her wrist, she ran from the room.

"There now, you eat this before you leave. It's a cold night for a wee lad to be running about in," Mrs. Dickens was saying when she arrived in the kitchen.

Melvin was standing by the door, eating a large slice of bread and jam.

"What has happened?" Harriet asked when she reached him.

"Your cheek, Miss Harry!"

"It's all right, Melvin. Tell me why you are here."

"It's Anna. She has a sore on her leg, and it's festered. She's hot and moaning, but no one is doing anything. I'm right worried she won't see out the night," he said, his narrow face pinched with worry. "She's breathing funny."

"How did you know where to find me, Melvin?"

The boy wore one of the knitted scarves she'd given him, and it was wound around his neck three times. Small, alert, and, like so many of the children in the Gail Lane orphanage, he was in need of more thick slices of bread and jam.

"Mrs. Secomb has a book. She keeps names and addresses in there."

"But you can't read, Melvin," Harriet said gently.

"Old Mr. Button can, and he's right worried for Anna, and the only nice person in that place. He got your address from that book."

"Right. Well, let's go then."

"But you can't go out there alone." Mrs. Dickens looked horrified. "Not in your condition and at this time of night. To an orphanage of all places!" Her words ended on a shriek.

"I'm fine. It is only a scratch to my cheek. I'll be back before my family," Harriet said calmly.

"Mr. Cuthbert will have something to say about that," Mrs. Dickens said. "You stay right here, and I'll fetch him."

"Go," Harriet whispered to Melvin when the cook disappeared. She nudged Melvin out the door before the cook and butler returned.

Why was her name in a book, and how had Mrs. Secomb known where she lived?

The only way could be if someone followed her. The

thought was not a happy one after what she'd endured tonight.

"Mr. Button said you'd know what to do, as you care for us," Melvin said.

"I do, very much," Harriet said, pushing the other thoughts away.

"I'm not rightly sure you should have come without your maid, Miss Harry. I think Mrs. Dickens is right there."

"And what do you know of needing maids, Melvin?" She looked at the serious little boy, who should be tucked up warm in bed with someone who cared for him, but instead lived in the Gail Lane orphanage.

"I know you live in a grand house and have plenty of staff. I know that Mrs. Secomb said your family are Yanks with more money than sense."

"Have you been listening to conversations again?" she said, wondering again how it was the matron of Gail Lane orphanage knew so much about her.

"I know that young ladies need maids for proper sakes. Old Mr. Button told me that."

People were fools if they thought children were not awake to what went on around them. They saw and heard much more than anyone knew.

"I don't need a maid, but thank you for your concern," she said gravely. Opening her reticule, she took out the bag of peppermint sticks she'd stuffed in there before sneaking out of the house. The boy's eyes went round as he took the treats she handed him.

"You've no notion of the bad people about, Miss Harry. You can't just be getting about London at night alone."

"Believe me, Melvin, I am very aware of the bad people, but as I'm in a hackney with you, I am safe."

His chest puffed out as he looked at her. "I won't let anything happen to you."

"I know that."

"What did happen to your face? It looks sore."

"I tripped and fell," Harriet lied.

"You need to take more care, Miss Harry."

"I'll try."

She watched him crunch on the sweet treats as she looked out the hackney window to the dark streets. The unease and tension inside her were a result of what had already happened tonight. Harriet did not want to believe she was any different from the woman she'd been before that man knocked her to the ground, but she'd be lying to herself.

She was scared now and hated that one man had given her that fear.

The streetlamps lit the way, but it was in the darkened corners and lanes that trouble would lurk for anyone in the wrong place. Harriet would ensure that would never be her again.

"And you say Anna is very warm and mumbling a lot, Melvin?"

The boy nodded. "I saw the wound before she got into her bed. It's festered."

"Why is no one helping her? Why hasn't it been cleaned, and a doctor called?"

"Matron looked at it yesterday. Poured something on it that made Anna scream, then wrapped a cloth around it. But it's got worse."

"And no one knows you slipped out to get me?"

The boy shook his head. "We always slip out. Besides, it's their meeting night. They don't let anyone stop that from happening, and we don't go to the building, or we get in trouble. Hamster did once, peeked inside, and got the birch."

It all sounded off to Harriet. "Surely someone is watching over you all?"

"They leave Melinda in charge on meeting nights, and she just tells us to shut up and go to sleep," Melvin said.

"It seems very late for a meeting, don't you think?" The clock in the kitchen had said it was 9:00 p.m. when she'd looked, which had been odd, because the day felt like it should be closer to midnight.

"I'm not sure how we will proceed once we reach the orphanage, Melvin, but I want to see Anna and will rouse someone to call a doctor if need be."

Harriet had passed the orphanage one day two years ago and found the children standing at the fence. Stopping to chat, she was soon inside and playing with them—much to the horror of the matron and staff who ran the place.

Since then she had visited each week. Harriet brought food when she could and had soon found women willing to knit for the children from her suffrage meetings. The staff might not like her visiting but knew the children did, and that she was doing what they could not be bothered to, so they relented and allowed her visits.

The matron, Mrs. Secomb, was a small, mean-eyed woman who stomped about the place saying it was her calling to cleanse the children of their bad habits so they might one day be fine upstanding citizens like her. Harriet despised her intensely. However, she was always scrupulously polite, so she didn't stop her visits.

When the hackney halted, she and Melvin climbed out, and Harriet managed to stifle the moan as her knees sent stabbing pains through her body.

"I will pay you to stay here," she said to the driver, wishing it was the man who had the gentle smile from earlier. This one had a hard look in his dark eyes. "I should not be long," Harriet added, handing over some coins. "I will give you more when I return."

"I'll be here" was all he said.

"That was a lot of money you gave him, Miss Harry," Melvin said as they walked up the narrow lane to the orphanage. "He's a mean one if you ask me."

"I want to make sure he stays, Melvin. I have no wish to walk home, and I may need to take Anna with me. Besides, we do not judge someone by the way he looks. He may be a very nice man." Harriet hoped she was right.

"I'm not rightly sure you can take Anna out of the orphanage," the boy said, looking worried.

"And yet you came to me, as you thought she wouldn't be alive in the morning. What is it you wanted me to do with that information?"

He thought about that as he crunched on another peppermint stick.

"I knew you'd know what to do," he said finally. "You always do when we ask you questions."

Why that made her want to weep she had no idea, but it was possibly to do with the fact she felt exhausted, and her body ached.

"Well then, how about we see how Anna is and then make a decision. I'm sure I'll think of something when I have a clearer idea of her condition. We now need to sneak inside before anyone sees me. Will that be possible, Melvin?"

"Yes, the doors are unlocked, and no one but us and old Mr. Button are inside, and he'll be sleeping by now."

And that was just wrong, she thought. The place was run in a shoddy manner, and since she'd been coming here, Harriet had wondered what to do about that. So far she'd come up with no ideas for change, as everything she put to Mrs. Secomb was ignored.

"No more crunching now, Melvin," Harriet whispered as they walked through the gates of the orphanage. The place was bleak during daylight hours, but in this light, it was worse.

The exterior walls she knew were once white were now a sooty gray. Faint light came from a window on the top floor, where the staff slept when they were in there and not in a meeting.

They took the stone path to the rear of the orphanage. It seemed very quiet considering there were many children inside those walls. And beyond Gail Lane, there were houses and carriages rolling through the London streets.

"Psst!"

"Don't you psst Miss Harry, Nigel," Melvin whispered loudly. "She's a bleedin' lady." A boy with the same look as Melvin stepped out of the shadows. "Are you snooping again?"

Nigel looked left and right, but as it was dark and he couldn't see that far, she wasn't sure what he was looking for.

"He's always slipping out to spy on things," Melvin said.

"And it's a good thing I do. Don't I always know what's happening before it does?" Nigel said, taking umbrage over Melvin's comments.

"Suppose you do," Melvin conceded.

"Mrs. Secomb has gone to a meeting at the other place, and Mr. Thomas and some of the others are here." Nigel pointed over his shoulder to a building at the rear of the property the orphanage sat on.

Harriet squinted and saw the small shaft of a light. She'd noticed the building before and simply thought it some kind of storage place for the orphanage.

"What did you hear?" Melvin asked, handing over one of his precious peppermint sticks as a peace offering to Nigel.

"There's bad skullduggery going on." Nigel pointed to the building again. "But we can't talk about it, as Janet never came back after she spied on them that night."

What?

Harriet looked to the moon, which was high in the sky. It

was said that a full moon turned people a bit odd sometimes. Was that what was happening today, and tomorrow she'd wake up and the world would be righted once more?

"I need to see Anna now, boys, but I wish to hear more about this missing child and the other business after." Harriet did not remember a Janet, so it must be before her time.

"We never saw her again. Told me she was going out to listen to their meeting and didn't return," Nigel said. "We think they saw her and killed her."

"You are not serious?" Harriet was shocked as they moved closer to the rear entrance of the orphanage.

"Tell her. Miss Harry won't speak to anyone about it, and it's time. They're threatening us and using some of the orphans to do things we don't want to because they know we got nowhere else to go," Melvin said. "She's a good one, and maybe she can help."

"It's dangerous," Nigel whispered. "I don't want to die."

"Tell me what you know, and I will decide what can be done, but I will not implicate either of you if the information you give me needs to be handed to the authorities."

Someone had threatened her tonight, and that should be her sole focus, but she couldn't walk away if these children needed her, as no one else seemed to care for them.

Puffs of white were coming from their mouths as the cold settled around them. Harriet wanted to stomp her feet to keep them warm, but as the boys did not seem similarly affected and were dressed in far less, she stayed still.

"They are thieving."

"What are they stealing?" Harriet asked when what she should be saying was, I don't want to know because right now I'm not entirely sure what is going on with my own life.

"All kinds of things, and they get some of the smaller children to do it for them. It's been going on for years. People tell them what they want, and they send us out to get it. We steal from all over London and sometimes take it to that other place. Them who are kin to Mrs. Secomb."

"What other place?"

"The academy for those young ladies."

The chill that ran through Harriet was not just from the cold.

"Which academy?"

"The Templar one. Him who runs it is Matron's brother."

CHAPTER THIRTEEN

"My nephews can fight each other, as both need venting before they take anyone else on. They can go first, and then I will fight you, Cam," Uncle Bram said.

"Gladly. After all, you have a few years on me. It should be an easy win," Cambridge said.

"Take your seats. It will be a good match," Uncle Bram said before turning to face Leo and Alex. Anger still smoldered in his eyes as it did in theirs. "It is done for now. I am proud of you both for coming here, and I'm sorry you faced Ellington, but more came out in support of you. Remember that and let go of the anger, nephews."

"You also, Uncle," Leo said, and Uncle Bram exhaled slowly. He gripped each of their shoulders before walking away.

"If I met that bastard in a dark alley—"

"Aye," Alex said, cutting Leo off. "The man is an eejit, as Mungo would have said."

Leo then did a series of lunges, swinging his arms.

"Are you so old now, brother, that you must loosen your

limbs like a peacock?" Alex taunted him as he swung his blade back and forth like a pendulum.

"Peacocks strut, and I am stretching. Please note the difference," Leo said as he dropped into a deep knee bend.

"I'll take the oldest," Alex heard Zach Deville say.

Looking to where the men all stood, he saw money was changing hands.

"He's got plenty of pent-up anger I'm thinking," Cambridge Sinclair agreed.

"My money is on Alex having fought him many times," Stephen said, pulling money out of his pocket.

"Can you believe we are back here, Leo?"

His brother, who was striding back and forth across the floor, stopped. "I find I am quite happy about that, Alex. Even considering Ellington."

"Me too." Alex smiled, surprised at just how much he meant that.

Their life was full now, and in so many ways far better than it once had been, but there were aspects of his old life he missed.

"Are you done playing the fool, Leo? I grow old waiting," Alex said.

"I am now limber enough to fence," his brother said. "And will take you apart."

"Did your knees just crack?" Alex taunted him.

While they debated and money changed hands, he and Leo circled each other.

"Remember to move your feet, Alex!"

"Yes, Uncle Bram."

"And focus, Leo. Do not let your mind wander."

"Yes, Uncle Bram."

Both smiled as the instructions came from their uncle. He had been fencing with them since they left society.

Alex lunged and Leo parried. He knew his brother's

moves as Leo knew his, and it felt good to be here doing this with him. A place that only a few months ago they would never have thought to return to.

"I say, Deville, are they sugarplums?" Alex heard Cambridge ask.

"How is it you can sniff out food, Sinclair?" Nathanial Deville said.

Soon Alex's shirt clung to him, and sweat dripped down his back. Neither he nor Leo were the soft noblemen they'd once been. Uncle Bram had made them strong with his insistence they learn to fight and trained them hard.

"Excellent riposte, young Nightingale!"

"Lunge, Seddon!"

Alex knew that everyone in the salon had now come to watch the spectacle, and he could see that Leo was equally as determined as he to win.

"I'm wondering if, in fact, we should have brought more food," Cambridge Sinclair said. "It could be a long night."

Leo's technique was different from Alex's. He was more aggressive, where Alex was technical. He bided his time, and when he saw the moment, he struck. Which he did now, and Leo cursed.

"You are both improving." Uncle Bram joined them. Both were bent, hauling in deep breaths. "And tonight, you were accepted again."

Alex looked at the men exchanging money. He wasn't sure he cared overly much anymore that he was accepted, but he knew it meant a great deal to his uncle.

"I will never walk in society again," Alex cautioned.

"Perhaps, but it is nice that if you wish to, you could," Uncle Bram said.

"I don't miss much of it." Leo mopped his forehead with his sleeve. "But this I missed. And some of my friends."

"You walked away from everyone; it is understandable you will miss some things."

"Bramstone, that man in the doorway is attempting to get your attention," Lord Sinclair said.

They looked and found Mungo. He was wearing his usual frown.

"If he's here, there's trouble," Uncle Bram said.

They hurried to the door and through it behind Mungo, who had disappeared as they saw him. They found him at the carriage.

"What has happened?" Leo asked.

"Mr. Peeky arrived at 11 Crabbett Close. He said his grandson is in trouble, and he's afeared that he'll not be alive by morning. The detective and Miss Ellen are awaiting you."

"Alex, what is your address? I will call to visit with you," Stephen said from behind him. After giving it, the Nightingales climbed into the carriage and were soon moving.

"Mr. Peeky does tend to panic when it comes to his family," Alex said.

"True, however, I doubt he'd involve us unless it was necessary," Leo added.

It did not take long to reach Crabbett Close. It was cold out, but that hadn't stopped a small gathering of neighbors waiting for them outside.

"Right, you'll all be quiet now," Ellen said. "Let Mr. Peeky explain the details to my uncle and brothers."

Everyone stopped talking.

"Joseph is my daughter Helen's youngest," Mr. Peeky said.

He was a tall man with stooped shoulders and a love of talking if you had the time. You never visited his house if you were in a hurry to go anywhere, as you didn't leave for at least an hour.

"He was a good lad until about four months ago. Got in with some boys who are stealing things. I don't know the details but seems like there's a few of them up to no good, and from what I hear, they are being controlled by adults."

"How is it no one comes to me with this information?" Gray asked. His wife shushed him.

"I got word from my Helen that her eldest boy, Johnny, came home and said Joseph no longer wanted to do what was asked of him, and now he's going to have to pay," Mr. Peeky said.

"How does Johnny know this?" Alex asked.

"He went to find Joseph when he didn't come home. Met up with some of the other boys in the gang, and they told him he was in trouble."

"So, he got cold feet at something they asked him to do, and now he's about to be punished?" Uncle Bram added.

"Aye, that's it," Mr. Peeky said. "My Helen is right fearful."

"Do you know where Joseph is?" Ellen asked.

"Gail Lane," Mr. Peeky said. "That's what them boys told my Johnny."

"Gail Lane," Leo repeated. "Why do I know that name?"

"There is an orphanage there," Gray said.

"That's the place," Mr. Peeky said.

"But why is your grandson there if he is not an orphan?" Gray asked.

Mr. Peeky looked at Gray like he had suddenly sprouted another head. "It's where some of them criminals go to lure them young'uns to work for them. The people who run that place are a smokey lot too."

"I should know that," Gray muttered. "Why has no one told me that?"

"Can we speak to Johnny?" Alex asked ignoring his muttering brother-in-law.

"He's at my house," Mr. Peeky said. "Mrs. Peeky is giving him a meal, as he was right starving after running here."

"The rest of you can head home now, and I'm sure there

will be an update in the morning of what has transpired this evening," Uncle Bram said loudly to the rest of the Crabbett Close residents.

There were a few grumbles, but they headed away to their beds. The Nightingales then made their way to number 2 Crabbett Close.

The street had an odd grouping of houses all circling a small park in the middle. It was a meeting place for residents, and events were often held there.

"Why are you and Gray here?" Alex asked Ellen. "Now you don't live with us, I thought you wouldn't be part of this."

He heard the hiss of angry breath his sister exhaled. It was never hard to draw one from her. Alex hid his smile.

"Just because I am no longer living here does not mean I have no wish to continue helping. As it happened, we were visiting with Aunt Ivy when Mr. Peeky called."

"It's very late to be visiting, don't you think?" Alex said.

"We were just about to leave actually," Gray said.

"But, of course, we stayed when I knew we were needed," Ellen said.

"I just bet Gray loves the fact you're out here and likely about to walk into danger," Leo added.

"I'm ecstatic as you can imagine," Gray drawled. "But my wife informed me she would go with or without me, so here I am. My hope is that no laws will be broken, as I have no wish for her to come to the attention of the authorities or for me to arrest anyone, because there will be questions I have no wish to answer."

"Of course we will all behave," Leo said, which had them all snorting.

"I mean it. I'm a bloody Detective. I will deal with this through the proper authorities if anything needs to be dealt with."

"Of course," Leo said. "You have our word."

"You'll forgive me if I don't believe you, because trouble does seem to follow anyone with the surname Nightingale," Gray muttered.

The Nightingales had learned to fight under the tutelage of their uncle, who had learned many different forms of combat on his world travels. He had decided that his nieces and nephews needed to learn how to defend themselves in every way possible and taught them what he knew. Now they were, for want of a better word, a vigilante group who helped people who needed them.

"I say, what has you all out here at this time?"

Gray moaned as Constable Plummy stepped into their path. Streetlights showed the biscuit clutched in his hand.

"Did you get that from the Varneys?" Ellen asked, looking at the house he'd clearly just left.

"Ah, Miss Varney had a small issue she wished my help with," he said quickly.

"I just bet she did," Leo said.

"I will be sure to tell Bud you are now getting your biscuits from the Varneys so she will not need to bake as many," Uncle Bram said.

The thud of feet had them all turning, and there was Mungo joining them after stabling the horses.

"Oh, there is no need for that. Miss Bud is unequalled in her baking, and I have no wish to upset her," the constable said quickly.

"Hello! What is going on? I have more biscuits would you need it."

"Run," Alex said as they found Tabitha Varney approaching.

"Can't stop, Miss Varney. We have official business. Plummy, you check the neighborhood is not under threat if you please," Gray said.

"Loath as I am to admit it, I think Gray may come in handy from time to time," Alex said to Leo.

"I live to serve you of course," Gray said.

They started walking again as Plummy hurried away to do what he was paid for, instead of visiting with Miss Varney.

Mr. Peeky collected Johnny when they arrived at his house. The boy looked nervous when faced with all of them.

"We mean you no harm, Johnny," Uncle Bram said. "We wish only to get Joseph back. You need to tell us everything you know to help us do that."

"Joseph has a friend, Toddy. He's an orphan. He works for these men, and they wanted to recruit more boys to steal for them. Joseph said he'd do it. I told him not to. I thought he'd listened until tonight."

"Not your fault, boy," Mr. Peeky said, putting a hand on his grandson's shoulder.

"And you believe the orphanage at Gail Lane is where your brother is?" Ellen asked.

"It is. Everyone knows what goes on there," Johnny said.

"Except me," Gray muttered.

"Carriage, Mungo," Uncle Bram said.

"I just put the bleeding thing away," the Scotsman muttered. But he started running back the way he came.

"There will be no rushing into things," Gray said.

"Of course," Uncle Bram agreed. "We always show restraint."

That was such a ridiculous statement they all started laughing, even Mr. Peeky.

CHAPTER FOURTEEN

Harriet couldn't believe what Nigel and Melvin had told her about the thieving and also the connection between the Templar Academy and the orphanage, through Matron and Mr. Templar. Plus, Harriet had seen Tapper and Mr. Sydney together.

What did this all mean if anything?

She couldn't think about that now.

"Nigel, I must see to Anna, as Melvin has said she is gravely ill." Harriet's voice was wobbly. Drawing in a shaky breath, she steadied herself. "But I wish to discuss what you have just talked about further sometime soon."

Life would have been a great deal easier if she had simply entered society, she thought as they climbed the steps to the solid wooden door. Or if, like her mother suspected, she read all day and went to the library.

"Nigel, you need to go to bed now," Harriet whispered. "No more snooping for tonight."

"I can't. I think they're up to something else. Not sure what's happening, but I heard the men talking about teaching someone a lesson. I need to watch in case it's one of us." He then slipped away before she could stop him.

"He'll be all right. No one ever sees him, and he'll come if there's trouble. He always gives us the heads-up. Now we needs to be quiet inside, Miss Harry."

"Need," she corrected.

She didn't see the boy's eye roll, but it was there. Harriet was always correcting their speech.

They entered through the door that led straight into a narrow hall and then climbed the stairs. It was as cold in here as outside. Quietly she followed Melvin to the top where they passed through another door.

One lamp lit the hallway up here, and she saw a long table lined with bonnets, caps, and gloves. Melvin then pushed open a door, and she followed him inside.

The sound of soft snuffles greeted them. Moving down the aisle created by rows of beds on either side, she kept close to Melvin. He stopped at the last bed closest to the window, and it was then she heard the weeping.

Harriet hurried to the little girl lying in the bed. She was rolling from side to side.

"Anna," Harriet whispered, bending over her. Tugging off her glove, she placed a hand on her forehead and instantly felt the fever burning there.

"H-help me," she whimpered.

"She's sick," the girl in the bed beside her said. "And keeping me awake."

"I'm going to help her now, Sally. You go back to sleep," Harriet soothed.

"Miss Harry, what are you doing here?"

She wasn't sure who it was but thought perhaps that voice had been Melinda's, as she was the most outspoken and seemed to be the head orphan, if there was such a thing.

"I was passing and popped in to see if you were all well,"

she improvised. Clearly not her best work, as the girl made a scoffing sound. "Go back to sleep."

She needed light to have a good look at Anna.

"We must take her out to the hall," she whispered to Melvin. Picking up the shivering child, Harriet then carried her from the room with her blankets still draped over her thin body.

"Move the things to one side on that table, Melvin," Harriet ordered the boy. He did as she asked, and she laid Anna on top. He then hurried to move the blankets and expose the bandaged leg. The cloth tied around the wound was dark with blood and ooze. Harriet bent to unwrap it, peeling it from the wound as Anna's head thrashed from side to side.

"Dear Lord," she whispered. A yellowish crust had formed around the injury, and poison was streaking up her leg in angry red lines. She would lose the leg if something was not done soon.

"I will have to take her with me, Melvin. This injury is grave and must be tended immediately. There is no time to waste."

"I don't want Anna to die, Miss Harry." Melvin's voice wobbled. "She's my friend."

"I will see she gets the help she needs," Harriet said. But she could promise no more, as she did not know what would happen to the child now, and that leg looked bad.

Picking up Anna, Harriet followed the boy back downstairs and had just stepped outside when she heard the thud of feet approaching. Before they could hide, a group of people appeared. Harriet could run fast, but she was now carrying a child.

"Miss Short?" A man stepped forward and moved to stand before her.

"M-Mr. Nightingale, why are you here?" Harriet stammered as relief coursed through her. Her bruised knees almost buckled as the fear she'd felt left her body.

"I believe that was to be my question," he said, looking at the child shivering in her arms and then back at Harriet. He leaned in closer, so his face was only inches from hers. "But a better one is what happened to your face?"

"She's saving Anna," Melvin said before Harriet could speak. "She's got a festered leg and fever, but no one would do anything about it. So, I sent word to Miss Harry."

"We will help her, Melvin. Have no fear. Perhaps you should return to your bed now," Harriet said.

Before she could move and walk around Mr. Nightingale, another man approached.

"Let me look at the bairn." He was huge—the biggest man Harriet had ever seen. She instinctively wanted to take a step back, but he was with Mr. Nightingale, so he would not harm the child.

How did she know that? Harriet rarely trusted people on such a short acquaintance, and yet, for some reason, she trusted him. Perhaps because of his connection to Frankie?

The big man smelled of woodsmoke as he bent over, his face close to Anna's. He placed a palm on the child's forehead.

"She's not breathing well," he said in a thick Scottish accent. "And her skin is on fire."

"Her leg. There is a sore, and it is infected," Harriet said.

"Give her to me." He took the child before she could say a word. "I will take her to the carriage and have a look."

"But—"

"Mungo will care for her. He is good with this kind of thing," Mr. Nightingale said.

"I don't know him," she whispered, watching the large back disappear. "I can't allow a stranger to take Anna—"

"I'll go with him," Melvin said, and before she could stop him, he'd run after the man.

"I will follow," Harriet said.

"Mungo is someone who has cared for me and my family for many years. The child will be safe. Now I have so many questions, I'm not entirely sure where to start, Miss Short, but first, what did you do to your face?" The fingers he touched to her damaged skin were butterfly soft and warm.

"I-I fell. Why are you here at the Gail Lane orphanage at this time of night, sir?" Harriet asked.

"Why are you?" He lowered his hand, and she missed his touch instantly.

Clearly, she was not herself.

"It is late, and you are alone, Miss Short. Care to tell me what the hell is going on?"

His voice was harder now, demanding an answer.

"Don't intimidate the poor woman," the lady standing behind him said. With her were Lord Seddon and two other men.

Suddenly a scream filled the air. It made the hair on the back of Harriet's neck rise.

"You gotta come!" Nigel appeared, running toward them. "They're hurting him!"

Harriet didn't hesitate; she ran in the direction of the scream.

"Stop at once!" She ignored Mr. Nightingale's roar. Someone was hurting a child, and she could not allow that. Would never allow it.

A large hand grabbed her shoulder, stopping her. "You will not run in there like the bloody cavalry!"

"Let me go. A child is in trouble!" She fought against him.

"Which is the reason we are here," he gritted out. "Return to your carriage at once, madam. We will deal with this; it is no place for you."

He nudged her back a step and then walked by with the others in his party. Lord Seddon smiled at her gently as he passed.

She needed to go to Anna, but if one of the orphans were hurt, she knew them and could help.

"Cor! He's an angry one, but I think he's the right of it. You shouldn't be here if there's trouble about to go down, Miss Harry," Nigel whispered, appearing at her side. "Come on, we need to hide." Harriet let him lead her to a pile of wood a small distance away. "Get down behind this, Miss Harry." He pulled her to a crouch, which sent shooting pains through her knees. "There's going to be trouble when they realize this lot are here, and we're a good enough distance away to watch it but not be seen."

"What are you talking about, Nigel?" Harriet whispered.

"Sssh," the boy hissed. "The door is opening, and them at the meeting are coming out."

"Who the bloody hell are you lot?" a man's voice roared into the night air.

Peering over the wood, Harriet could see a group of men walking from the building. Mr. Nightingale's party was standing in a wall facing them.

"Hand that boy to me," he said. "Now." His voice made her shiver. It was hard enough to cut glass.

"Is he from the orphanage?" Harriet whispered.

"No. Never seen him before," Nigel said.

Harriet crawled to the right to get a better look. She saw a child standing beside one of the men, a large hand gripping his shoulder.

"That boy was being disciplined in there for not stealing what they asked him to is my guess," Nigel said.

"We've come for Joseph and are not leaving without him," one of the men with Mr. Nightingale said. "I also want to know why you think it's acceptable to mistreat a child."

"They'll be scared," Nigel whispered. "They've been hiding what they do for years. If them nobles expose them, they won't be happy."

"How do you know they're nobles?" Harriet asked, nodding to where Mr. Nightingale stood.

"They got the look, and then there's the snooty way they talk like you, except you got that other thing," Nigel said.

"Thing?" Harriet whispered, keeping her eyes on the scene playing out before her.

"The American thing."

"Give us the boy," Lord Seddon demanded.

"Or what?" someone replied.

"Or I'll arrest you," another of the men with Mr. Nightingale said.

Harriet watched as Mr. Nightingale looked around him as if he was searching for something. His eyes landed on the wood she hid behind. She dragged Nigel out of sight with her.

"That look was a mean one." Nigel sounded impressed. "I hope he punches Mr. Thomas. We hate him."

Harriet hoped so too; she'd never liked the man when she came to visit the orphanage. He was always rude to her. Rising again, she tried to identify the men. Mr. Thomas was the only one she recognized.

"Give us the boy now," another in the Nightingale group demanded. "You'll need all your men to defend yourself, and even then, you won't win."

"You don't scare us. We work for a living, unlike you toffs," Mr. Thomas said.

"Yes, I can see how you work for your living," Mr. Nightingale said. "By hurting children, and from the reports we've had, stealing."

"Which I will be following up on," the one who'd spoken about arresting them said.

"Oooh, look at Mr. Thomas's face. He's scared now," Nigel hissed with glee.

He was right; he did look fearful.

"What the hell are you doing on private property? Leave now," another man said. "This is none of your business."

"His name's Joe Clancy," Nigel whispered. "He's a nasty one too."

"We came for the boy. His family alerted us where he would be," Mr. Nightingale said in a hard voice. "Release him now."

The man who held the boy shook him like a piece of cloth. The child raised his head, and Harriet saw blood dripping from his nose.

Mr. Nightingale moved fast and was before the man in seconds. Drawing back his fist, he slammed it into his face before anyone realized what he was about. The boy fell forward when the man stumbled back clutching his nose. Mr. Nightingale caught the child and brought him to where she stood.

"Seeing as you can't obey orders, take care of the boy, but stay back." He growled the words at her. Harriet rose and took the child, pulling him quickly down beside her.

"In my pocket there is a handkerchief. Left side of my cloak, Nigel. Retrieve it please." He did as she asked, and she pressed it to the boy's nose.

"It's all right now. No one will harm you again," she vowed, needing to reassure him in that moment. He rested under her arm, his face pressed to her side.

She could do little for him but offer comfort, and that she would do. Harriet raised the edges of her cloak and wrapped them around the shivering boy.

A loud grunt had her looking to the people before her again. They were fighting each other. Harriet watched in awe as the woman pulled out an umbrella and wielded it like a sword.

"Wow," Nigel whispered as she did a series of maneuvers and then jabbed one of the men in the stomach, sending him to the floor.

"Oh, I say, that was excellent," Harriet whispered.

"Blimey, I ain't never seen anyone fight like them," Nigel said.

Mr. Nightingale now had two sticks in his hands, which she hadn't seen until that moment. They were attached by a rope. He was moving them about with amazing speed that seemed to be frustrating his opponent, who lashed out with a fist.

"Duck," Nigel encouraged, but it was not required, as Mr. Nightingale blocked the move with a stick. He jabbed and kicked out with a foot, and his opponent dropped like a stone to the floor at his feet.

Lord Seddon was swinging his cane about and felling men also.

The fight did not last long, and the Nightingale party were soon the only ones left, as the other men had fled into the night. Harriet struggled to her feet and then helped the boy to his as Mr. Nightingale headed her way. Nigel, she noted, was now pressed to her other side.

"You must leave at once, Miss Short," Mr. Nightingale demanded, "but when you call at 11 Crabbett Close, there will be much for us to discuss."

He was close enough now that she could see the dark expression on his face. Anger poured off him in waves.

"Hello, Miss Short, lovely to see you again so soon after the meeting," Lord Seddon said, joining his brother. He then reached for the hurt boy, putting an arm around his shoulders to support him.

"Now is not the time for civilities, Leo," Mr. Nightingale snapped.

"There is always time for civilities. There now, Joseph, all is well. We will have you home to your family soon."

"Do either you or the boy know what is going on here, Miss Short?" Mr. Nightingale demanded.

"Adjust your tone, Alex. I doubt very much if Miss Short is the villain here," Lord Seddon said.

"She shouldn't be here!"

"Perhaps, but now is not the time for this conversation. The injured children need tending, and Miss Short, may I suggest you get that nasty cut on your cheek seen to also when you get home, which should be sooner rather than later," Lord Seddon added.

"I will," she said to his back as he walked away with the boy.

"Nigel, make haste to find your bed, please," Harriet said quickly. "But don't let anyone see you."

"I know things," he said.

"What things, boy?" Mr. Nightingale demanded.

"About what goes on around here."

"Then you must speak with my brother-in-law, he is a Detective at Scotland Yard, and will be looking into this evening's events.

"I will find out what he knows, and pass the information on to you," Harriet said quickly. "You need to get to bed now, Nigel." He would not be safe until he was back inside the orphanage. Melvin too. In fact, she wasn't sure they'd be safe even then, considering what she'd learned tonight.

"Good night, Miss Harry." She watched him scamper off. Harriet was about to leave too when a large hand wrapped around her wrist.

CHAPTER FIFTEEN

"Are you mad?" Alex said as he towed her in the direction his family had taken, and where Anna hopefully waited with a large man called Mungo. "What possessed you to be here at such an hour?"

Alex had not believed his eyes when he'd seen Miss Short with that child in her arms and her swollen cheek. He'd felt a burst of rage that someone might have hurt her.

"I-I spend time here often with the children and—"

"Not at this hour, I'm sure." He didn't seem capable of speaking in a calm tone.

"No, but one of the children called at my house to tell me Anna was unwell, and no one was tending her. I came as soon as I could," she said in a haughty tone that he guessed was meant to put him in his place. It failed.

If they hadn't arrived, she would have been here with two boys and those men in that building not far from her. Anything could have happened, and who would have known?

"It would be reckless and foolhardy for anyone to come here alone, but you, a lady, doubly so," Alex snapped.

"I am more than capable of looking after my-myself." Her voice wobbled, which told him the words had been a lie. "Unhand me if you please, sir. Your legs are a great deal longer than mine, and I am struggling to keep up."

"Are you limping?" He slowed his pace slightly but did not release her.

"No." Alex was sure she was lying.

"Why did you not bring someone with you?"

"Who, pray tell?" she snapped. "Clearly I am here without anyone's knowledge. Had I alerted someone, they would have felt as you do and likely stopped me from coming."

"Then at least you know some rational-minded people, madam."

"I am entirely rational. My actions are no concern of yours."

"Your actions suggest no one in your family is keeping a close eye on you, or they are far too liberal minded considering what I have seen you doing since our very brief acquaintance began."

The breath hissed from her throat. "My family is no concern of yours."

"Because they have no idea what you are about, I suspect," Alex said.

"They would not understand," she added in that snooty tone.

"How many of you are there?" Alex asked because the woman intrigued him. Even if the temperature was close to freezing and he was tired and hungry, he wanted to know about her. The anger still lingered too, for what those men had done to the boy, and why Miss Short had taken such a foolish risk coming here.

"What bearing has that on anything?"

"Nothing at all, just curiosity. But I will hold all further questions until you call at Crabbett Close."

"I'm not sure—"

"Yes, you will call, as I believe there is a great deal more afoot than either of us know, and my brother-in-law will want all the details you have. My advice to you, Miss Short, is to order your thoughts, as we will have much to discuss, including Frankie."

"We?"

"As I have already stated, Gray, my brother-in-law, is a detective at Scotland Yard."

That silenced her, but he doubted it would for long. "Your grandfather is showing me an apple tree, Miss Short. Care to tell me why?"

He looked down at her when she did not speak, but her bottom lip was now firmly clamped between her teeth, and her face slightly averted from him.

"I'm sorry if that upset you."

"M-my grandfather used to make me stand under the apple tree when I was naughty. It was his form of punishment."

"Ah, well then it all makes sense, as on your current record, I should imagine you were a challenging child."

"I was not!"

"Is that your hackney next to our carriage?" he asked.

"It is, and now I must see to Anna."

"Did you abduct that child from the orphanage, Miss Short?"

"No... well, yes, actually, but only because she is extremely unwell."

"And where were you taking her?" Alex asked, looking down at her, taking in her damaged cheek. She said she fell. *Was that the truth?*

"Well, as to that, I'm not entirely sure, but I will find someone to care for her."

She pulled away from him as they reached his carriage

and the rest of his family. Leo and Ellen were inside with Mungo, looking after the injured children.

"How is Anna, Melvin?" Miss Short asked the boy who stood outside wide-eyed, watching everything.

"She needs a doctor and fast. I fear she will lose the leg if the infection is not removed soon!" Mungo barked from inside. "She's not woken once and in a fever."

If he was a betting man, which he definitely was not considering his father's gambling habits had brought his family to their knees, Alex would say no one knew where Miss Short was, and that she was used to doing what she wanted without being questioned.

"Please bring the child to the hackney, Mr. Nightingale. I will find a doctor to—"

"I know someone who can care for her. Tell me her situation," Alex interrupted her.

"Oh, I couldn't. She doesn't know you." She turned those amazing eyes on him.

"She's unconscious with pain, and I can get her help fast. Can you?"

She looked ready to argue but then shook her head.

"I promise my family will make sure she is well tended. Now come to your hackney, Miss Short, and home with you." He pulled her with him to the waiting hackney.

"Wait!"

"What?" Alex demanded.

"Release me," she hissed. Reluctantly he did so. He then watched her go to the boy.

"Melvin, go back to the orphanage, but be alert, as I don't want anyone to see you."

"He will make his way back inside undetected. Won't you, boy?" Alex asked him. The child nodded and then disappeared into the dark as the other child had minutes before.

"Had anyone seen you, it would be abduction, Miss

Short," Alex said as he led her to the waiting hackney. It didn't sit well with him to put her inside and send her home alone, but he doubted she'd make it easy for him to accompany her.

"That place is not fit to house the children in it. No one cares for them, so I do. And I will steal a child from her bed if she needs it." She glared up at him.

"Very commendable and also reckless, but I promise the child will be well tended, and if you furnish me with your address, I will send word to you with details on her condition."

"I will call at your address tomorrow, Mr. Nightingale, as we originally planned."

"Very well," Alex said, knowing she did not want to furnish him with her address. "I'm not sure what is going on, as your friend Frankie is still hounding my thoughts."

"She was like that in life," Miss Short said softly. "I will call at 2:00 p.m. if that suits you, Mr. Nightingale?"

"Yes, that will be fine. I will see you home," he added, making the decision.

"What? Absolutely not."

"It's dangerous."

"I am more than capable of traveling across London in a carriage, sir." She opened the hackney and prepared to climb inside, but he beat her to that and picked her up. Stepping into the carriage, he lowered her onto the seat. Bracing his hands on the seat beside her, his face was now close enough that he could see her eyes.

"It is after midnight; you are a beautiful woman alone. It is not safe."

"I—Please move back."

"What happened to your face?" Alex had seen her at the meeting earlier. She'd not been injured then.

"I fell." Her eyes moved slightly.

"I don't think you're telling me the truth, Miss Short." He didn't seem capable of moving away from her.

The small sob surprised him. "Pl-please, I just want to go home, Mr. Nightingale. It has been a trying night."

"Did someone do this to you?" She didn't answer his question, but he read it in her eyes. "Who?" he demanded.

"Alex, we need to get this child medical help!" Leo's voice reached him.

"Go... please go. I shall not leave the hackney until I reach my doorstep. I promise." Her hand touched his chest fleetingly and then dropped back to her lap.

He had no idea why he did it, but in that moment, he had no strength to deny the need inside him. His lips brushed hers softly, and then he climbed from the carriage.

"Tomorrow at 2:00 p.m., Miss Short. Be there, or I will come looking for you." Alex shut the door.

"See that you take her directly home and watch as she enters her house," he said to the driver after handing him money. He fought with the need to question what address the man would take her to. Alex would get that from her tomorrow.

"I will, sir. Thank you." He stepped back, and the hackney rolled away.

There was a mystery around Miss Harriet Short, and Alex found he wanted to know what it was. Someone had hurt her tonight. He wanted the name of that person, and that, too, he would get tomorrow. But right now, he needed to get Joseph home and help for the poor child Miss Short had rescued.

"Come into the carriage. We will get these children the care they need," Ellen said to him as he returned to his family.

He climbed in with Leo, Gray, Ellen, Joseph, and the girl. Uncle Bram was seated up beside Mungo now.

"The lad is bruised and beaten, but I don't think anything is broken," Gray said. "The little girl is in a worse state."

They'd turned up the lamps, and now Alex could see the sheen of feverish sweat on her forehead.

"It's all right," he said as she opened her eyes to narrow slits. "I am Alex, and a friend of your Miss Harry. She asked me to help you."

Her eyes closed again on that, which he hoped meant she felt safe with him. But then, why would she? The child lived in an orphanage that, by the sounds of it, was run terribly, and the children neglected, which he knew was often the case.

"Something is not right about that place," Gray said. "What was going on tonight? We need to speak with Joseph about what happened when he is feeling stronger."

"Miss Short has some answers I believe. She is coming to Crabbett Close tomorrow, and we will get them from her and discuss her friend who loves lemons."

"I will be there," Gray said. "I have a feeling we are about to uncover something distasteful, and my instincts are rarely wrong."

Alex agreed, but he sat back and thought about Miss Short for the remainder of the journey to Crabbett Close.

When they arrived at number 2, Gray and Ellen took Joseph inside while the carriage continued to the Nightingale home.

"I'll get Ivy," Uncle Bram said as he climbed down from the driver's seat. "I'll send Jack out to put the carriage away, Mungo. Then you rouse Bud."

They all moved at once, and Alex followed Leo up the stairs to the bedroom that was no longer inhabited by Ellen. He lowered Anna onto the mattress. The girl's eyes flew open as he released her and locked on his.

"'Tis all right," he said, crouching beside the bed so their eyes were level. "We are going to make you feel better." He touched her shoulder gently. Her hand grabbed his. The chilled fingers wrapped around three of his and held them in a tight grip.

"Hello, Anna. I am Leo." Alex felt a hand settle on his shoulder as his brother leaned closer so the child could see him. "Will you let us help you?"

She was shivering from the fever but managed a nod.

"It's cold in here," Gray said, arriving. "I will light the fire."

Uncle Bram appeared next with Aunt Ivy in her dressing gown. They took the opposite side of the bed.

"Anna, all my family is here to look over you. This is my aunt and uncle, and Gray is tending to the fire," Alex said as he stroked his free hand over her clammy forehead. "They are good people."

Her eyes went from him to the others, slowly circling the room.

"Bud is bringing supplies," Mungo said. "I have blankets." He placed them at the foot of the bed, and Anna's eyes widened as she took him in. "I'll get some lamps set up, and I've sent for Mr. Greedy."

"Yes, he will know what to do," Alex said. The elderly man had many potions and cures for just about anything.

"How is she?" Ellen appeared next. "I doubt we can rouse a doctor at this hour, so I've sent a note to Essex Sinclair. If it is possible, she will come at once."

Aunt Ivy covered the little girl with blankets as Bud brought in a steaming bowl of water.

"Now, Anna, we need to have a look at the wound on your leg," Aunt Ivy said. "You just squeeze Alex's hand if you need to."

"What's going on?"

Alex turned to find the youngest Nightingale sibling in the doorway. Matilda wore her white nightdress and a thick blue shawl around her shoulders. Her dark hair was in a long braid. His sweet little sister was growing up, he thought looking at her.

"This is Anna, Matilda. She has injured herself, and we are going to help her." He held out a hand. She came to his side slowly and took it. "Anna, this is my youngest sister, Matilda."

"Is she very sick, Alex?"

"We are not sure yet, but perhaps you could stand here and talk with her while we have a look at her injury."

Alex rose and eased his hand from the grip Anna had on his fingers. "Hold her hand, Matilda."

She moved to the side of the bed and took Anna's fingers. The two girls then stared at each other.

"I have a dog called Chester," Matilda began.

Aunt Ivy raised the blanket and the hem of Anna's thin nightdress. Alex kept his expression clear as did the others when they saw the festering wound.

"I can't imagine the pain she's in," Gray said softly.

"I fear the infection is spreading," Aunt Ivy said. "Bram, get the bottle of laudanum. The cleaning will be painful for her."

His uncle ran out the door.

"Well now, here I am." Alex watched Mr. Greedy stomp into the room with his cane in one hand and a large leather satchel slung over one hunched shoulder. Like the other residents in Crabbett Close, Alex had no idea of his age, only that his hair was snow white and his shoulders stooped. He'd been treating the residents for years.

"It's all right now, Anna," Alex said, stroking the girl's damp hair back from her face. "Mr. Greedy is going to help you."

Over the next hour, he held the child as she writhed in agony while they cleansed the wound of all the poison.

Finally, when she slumped unconscious to the bed, he was able to take a deep breath.

"It will be easier on her now," Ellen said from the other side of the bed.

Looking down at the child, he thought that Miss Short's actions tonight, reckless though they were, had saved Anna's life.

"I came as fast as I could." Essex Huntington ran in the door. Behind her followed her large, powerful husband, Max. A man of few words, but when he spoke, people tended to listen.

She was soon talking with Mr. Greedy about how to treat the child, and Max was lured away with offers of brandy. Alex stayed with the child, as they'd sent Matilda to bed.

Finally, when they were finished, Anna seemed to sleep deeply with whatever Essie had given her. Bud was happy to watch the child for a while to ensure she did not wake.

After thanking Mr. Greedy, Essie, and Max, they left for their homes. Alex said good night to his family and fell into bed, exhausted. His last thought was that he was looking forward very much to seeing Miss Short again tomorrow. Closing his eyes, he fell asleep with the feel of her soft lips against his.

CHAPTER SIXTEEN

Harriet had woken the morning following the day she was sure she'd never forget with a stuffy head and sore body. After lying in her bed going over everything that happened yesterday and still not quite believing it, she rose feeling like a piece of chewed straw.

Dressing was a slow process that eventually, breathless, she had achieved with a lot of grunts and moans. Sadie told her she was to appear downstairs to eat her morning meal with her family. Harriet had thought about refusing but then dutifully appeared at the table for breakfast.

She wanted to leave the house later, so she would need permission to do that. If she stayed in bed, she could not get it.

Her family's shocked faces told her just how bad she looked. After explaining she'd fallen down the stairs, Heloise Shaw, in a rare burst of maternal concern, had directed her back to her room. Harriet's protests that she was quite well had fallen on deaf ears, and to bed she had gone, where she had stayed for two days.

Lying there while being force-fed broth and invalid food

had allowed her too much time to think, which was not at all welcome. She'd worried over Anna and who was following her and why. She'd also dreamt about Frankie and the night she'd found her floating in the river behind the Templar Academy. Harriet wasn't sure what her next step should be, if any, but believed meeting with Mr. Nightingale would be a start. His brother-in-law was a detective at Scotland Yard, and he might be able to help her.

Clearly she would need to tell them everything that was going on with her, and the truth. The thought made her nervous, but she also knew that whatever this was, she could not deal with it alone.

She'd also thought endlessly about that kiss. Mr. Nightingale's lips touched hers for no more than a second, possibly two, and likely had meant nothing to him. It most certainly had meant something to Harriet. Every time she remembered that moment, she smiled. A soft, dreamy one because she'd checked in her mirror.

Harriet should be furious at the liberty he had taken; unfortunately she had yet to find that emotion.

She had sent him a note explaining why she could not make the appointment at 11 Crabbett Close. She had also asked after Anna. Sadie had handed it to Percy who would wait for a reply. It had come two hours later.

M*iss* H*arry*,

I am *sorry to hear you are unwell, which Percy assures me you are, and this is not a tactic to avoid further contact with me.*

Anna's infection has been treated, and we are hopeful of a full recovery. She is now resting comfortably. As for her circumstances, she cannot go back to the orphanage in her current state, and we will discuss what is to be done when we meet. She is safe here for now, so rest easy.

It's my hope you will be able to leave your sickbed soon to resume your reckless and foolhardy midnight adventures and once again march for the rights of women.

Strength will win out. Determination will succeed.

Yours, *Alexander Nightingale*

Harriet had reread the note several times. She could concede to being reckless and foolhardy going into the narrow opening to search for that man, but she would never regret rescuing Anna. Tucking the note into the box she kept under her bed, she'd tried to work out what her next action should be. If that man was still following her, what would she do?

She'd fallen asleep thinking about her dilemma and slept the entire day and night away and much of the following.

The second day had her feeling marginally better, and she'd dashed off another note for Percy to deliver to Mr. Nightingale. The reply had said:

Miss Harry,

Percy has assured *me your illness is not grave, and you will live to partake in more reckless escapades. He really is a wonderful font of information and quite willing to discuss your inability to see that a woman, alone, should not jaunt about London, especially in the middle of the night to areas frequented by those with nefarious intentions. According to Percy, you have a willful nature. Imagine my shock!*

As for Anna, she is doing exceptionally well with that resilience children often have. My younger siblings have been keeping her company, and she told me to thank you for rescuing her, even if you put your life in danger to do so.

Strength will win out. Determination will succeed.

Yours, Alexander Nightingale

Harriet, believing she was neither reckless nor willful, had felt her anger rise at his unjust accusations and wrote a reply.

Mr. Nightingale,

Thank you. I am recovering and have hopes to visit you tomorrow at 2:00 p.m. if that would suit?

I am grateful to you and your family for caring for Anna and relieved she is recovering. During our visit, we will discuss options for her future.

As to your claims of my willful and reckless nature, I can assure you they are false, and your defamation of my character is unjust, as you know little about me, and I will add that if I were Mr. Short instead of Miss Short, you would not even question my actions.

Sincerely, Miss Short

. . .

She had not expected a reply, but one arrived later that day, delivered to her by Sadie, who said Percy had told her that Mr. Nightingale was a top-notch gentleman, as is Mungo, and that someone called Bud makes the best treacle cake he's ever tasted.

She had no idea who Bud was, but Mungo was the large fierce man who had cared for Anna.

Miss Harry,

Had any of my brothers or sisters undertaken such reckless acts as you have, alone, I assure you my opinion would have been equally as harsh. But I have written this in a stern voice: a woman does not have the strength of a man, and nothing you can say to the contrary will convince me otherwise. A man may fight his attacker and win; I doubt the same could be said for most women. Mavis Johns, of course, is more than capable of looking after herself, as we both know, and is the exception.

I look forward to debating the matter further with you tomorrow.

Yours, Alexander Nightingale

Harriet had come to the conclusion the man was extremely vexing, and she had no doubt that he liked to have the last word in most things, as was evidenced by that final note. Everything in her had wanted to reply, but she would not stoop to his level. It was a Herculean effort.

CHAPTER SEVENTEEN

After two days in bed, she woke feeling a great deal better and determined to carry on with her life as it had been. Harriet would show more caution of course. Clearly she could not get about alone in the dark—in fact, at any time if she was being followed. But she would not let whoever had pushed her to the ground intimidate her.

A tap on her door had her rising. Walking slowly as her sore muscles tugged at her, she opened it. Sadie stood there.

"Mrs. Shaw would like you to come down to the parlor this morning, Miss Shaw," Sadie said with her arms full of dress. "She said at once."

"Why are you carrying that?" Harriet asked.

"She wants you to wear it."

"It's not mine."

"She had it made for you. Now, there is not a moment to lose according to Cuthbert," Sadie added, waving Harriet back into the room, waggling the fingers poking out beneath the rose fabric. "Come, we must get you dressed."

"But why? Mother could come here if she needs to speak with me."

"It's not my place to question, just get you ready, and it will be nice to do so and have you looking like a lady finally."

"I don't want to dress like a lady, as I have nowhere to go," Harriet protested.

Sadie ignored her. A bath was brought in, and Harriet forced into it. If she was honest, she did not put up a great fight, as it was wonderful on her sore muscles. She then dried herself, and Sadie threw a clean chemise over her head, followed by the rose dress.

It fell from a satin bow beneath her breasts to the floor in soft folds. The sleeves were long and fitted, and as far as day dresses went, it was lovely, and nothing like she usually wore. Harriet was suddenly extremely nervous.

"What's going on, Sadie?"

"Oh, now look at you," her maid said, ignoring the question. "You should be wearing dresses like this more often. Sit, and I will style your hair."

"I don't want my hair styled; I like the bun at the back of my head."

A hand nudged her down into a chair before the mirror, which allowed her to see the dark bruise on her cheek and her pallor.

"Just a bun, Sadie," Harriet repeated. Her maid made a sound she couldn't understand.

The end result was a bun, but there were also curls on either side of her face and a matching ribbon tied in a bow on the side of her head. Harriet's stomach clenched. Something was afoot.

"Lovely," Sadie said when she was finished. "Off you go now."

"To take tea with my mother you had to dress me like this?" Harriet asked.

"Off with you now," her maid said, opening the door. "Your mother is waiting."

She was reluctant to go but knew her mother would come and get her when she failed to arrive. What she didn't know was why.

Entering her mother's favorite parlor minutes later after a slow walk downstairs, Harriet found her with two guests.

"Here she is, my darling daughter. She had a terrible fall, you understand, but is recovering with our care. Come, Harriet, and meet Lady Smitherton Howard and her dear son, Lord Talbot."

She didn't react to seeing her mother had company; Harriet had learned long ago how to hide what she was thinking.

"Her poor cheek is quite bruised," her mother cooed. Heloise Shaw was using her society voice, and Harriet fought the urge to turn and run from the room.

The man gave her a tight smile and looked as comfortable as Harriet felt. He bowed; she curtsied, her knees sending stabbing pains through her body.

"Please sit, everyone," her mother said. "Harriet, you here," she said, waving to a seat. The others all retook theirs.

What was going on?

Cuthbert brought a tea tray and avoided her eyes, which told her something was definitely afoot.

"Would you like a piece of cake, Harriet?"

"No, thank you, Mother."

"My eldest daughter is quite accomplished at painting, you know," her mother said from the seat beside her, where she was placing cake on small gold-rimmed plates.

"Hand this tea to Lord Talbot, Harriet."

Heloise Shaw was dressed elegantly and wearing what she called her occasional pearls, which Harriet thought silly. Most things were worn occasionally after all.

She took her mother's favorite teacup in deep blue with a gold handle and handed it to the man, wondering why her mother couldn't, as she was closer and pouring the tea. Granted, he was between Harriet and her mother, and close enough that his chair almost brushed the arm of hers, which was odd, as she'd thought that chair some distance away yesterday. But still her mother was closer.

"My daughter is quite the wonderful hostess," her mother said to Lady Smitherton Howard.

As far as whopping untruths went, this was a good one. Harriet did not take tea with anyone but family, nor did she ever play hostess. That role was solely Heloise Shaw's.

"Well now, isn't that wonderful to hear, Bertram?" Lady Smitherton Howard said, smiling at her son, who looked like last night's fish was not sitting well in his belly.

Dressed in thick forest-green brocade, Lady Smitherton Howard looked imperious like her mother, and there was every chance, also like Heloise Shaw, that she was strong-willed, determined, and used to getting her own way. Perhaps it was unjust to have this opinion on such short acquaintance, but she was an astute judge of character.

"Your poor cheek, my dear. It must hurt terribly."

"Thank you, it is much better now," Harriet said.

"Your daughter has rather unusual eyes, Heloise." Lady Smitherton Howard peered at Harriet like she was a specimen to be viewed.

Heloise trilled out a fake laugh. "Aren't they simply darling eyes? She is a rare gem, our Harriet. An original, some would say."

Some might say that; however, her mother had never been one of them, Harriet thought. She loathed her daughter's less than perfect eyes, as they were a reflection on her. Plus, there was the small matter of her disgrace at the Templar Academy and resulting gossip.

Her mind wandered as the two women started chatting

about people she did not know and never wanted to while their children sat in uncomfortable silence, forced to listen.

"The decor in this room, Mrs. Shaw, is really quite something," Lady Smitherton Howard cooed. She then raised her teacup, little finger aloft, and sipped.

"Thank you. Harriet, of course, had much to say when choosing the decorations in here," her mother said, which drew a look from Harriet.

Another lie. What was her mother's game, and why did the sinking feeling in her belly tell her she did not want to play it?

"The wainscoting," Lady Smitherton Howard said. "It's simply delicious."

Harriet thought delicious was a term used for things like almond slice and coconut tartlets. Not the pale lemon decorative wood paneling her mother had put in here.

It was a nice room considering some of the hideous and yet highly fashionable decor on display in other areas in the house she supposed. The rugs were patterned in black and gold, and the window wide enough to let in lots of light. The walls had two large gilt-framed paintings on display. Her mother liked people who came here to see she had the wealth to own expensive artwork and furnishings.

The chair Harriet sat on was inspired by her mother's love of all things Egyptian. Low at the back, which forced her to sit very straight, it was extremely uncomfortable and embroidered with ancient Egyptian symbols. She was currently leaning to the right on the scarab beetle, a species of dung beetle that symbolized resurrection and regeneration, to avoid Lord Talbot, because she'd added one plus one and come up with the fact her mother, for some reason, was pushing her at him.

"Perhaps you and dear, sweet Miss Shaw could go driving in the park soon, Bertram?" Lady Smitherton Howard said.

Her son looked like he'd rather have a tooth extracted without the benefit of whisky to numb the pain like her father had two months ago.

"I'm sure Lord Talbot has more than enough to occupy his time that he has no wish to take me driving."

The man shot her a look, clearly surprised by her words. Harriet sighed silently. Here was yet another man who thought all a woman wanted in life was to garner the attentions of a man, which would eventually lead to a proposal.

"Nonsense." His mother brushed aside her words. "He would love to take you driving."

She caught Bertram's eyes and shook her head slightly. He nodded, just a small gesture, but she saw it.

"Harriet, take Lord Talbot to the conservatory and show him your petunias," her mother said.

"They are not—"

"Now!"

Bertram rose and held out a hand. Harriet took it and let him lead her from the room and away from the two smiling, conspiring women.

"It will be frigid in the conservatory," Harriet felt she needed to say.

"We shall keep moving" was his brusque reply.

"But not too fast," Harriet added.

"Forgive me, I see you are sore. Perhaps we should find a place to sit."

"I'm quite well. I am simply a bit stiff."

The conservatory was a long, narrow room off the end of the hallway on the lower level. It was her mother's pride and joy, and contrary to what she'd just said, it was she who nurtured the petunias, as Harriet could kill a weed.

"I would like to speak frankly if I may, Lord Talbot?" Harriet said when the door was partially closed and they'd moved deeper into the room. Color, greenery, and the earthy scents of being outside but not quite outside filled the air.

"Please do, Miss Shaw."

Removing her hand from his arm, she faced him. "It seems our parents are conspiring to throw us together." There was no point in dancing around the matter when it was such a serious one. "I have no wish to offend you, sir, but neither do I have a wish to marry you."

"Thank God." The words came out followed by a large exhale. "My bloody meddling mother," he added.

"Agreed, and I'm not sure why now she wants me to wed, but there you have it. I have never understood how her mind works. It's not like she doesn't have two other children who actually want to fall in with her wishes of connubial bliss to titled spouses," Harriet muttered.

"I'll be blunt, Miss Shaw—"

"Call me Harriet."

"I'm Bertie, which I honestly loathe, but there you have it." He shrugged. "Anyway, I have no wish to wed either. I have given my heart to another who my family does not see as a suitable connection and so are thrusting other women at me."

"She must be desperate if she's thinking I'd be suitable," Harriet said.

He barked out a laugh at that. "She did say on the way over that I was not to believe a word about anything I'd heard in connection with you."

"I don't walk in society, and there is something murky in my past." She waved his enquiry away. "I did not run away to get married. It was nothing like that, but my point is I would not be a very comfortable wife for anyone."

"My Amelia is the daughter of a shopkeeper," Bertie said softly.

"Well then," Harriet said, the romantic inside her rising. "You must do something about that."

"Believe me, Harriet, I have tried everything. You'll forgive me for speaking in such a direct, vulgar manner. However, I feel that honesty is important between us."

"Speak freely. Direct and vulgar do not bother me," Harriet added.

"I believe my family are after your money. It is not that our pockets are let, you understand, but my mother wishes for more, and you can offer her that. We, in turn, can offer your mother a title."

On any other day and under different circumstances, Harriet thought she might quite like Bertie.

"Aren't mothers horrid." She sighed.

"Perfectly horrid, and yet we love them." He sighed too. "Your face really does look sore."

"Only when I squint. Now, Bertie, I shall think on your dilemma and send word if I come up with any solution, but you must prepare yourself for the option of fleeing London for Gretna Green if all else fails."

"Amelia said she won't allow me to do that."

"You may have no choice if you want to live your life with her."

"I won't live without her," he said suddenly, looking exactly like the lord he was.

"Excellent. But for now, if we are at least occasionally seen in each other's company, they will stop throwing others at us, which I must admit my mother has not done until now."

He smiled, and she saw another reason Amelia was in love with him. Not that he was for her, but still, he was handsome in a boyish way. A vision of Mr. Nightingale slid into her head. He was most definitely not boyish. Thinking about him reminded her that she was due to leave the house shortly.

"Send me a note, and we will go driving and plan our next move," Harriet said, grabbing his arm. "When we get back in the parlor, try to appear a tiny bit smitten. In fact, think of Amelia."

"I can do that," he said with grim determination.

CHAPTER EIGHTEEN

*A*n hour later, their guests had finally left the house, with both mothers thinking their plan was working… which it absolutely was not because their children weren't fools. What she couldn't fathom was what her mother's game was?

Having no time to contemplate that, she had rushed back to her room to collect her things before leaving for her appointment with Mr. Nightingale. She had no time to change because of her mother's silly matchmaking.

Finding her long gray jacket, she pulled it on and then her bonnet.

She absolutely did not feel a flutter of excitement over the prospect of seeing the man again. After all, Harriet did not like people she did not know—well, any people, actually—taking her to task over her actions. She'd been making her own decisions for a long time now, even if her family thought they made them for her.

Harriet was very good at deception.

Why had he kissed her?

"Harriet!" This was followed by a tap on her door. She

froze. Why was her mother up here standing outside the door to her room when she'd just spent time with her? In the normal course of a day, they were lucky to spend more than a few minutes in each other's company, and that was forced and uncomfortable.

"Open this door at once!" her mother demanded. The handle rattled, and then to her horror, it was opening before she could take off her outer clothing, and there stood Heloise Shaw.

"Harriet, why are you dressed to go out? We have visitors arriving this evening, and I wish to—"

"Again? I thought you just had visitors—"

"I like to entertain," her mother cut her off. "And I want you to join us."

"Why? I thought you decided when I returned from the Templar Academy that I was the disgraced Shaw and as such not to be seen in society again. The daughter that had a hand in her dearest friend's death—oh and let us not forget the thievery I was accused of."

"We do not speak of that time." Her mother's lips thinned.

Heloise Shaw was the strongest woman Harriet knew. She loved her children the only way she knew how. By providing them with everything they needed except a hug or words that spoke of her love.

When Harriet had returned home in disgrace, her mother had simply said, "Well that's done with, and we will not speak of it again." And that, as far as she was concerned, was that.

This refrain was hammered home until Heloise Shaw thought her daughter believed it.

Harriet hadn't, but she knew the path of least resistance was the best one for her life to run smoothly. After two years where she had done little but walk, read, and think, the Shaws had moved here, and then her life had really started. She had stuffed down her pain and decided to live.

"Do you understand, Harriet? Never again will you mention that time!"

"Just because it is not spoken of around you, Mother, does not mean it is forgotten," she muttered, feeling the rage and frustration she'd never quite been able to squash rear its head.

"Enough!" her mother said, holding out a hand as if she could halt Harriet's words.

"I will never forget that you, Father, and Oscar, along with society, believe through my reckless behavior that I was in some way responsible for Frankie's death. I lost a friend. Someone I cared very much for." The words came out an angry snarl. But that was how she felt. For years she'd had to keep the memory of Frankie alive in her head, as no one would talk about her.

"Desist at once! We do not speak of that time." Her mother's cheeks were now red. "You are to present yourself downstairs later to meet the guests when they arrive."

"I will not, just as I will not allow you to hurl me into the path of single, unattached men like Lord Talbot simply because you and his mother have concocted some plan to wed us for whatever reason."

She didn't often stand up to her mother; no one in the family did, and that was mainly because, for the most part, they rubbed along together leading their own lives. Her mother was clueless as to what Harriet got up to, and she was more than happy with that… or had been until now.

"How dare you, a child of mine, suggest I would do such a thing!" But the guilty flush of deep red color gave her away.

Harriet didn't roll her eyes, but it was a near thing.

"I will not be sold to a man like Lord Talbot because Father has offered a large dowry and you wish for a title in our family." She knew she'd hit the mark when her mother clutched her chest dramatically, beneath which beat one of the strongest hearts in England.

"Harriet, how could you speak to me in such a way?"

Ignoring that question, she asked one of her own, "Why now, Mother? You have not wanted me anywhere near you or your guests for years. Why now?"

"Is everything all right, Mother?" Harriet's sister appeared.

Catherine Shaw was the youngest sibling. She had hair the color of sunrise and was the epitome of how a young society miss should look. Her face was pretty, she wore what her mother told her, and had taken to her etiquette lessons with enthusiasm. After the disaster at the Templar Academy, it was decided not to send Catherine anywhere but have a tutor come to the house.

"Your sister is being vile to me," her mother said theatrically. "I was merely explaining that she is required to assist with entertaining our guests this evening."

"Really?" Catherine looked understandably shocked, aware that Harriet was never there when they entertained. "But that is exciting, Harry."

"No, it is not," Harriet replied.

"Harriet!" her mother snapped. "Harry is a man's name."

Catherine smiled and patted her mother's hand. She was the peacemaker in the family.

"Will you come and help me choose which dress to wear, Mother? I can't decide and have three laid out on my bed."

The scowl fell from Heloise Shaw's face, and she smiled at her youngest child. "But of course I will. I will return to speak to you shortly." She shot Harriet a hard look before walking away. "Do not leave this house."

Catherine turned to look at Harriet and mouthed the words, "you owe me," before leading their mother to her room.

Harriet liked her youngest sister the most of all the Shaws. She'd been the only one who believed her story when she returned from the academy.

Collecting the small black bag that had her journal inside, she then hurried from the room. There was no sign of her mother, so she ran, which was not easy with sore knees, down the stairs. Reaching the kitchens, she hurried through. Cuthbert stopped her before she could open the door.

"Is all well, Miss Harry?"

"Perfectly, thank you, Cuthbert, but I should be excessively pleased if you did not tell my mother you saw me." She didn't wait for his response, simply opened the door and fled.

"Why now?" Harriet muttered as she hurried down the path to the gate. Why was her mother wanting to marry her off? It made no sense, but she also knew her mother, and there had to be more than one reason. Yes, the title was a lure, but Harriet had a feeling there was more to it but as yet did not know what.

But she would.

Reaching the rear gate, she did not encounter Percy; another good thing, as he'd told her that Mr. Nightingale said he should ensure she did not leave the house alone.

Suddenly it seemed she was everyone's business, and that would not do. She had the suffrage movement and the march and rallies. She had the orphans and the students she taught. If her mother started watching her movements, Harriet would have to stop, and that would never do.

Clearly she needed to be sneakier.

CHAPTER NINETEEN

The hackney dropped her a short distance from Crabbett Close, as she wanted to walk to the house rather than announce her arrival with the clop of hooves. She'd been there twice before to visit with Miss Alvin and pick up the knitting she and her friends had done for the orphanage. Harriet also met a few of the locals, but not once had she seen Mr. Nightingale. Of course, not that she'd have known him then, but still Harriet was sure she would not have forgotten him.

She loved the street, as there were always people outside their houses talking or children playing in the park. It seemed a comfortable place to live and grow up unlike the location of the Shaw town house, which was all about status and appearance.

The wind was cool and slapped her hard in the face as she studied the three shops before her. She'd looked at them a few times but always been in a hurry with no time to stop.

Pulling out the watch she carried in her pocket, Harriet saw she still had twenty minutes before she was to present herself at 11 Crabbett Close. Eager as she was to find out about Anna, it was rude to arrive before you were expected. Her mother had hammered those manners into her since she was a child.

Taking the stairs up to the bookstore, she entered. The sign said Nicholson's Books. Entering, she inhaled the wonderful scent.

"Good day to you," a woman said from behind the counter.

"Good day."

"If you need help with anything, please let me know."

"Thank you, I will."

A few people were in here browsing at the selection of books, and Harriet told herself she would return when she had more time, as she could always add to her collection.

"That was my brother," the woman said from behind her. Harriet had stopped to look at a framed painting of a man that hung on a wall. "George is no longer with us, and we miss him every day."

"I'm sorry for your loss." She might not like her family very much at times, but she still loved them and could not imagine life without any of them.

"Thank you." The woman went back to the counter, and Harriet wandered for a few more minutes, stopping before a shelf to study the titles.

"That is an excellent book. I have read the entire series," a man said from behind her. Studying the binding, she read the title. *Captain Broadbent and Lady Nauticus: The Egyptian Adventure.*

"I have not read them, sir." She turned to face him.

"Ouch. I bet that hurts." He pointed to her cheek.

"Only when I squint," Harriet said.

"May I suggest you don't squint then."

She smiled, as the conversation was silly, but she felt relaxed for the first time today.

"What happened?"

"A fall."

His smile was gentle. Tall with dark hair that was graying at the temples. He had the greenest eyes of any she'd seen before.

"I have a brother who lowers his eyes when he's not telling the truth."

Harriet sighed. "The story is a long one, sir. I'm not sure, as you are a stranger, that it would be of interest to you."

"Did a man make that mark?"

"I—pardon?"

"I do not like to hear a man has raised his hand to a woman, madam." His eyes, if possible, had become greener, and he was staring at her intently.

"No, it was not from the hand of a man." Not exactly a lie, and why did his words have her wanting to weep? Perhaps because her own brother was not as protective of her as this man was—a total stranger.

"Very well, now back to the book. It is pure escapism, and well worth your time, I promise you," he said.

"He has read the entire collection of those books many times, even though he will deny it with his last breath," an elegant blond woman said, moving to his side.

"My name is Lord Sinclair, and this wonderful woman is my wife."

"Hello," Harriet said, not wanting to give them her name but not wanting to lie either. "I am Miss Short." It was easier, she told herself, as they may know her family.

"Miss Short has hurt her cheek, my love. Do you see?" Lord Sinclair said.

"Indeed I do." Lady Sinclair really was beautiful. That classic beauty that was bone-deep. They were a handsome couple and very clearly in love. "I know a bit about healing,

Miss Short." The woman tugged off a glove and moved closer to Harriet.

"Ah, what are you doing?" Harriet asked.

"Let her inspect your face, Miss Short. She will not hurt you, and in fact you will feel a great deal better."

The fingers that touched her were warm on her damaged skin, and then she pulled away, and Harriet no longer felt the deep, throbbing ache in her cheek. *Odd.*

"There now, you will feel a great deal better soon I am sure," Lady Sinclair said.

Her husband moved to her side and slipped a hand around her waist.

"Buy the book, Miss Short, and find a group of people you like and read it out loud. It is a great deal of fun, I assure you. Good day to you," Lord Sinclair said. He then led his wife away.

Harriet watched, not entirely sure what had just happened. Touching her cheek, she thought the swelling had gone down but knew that was not possible. Deciding her life was filled with things she couldn't understand at the moment, and that was yet another, she picked up the book and made for the counter and purchased it.

Stepping outside the shop, she inhaled deeply to steady herself and breathed in a delicious scent.

Harriet had not eaten this morning, as she'd slept through breakfast and then had tea with her mother, but nerves had not allowed her to even nibble on the cake. Perhaps she could eat something on the walk to 11 Crabbett Close, as it would not do for her stomach to rumble when she arrived.

Entering the store, she was bombarded with delicious scents. A man stood at the counter, tapping his hand against his thigh as he studied a tray of food. He turned to look at her and smiled.

"If I may help you with your selection, I would try an apricotine. They are the best in London."

He was tall and dressed like Lord Sinclair had been. His overcoat was a deep gray, and his trousers black, as were his polished shoes. One large gloveless hand held his hat. His hair was the color of chestnuts and tousled.

"There are ten left. How many do you want? I will take the rest, as I am to visit family," he continued.

"Ah, well, I'm unsure if I want an apricotine," Harriet said.

The man was shocked. "Not want an apricotine? Are you unwell?" As this was said with a smile on his lips, she did not take him seriously.

"No indeed, but I find I am leaning toward the fruitcake."

"Are you really?" He studied the cake Harriet was pointing to. "I've not tried it if I'm honest."

"It's good," the man behind the counter said. "Best in London, Mr. Hellion, as I've told you a time or two."

"I know you have, Mr. Eccles, but I'm not sure anything can replace an apricotine in my life."

"I will take a slice of fruitcake if you please," Harriet said, enjoying the ridiculousness of the conversation. There were not many people in her life who made her laugh in such a way, especially lately.

"And I will take ten apricotines," Mr. Hellion said.

"And a piece of fruitcake, as you really should try it," Harriet added to his order.

"Should I?" He looked at her.

"Indeed you should. It is important, as what would happen if you came in here one day hungry and all the apricotines were sold?"

He shuddered. "Just the thought makes me feel nauseous."

Harriet laughed.

"Ramsey Hellion." He bowed before her.

"Harriet Shaw—Short," she added quickly. This was the

problem with using two names—you were never sure which one to give to people. But to be fair, she didn't often have this problem, as she did not converse with many people she did not already know. It was only recently that had been happening.

"Shaw or Short? You seem confused," he asked, smiling.

Harriet had a feeling this man smiled a great deal and used it to get exactly what he wanted in life, as it was a nice smile.

"Ah, well, as to that—"

"Say no more. We all do things we have no wish for others to know. I shall instead simply call you Harriet."

"Shall you?"

As Mr. Eccles arrived in that moment, she was spared further comment. Taking her cake after handing over some coins, she drew it to her nose and sniffed.

"Did it pass?" Mr. Hellion said, following her out the bakery door with his large package of apricotines.

"The sniff test?"

He nodded.

"Indeed it did. It's exactly as a fruitcake should smell." She took a bite and hummed her pleasure.

"Oh, very well," he said, looking at the slice of fruitcake he held in the hand not clutching the package of apricotines. He took a small bite—unlike Harriet who was still chewing her mouthful. His sigh was loud after he'd swallowed.

"Come now, you have to concede it is excellent fruitcake."

"I did not want to like it, but unfortunately it was very good."

Harriet laughed. "Well good day to you, sir. I am to head this way, as I have an appointment at 2:00 p.m. and have no wish to be late."

"Crabbett Close is your destination?"

"It is."

"Excellent, we shall walk together and eat our cake in silence, and you can protect me from the rather unusual inhabitants."

"I know the Alvins," Harriet said. "They knit for the children, as do a few of the others who live there."

"How many children do you have?"

"Oh, haha, no, they are not my children. I visit the Gail Lane orphanage."

"Do you really? How wonderful. I've never been very charitable, but I really should try harder."

"Well now, it's a good day to you, Mr. Hellion, and you also, Miss Short."

"Good day, Mr. Peeky," they both said.

The elderly man stood on his front step smiling. "There be a bite in the air today."

"There certainly is," Mr. Hellion said politely.

"How is it you know our Miss Short, sir?" the elderly man asked. His cap was pulled lower over his eyes, and he was wrapped in a brown woolen scarf.

"We are old friends through our families," Mr. Hellion lied before she could speak.

"Friends." Mr. Peeky rocked back on his heels. "We all need them."

"That we do," Mr. Hellion said, raising a hand. He then walked on, and Harriet did the same.

"That was a lie."

"We've known each other for at least twenty minutes. That is old friends by now, surely?" he teased her.

"Hello, Mr. Hellion! I wonder if you would come and see to my window. It appears to be stuck!"

These words came from the young woman hanging out an open window who Harriet also knew. She seemed to have a great deal of her chest showing even considering the cool weather.

"Sorry, I have an appointment, Miss Varney," Mr. Hellion replied.

"Oh, hello, Miss Short," Miss Varney said, clearly unhappy to see her walking with Mr. Hellion.

"If I may suggest you get a shawl, it's quite chilly out," Harriet called to the woman.

Mr. Hellion snorted as he increased his pace, and Harriet struggled to keep up.

"If you wish to rush, sir, do not let me stop you."

"Are you injured? You appear to be shuffling, and there is that fading bruise on your cheek."

"I had a fall."

"Well, as you saved me, I will slow my pace. That woman is hunting for a husband and any man will do," he added.

"Yes, she is a member of the women's suffrage movement that I belong to. She spends a lot of time while marching chatting to men."

"You're a very busy woman, Harriet."

She felt his eyes on her.

"I like to keep busy." Looking at the numbers, she saw they had reached 9 Crabbett Close.

"There are not many more prospects for some women, sir," she felt compelled to say.

"No indeed. It is not an easy lot for some, but that one is terrifying."

"Well then," Harriet said when nothing else came to mind. "I'll bid you good day, as the house I am calling at is there." She pointed to a three-story redbrick house.

"You're visiting the Nightingale family?"

She nodded.

"How fortuitous, so am I. You will be able to experience the delights of an apricotine after all. Come along, Harriet."

She watched as he opened the black iron gate between the brick fence to the right and left. He then waved her through.

"How is it you know the Nightingales?" he asked.

"As to that, I don't... not really. They are to help me with something."

He nodded. "They're very good at that. Helping is a particular forte of the people who live within these walls. My cousin is married to one. Come, Harriet, no need to skulk about in the gate. They will not bite you."

"I was hardly skulking. I took a mere few seconds to look at my surroundings, surely?"

"Are you a literal creature, Harriet?" Mr. Hellion asked as he bounded up the steps and thumped his fist on the front door.

"Usually, yes." Harriet wasn't sure if she wanted to turn and flee or stay, but then she remembered Anna and knew it would be the latter. Of course, there was also the matter of what happened when last she saw Mr. Nightingale, and the fact that seeing him again would make her heart thud a little harder no matter how much she willed it not to.

The door swung open, and the large man who had carried Anna to the carriage a few nights ago stood there dressed in a kilt.

"Do you know, Mungo, I don't think I've seen you in a kilt before today. It's quite the look and adds to the ferocious Scotsman persona you carry off so well," Mr. Hellion said.

"Why are you here... again?" The kilt-wearing behemoth scowled. His accent was thick enough to cut with a knife.

"I know you don't mean that, and as I brought you apricotines, you had better be a great deal nicer to me."

The Scotsman's eyes went to the package Mr. Hellion carried. "Well then, I suppose you can come in."

"Gracious as always, Mungo." Mr. Hellion bowed. "And this beautiful lady is Miss Harriet Short or Shaw, as yet I am unsure which. She is here... actually I'm not entirely sure why she's here, or who to see."

Both men looked down at Harriet, where she still stood on the path. The Scotsman did not by a flicker of an eyelash acknowledge they'd met each other before.

Would the others inside this house pretend too? For some reason, she did not want that to be the case, as she was ignored by a great many people already.

CHAPTER TWENTY

"Mr. Alexander Nightingale," she said quickly. "I have an appointment at 2:00 p.m. with him."

"Do you really?" Mr. Hellion asked, looking down at her. "What for?"

"I would rather not say."

"Which simply makes me even more curious, but I shall hold it in and then ask Alex later." He smiled again, and Harriet thought this man did that often.

"Well then, Mungo, lead on and have Bud immediately take down the large teapot, as we are to drink lashings of it with our apricotines."

Harriet watched Mungo roll his eyes, but he did step back. Mr. Hellion entered, and she wasn't entirely sure if she should follow or wait to be called in. After all, usually in such circumstances the person you were to meet was notified you were there, and then you waited until they were ready. She might not walk in society, but she knew how to.

"Harriet, enter the house please!" Mr. Hellion called from inside.

Her eyes went to Mungo.

"Are you intending to cause trouble for anyone inside, Miss Short or Shaw?" Mungo said solemnly.

"No indeed. I wish to enquire how the girl, Anna, is doing and am also to meet with Mr. Nightingale to discuss a matter of importance."

The man's face softened, and it was really something to see, as he seemed more approachable suddenly.

"The wee lass is doing well, and it was a good thing you got her out of that place when you did. It has been a rough few days for her, but the infection is gone, and now there is just healing to be done."

"She's still here?"

"And where else would she be in the condition she is?" The soft look was gone, and he was scowling at her again. "She cannot be moved."

"Of course." Should Harriet have contacted the orphanage? What would she say, as surely what she had done was illegal. These thoughts and many more had plagued her for the last few days. "I was very worried for her."

"She's going to be fine," he said. "Now come inside, as it's a mite chilly out today, and that fool is here, so you can be no worse than he."

"I heard that!"

Mungo's face changed subtly. Just a small grin, but Harriet saw it.

"Come along with you," he said, waving her up the steps.

It was all very odd if you asked her, but then what else was she to do but enter the house. And surely odd was commonplace here; after all, Mr. Nightingale talked to the dead.

"Is Mr. Alexander Nightingale home, Mr. Mungo?" she asked when she reached the top step.

"He is, and I'll tell him you're here, Miss Short or Shaw."

"Short," she said quickly. After all she'd been introduced to Mr. Nightingale that way, so she should continue to do so.

The large Scotsman waved her inside, so she walked through the door and stopped, letting her eyes take in her surroundings. Of Mr. Hellion there was now no sign, but she could hear him barking out a loud laugh.

"I'll take your things," he said, holding out his hand.

Harriet removed her outer clothing and handed it to him.

"Head toward the laughter, Miss Short," Mr. Mungo then said. "I shall inform the housekeeper we need tea and take her these apricotines."

"Is it possible to see Anna first, Mr. Mungo? I can then wait here for Mr. Nightingale, as the voices suggest there are visitors."

"Just family. I'll take you to the girl, and then you'll come down and join the others," he said, and Harriet thought not many would refuse this man.

After placing her things on a side table, he started for the stairs. Harriet hurried to catch up, ignoring the twinges in her muscles. Her eyes took in everything as she rose and then walked along the hallway behind the Scotsman. Unlike her family's town house that was immaculate, this had a homely feel. She found a pair of shoes against a wall and some books in a pile. Her mother would never have allowed that.

"She's in here." He opened the door and entered. The room was large with a fire crackling in the grate. Her eyes went to the bed. Anna lay there sleeping. Beside her sat a young girl reading.

"Matilda, this is Miss—"

"Anna's Miss Harry," the girl said. "I've heard all about you. She said you had lovely eyes, one green and one blue, and were very pretty."

She could see Mr. Nightingale in the face of the girl before her.

"Did she? That was very kind of her. How is Anna doing?" Harriet spoke softly as the girl had. Moving to the side of the bed, she looked down at the slumbering patient. Her cheeks had color now, and her breathing was not labored. Anna was sleeping peacefully.

"She's doing marvelously well considering what she's been through," Matilda whispered. "Sleep is the best thing according to both Mrs. Huntington and Mr. Greedy who are the ones caring for her."

"Well now," Mr. Mungo whispered from behind her. "As you can see, she is recovering, so you come away, Miss Short, and we'll see about getting you a cup of tea. Perhaps when she wakes you can see her again."

"I cannot thank you enough for sitting with her," Harriet said to Matilda. "Anna does not have the best life, you see."

"I know. My family told me she is from an orphanage."

Harriet touched the girl's hand. She wasn't a person for large gestures. Rarely did she hug or touch, but she felt the need right then. With a final squeeze of Matilda's fingers, she left the room. Her heart felt full from what these people had done for Anna. What she should have done if her mother wasn't the way she was.

Heloise Shaw did not have a benevolent nature. She would never have allowed an orphan into her house to be cared for.

"I will see to the tea," Mungo said when they reached the bottom of the stairs once more.

"Thank you for helping Anna. What you are doing for her is very generous."

"'Twas all of us," he grunted and then left her standing in the front entrance confused and feeling too many emotions. She also had no idea what to do now.

A loud woof had her eyes traveling up, and at the top of the stairs, she found a big white dog with black circles around his eyes. Harriet had not had a great deal of experience with dogs in her lifetime, except those she encountered on the streets, but she had to say she liked them. They were not taxing like people and rarely wanting anything but a pat or food from her.

With another woof, he bounded down the stairs. The dog leapt off the last two and galloped toward her.

"Chester, do not jump all over Miss Harry!"

The words had the dog attempting to stop its progress, but it collided with her, clipping her legs and sending her backward. She fell onto her bottom. The dog woofed again and planted two large paws on her chest to peer down at her.

While Harriet grappled with the need to haul in a breath, a large pink tongue licked her cheek. Muscles that were already sore screamed at her in pain. Her breath wheezed as she tried to haul one in.

"Chester, off!"

The weight on her chest was suddenly removed and hands lifted her to her feet, and there he was again—the handsome, disturbing Mr. Alexander Nightingale.

"Are you all right, Harriet?"

She attempted to speak but didn't seem able to make her vocal cords work.

"There now, take a deep breath and try again. You are unhurt?"

She nodded and focused on his deep gray trousers, pristine white shirt, and waistcoat of emerald green with silver flowers all over it. Unlike her father and brother who always wore their jackets, he did not have one on.

"Your cheek looks a great deal better." He touched it softly, just a light brush of his fingers on her skin. It made her shiver. "But I can tell you are still sore in other places by the way you move."

He really did have a lovely smile like Mr. Hellion. It filled his entire face and made his brown eyes come to life. He had not been smiling that night at the orphanage, however; then his look had been almost savage.

"I am well, thank you, Mr. Nightingale, and I must also thank you for your care of Anna."

"She is a very brave, sweet girl considering the life she has likely endured," he said solemnly.

Harriet nodded.

"Most of us face adversity at some stage, but to do so at her age must have been harrowing."

Harriet wondered what adversity he had been faced with.

"Did you make it home without detection?" he asked her.

"I did, yes."

"Well, that was extremely lucky considering you should not have been out alone in the first place."

"Yes, I believe you made your displeasure for my actions felt in those notes. But as what I do is no concern of yours, I chose to ignore them."

"Percy agreed with me." His look was smug.

"Only because you bribed him with treacle cake and questioned him."

"It is good treacle cake," he said, still standing close to her. "And Percy is simply worried about your reckless behavior resulting in injury or worse."

She wondered just what Percy had told this man about her circumstances. Did he know about the Shaw family?

"There is much for us to talk about, Harriet, but first we will take tea and have apricotines."

"I am unsure how next to progress with Anna, sir," Harriet said quickly. "Should I tell the orphanage where she is before they start searching?"

"My brother-in-law had someone call in to the orphanage to see if there was anything amiss under the guise that he'd heard there was trouble there with children going missing. The matron, Mrs. Secomb, said nothing was wrong, and the children were all doing wonderfully well. He did add that he thought she looked nervous, however."

Anger shot through her. "How dare they not care that one of their children has gone missing!"

"Gray has started investigations into the orphanage."

"Good, as I fear there is more going on, which I would like to speak to you about."

"Very well, but for now no one is looking for Anna, which is a good thing."

"Yes," she said. "I will, of course, take her back when she is well. Or perhaps find her somewhere else that is a better arrangement?" Surely, through the suffragettes, she would be able to find a home for the child.

"Yes, sending her back now would not be easy, as there would need to be excuses formulated. But it could be done, as I'm sure children come and go from that place regularly," Mr. Nightingale said.

"They do."

He leaned in closer—so close that his face was soon only inches from hers.

"Wh-what are you doing?"

"You really do have lovely eyes."

"Which one?" Harriet snapped. People had made fun of her different colored eyes since she'd been born. Her mother loathed them, and her brother teased her constantly.

"Both." He smiled. "They simply add to your beauty." He straightened, and Harriet could breathe again.

"There is no need of flummery, sir. Now I wish to discuss the matter of Frankie with you please."

"Flummery certainly has its place, and I'll thank you for

that word, as it will be a good one to throw at my siblings for word of the week." He continued to smile. "But I assure you I speak the truth."

"Word of the week?" she had to ask.

"It is a family thing. Whoever chooses the word of the week, also chooses an action that must be performed when the word is spoken."

"Well then" was all she could come up with for that. She'd never met someone like this man. He disarmed her, and that was unsettling.

"Now, before I take you in for tea, I would just like to clear up a matter if I may?" he added.

"I do not need tea but thank you."

"There is always a need for tea, and if we do not make it back into that room soon, all the apricotines will be gone."

"What is this fixation with apricotines?"

"Yes, I heard you arrived with Ramsey, and that man certainly has an unhealthy appetite. Food of any sort is important, but food as delicious as those delightfully tasty treats are even more so."

"I will wait here."

"No, you will not."

"I have no wish to intrude on your family's afternoon tea."

"I insist. Besides my family do not stand on ceremony."

Her mother was an absolute stickler for ceremony. In fact, Harriet was sure she could write a book on it should she be asked to.

"It's not like I'm asking you to venture out at night and into an orphanage to steal a child. Or for that matter face down several criminals who could easily have gobbled up a morsel like you, Harriet."

"Miss Short," she snapped. "And you are not my keeper, sir. Should I choose to walk the length and breadth of this country at midnight, alone, there is little you could do to stop me."

His smile was more a knowing smirk. "I'm sure your family would have something to say about that, as they would over your antics the other night... that is if they knew."

Bloody bothering hell. Harriet hated that he was right.

CHAPTER TWENTY-ONE

Miss Harry was rather sweet, Alex thought. She was small and delicate when not bundled in her outer clothing, which is how he'd always seen her. Taking her arm, he started walking, and she had to follow. He was surprised to see her in a dress the color of a blush-pink rose. He'd thought she would lean toward browns and grays. It cupped and caressed her lovely body, and he'd needed no further reason to be intrigued with this woman, but now he had one.

What was her story?

While he had tried to coax information out of Percy, he hadn't been entirely successful. The man was loyal to Miss Harry, as he and the orphans called her, but had let his displeasure at her reckless behavior be known.

She had a backbone, which was pleasing to see, but then he knew she must. Firstly, there was the marching with the suffragettes and then rescuing Anna.

"My sister, Ellen, shows a willful disregard for rules and her own safety like you," he said, walking with his hand still around her wrist.

"Independence is not a disregard for safety," she snapped, trying to get away from him.

"Stupidity is."

The breath hissed from her mouth like a pot expelling steam. "Why are you pushing me about again? I did not like it at the orphanage. However, I understood your reasons. Today I do not."

"I am not pushing you. I am assisting you, please note the difference," Alex said, thinking her wrist felt delicate enough for him to crush if he squeezed too hard. Appearances were deceptive, as this woman was in no way small or weak. "If I didn't drag you, you would stay in the entrance, where it can be drafty."

"I have a coat."

His eyes ran over her dress again, which was no hardship, as the body it covered was lush. "You are in a dress."

"My coat is…" She turned to look behind her. "There." She pointed to where Mungo had placed them.

"We do not bite, so come along and formally meet the people you were not properly introduced to the other night."

"Must I?"

"You must."

At a guess, he added scrupulously polite and honest to what he knew about her. He'd been right about her hair color, it was brown. A deep chestnut shot through with strands of copper. Pulled back into a simple bun, several wisps had broken free when she removed her bonnet. The picture she presented was entirely too disturbing for Alex's peace of mind.

Chester woofed, which had her looking his way. The dog sat between the parlor and the stairs. His people were dotted all over the house, and he was torn which way to go. Alex thought the parlor they were approaching would win, as there was food.

"He is a large dog."

"But would never willingly hurt anyone." Alex stopped and clicked his fingers. Chester came to stand before them and plopped down on his bottom. He then gazed at Harriet, his tail swishing from side to side. "Now, Chester, you have upset Miss Short—"

"I am not upset, I assure you," she cut him off.

"Say sorry, boy." The dog hung his head.

"Oh, now there is no need for that, I assure you, Chester. It is merely that your size surprised me."

Alex watched as she leaned over the dog, patting his large head. "Now a lovely big boy like you has no need to hang his head."

While she'd not talked freely with him, she did with Chester, which he found interesting. She spent time at the orphanage too, which told him she was comfortable with animals and children. Alex wondered what had happened to put her off people. *Not all people*, he added, as she did march and meet with the suffragettes. Plus, he'd taken tea with Mr. and Miss Alvin and subtly asked questions about her. Miss Alvin said she was a shy, lovely girl who did not speak about herself, and he'd do worse than stepping out with a fine young lady like Harriet. Clearly his subtlety had not worked.

"I know you're sorry for knocking me over." She patted his head again, and the dog gazed at her adoringly. "I am quite well."

She then did something that surprised Alex, as he'd not thought her a demonstrative woman. She placed a kiss on the top of Chester's head.

The dog made that funny little sound he reserved for his family and continued to gaze at her.

"He is your servant for life, Miss Harry."

"He's lovely. I have never owned a dog but think I would quite like to." She bit her lip after that statement, and he thought it was to stop any further words spilling from her mouth.

They then made their way toward the voices.

"How long have you been in London?"

"Many years. Are you sure we cannot go somewhere to discuss Frankie and the other matters I wish to speak about?"

"We will do that, but there are apricotines in there"—Alex pointed to an open door—"and with them unfortunately come my family, but what can you do. I promise we will get to your story."

He could tell she was reluctant to enter the room. Alex nudged her through, and the brief contact with her spine told him how tense she was.

"And here she is, Miss Short or Shaw," Ram said, rising with the other men as they entered.

"I'm Miss Shaw, but I do use Miss Short," she said quickly, clearly uncomfortable to be here with people she did not know.

"I'm sure your reasons for the double names are good ones, and I will try not to pry, but when you get to know my nature, you will understand why that will come hard for me," Ram said.

She smiled. Small and over in seconds, but Alex felt annoyed that Ram had achieved it and not him. Which said what? That he was jealous because his friend had made a woman smile?

"Family, if I may have your attention," Alex said. "This is Miss Harriet Shaw—"

"My friend," Ram added.

"We will get to how you two met," Alex said. "But first, introductions. You met Ellen and Uncle Bram briefly the other night, but now we can deepen that acquaintance." He waved a hand their way. "The eldest of my sisters, Mrs. Ellen Fletcher. And her husband, Gray."

Alex looked at Harriet and saw she was unsettled meeting his family. He had to admit, they were quite the force at first glance, but the very best of people.

"Ram you apparently know, but not Aunt Ivy."

Where Uncle Bram was large like the other Nightingale men, his wife was not. She was slender with a personality that made her seem a great deal bigger. Alex would do anything for his aunt and uncle.

The men bowed.

"Hello, Harriet. I hope you don't mind our familiarity, but I find it makes a person more comfortable, and seeing as you are a friend of Ram's, it's my hope you'll be ours too," Aunt Ivy said, taking Harriet's hands.

"We're not exactly friends," Harriet said, clearly a stickler for the truth, unlike Ram, who could stretch it in many different directions.

"I'm wounded," Ram said. "But here is Bud. My day is complete."

Aunt Ivy waved Harriet into a seat. "I know you're actually here to see Alex, but perhaps you could take tea with us first?" Aunt Ivy continued chatting as she nudged Harriet into the seat next to Uncle Bram on the sofa. "I'll pour. How do you take it?"

Harriet managed to rally and stammer out, "Milk and sugar please."

He was used to his family now. Once they'd not behaved like this and were all that was proper and expected in society. However, that was no longer the case. They weren't sticklers for much except being exactly who they wanted to be. Alex had to say he liked this way of living a great deal more.

"Did Ram eat all the apricotines?" Theo, his youngest brother, wandered in. He was an exact replica of Leo and could sniff out food from a great distance.

"Very well, brat, you may have one," Ram said. "But before that, bow to Harriet."

Theo did and then headed for the food tray.

"Are you related to Mr. George Shaw, Harriet?" Uncle Bram asked.

She didn't want to acknowledge the connection, he realized, but manners dictated she must. His curiosity about this woman climbed.

"He is my father."

Uncle Bram smiled gently. "A wise and astute man, your father. He is admired by many."

"Thank you."

Alex would need to question his uncle about the Shaw family after Harriet had left.

"So how do you know Alex, Harriet?" Ram asked, reaching for an apricotine.

Knowing the man had a large appetite, Alex did the same, as there would not be many left on the plate shortly.

"I met Harriet at the women's suffrage society meeting," Alex answered for her.

"I wanted to go to that," Aunt Ivy said, "but unfortunately Lottie, our daughter, was unwell."

"We will go to the next one," Ellen said.

Alex was fairly sure she heard Gray say, "not bloody likely," under his breath. Uncle Bram just nodded, knowing his wife would do what she wished.

"Do you not support the rights of women to have more freedom to make decisions in their lives as men do, Detective Fletcher?" Harriet had clearly heard Gray's words. She wasn't exactly glaring, but it was a near thing.

"I do of course. I just have no wish for the woman I love to be verbally abused by shortsighted people. It's purely selfish on my part, Miss Shaw. But I would not care to see her treated in such a way."

Alex rolled his eyes, as did Ram. Ellen sighed and then planted a loud kiss on her husband's cheek.

"But I wish to show my support in some way," Ellen added.

"We are always looking for support, Mrs. Fletcher, in many ways," Harriet said. There was color in her cheeks now, as clearly she was passionate about the suffrage movement.

"Wonderful, and my entire family would love to support your cause, as it affects half of us," Ellen said.

Harriet sat on the edge of her seat sipping tea and not eating while around him his family—he included Ram in that, as he was a constant visitor—talked.

"There is a single apricotine left. Will you take it, Harriet?" Alex asked.

"No, thank you."

"She ate a slice of fruitcake on the way here and forced me to try some too," Ram said.

"I don't believe force was used," Harriet said.

"Coerced then." Ram smiled at her. "And the hell of it is, I enjoyed it."

"Food does not have feelings, Ram," Gray said. "You are not betraying the apricotines because you like fruitcake."

"If you say so. Now I'm curious about why Harriet has an appointment with you, Alex."

"We are to discuss a matter we talked about at the women's suffrage society meeting," Harriet said quickly before he could speak.

She'd put her teacup down on the table before her and now sat legs together, hands clasped in her lap, back straight. Alex had the urge to mess her up, or at least get his hands on her.

She was nothing like the confident women that usually interested him. Prim, uptight, and usually dressed in large, drab clothing, Harriet Shaw was, in fact, the exact opposite.

"Hello!"

Aunt Ivy and Uncle Bram's daughter, three-year-old Lottie, came into the room as she did most things—in a hurry. She was a delightful little bundle of sunshine who he and his siblings loved and doted on.

"Uncle Alex!"

"Hello, brat," he said, catching her as she ran at him.

"It's always him she runs to first." Aunt Ivy sighed. "You'd think seeing as we are her parents it would be us, but no."

Alex whispered in Lottie's ear, and she slid out of his arms and ran to the table. Picking up the apricotine, she brought it back to him. He gave her half and ate the other in a single mouthful.

"That's hardly fair," Ram protested.

"You would take food from a child?" Alex asked as Lottie left him again. He watched her walk to where Harriet sat.

"Hello."

"Hello." Her smile was genuine like it had been with Chester. It made her look softer. "I am Harriet."

Lottie was a charmer, and anyone who entered the house fell under her spell; it seemed Harriet was no different.

"Now you have another wrapped around your finger, Lottie. You will excuse Gray, Miss Shaw, and me, as we need to discuss something in private," Alex said, rising.

They left the room, leaving silence behind. It would not last; they would be discussing scenarios as to why both he and Gray were talking to Harriet until they returned. He would then be expected to tell them everything.

CHAPTER TWENTY-TWO

Alex led the way to the office library all the occupants of the household used. He opened the door, and Harriet entered with Gray on her heels. A large desk was littered with papers, and shelves filled with books. There were two chairs.

"Please take a seat, Harriet," Alex said. Gray took the other, and he sat on the edge of the desk. "Begin when you are ready."

"I have so many things I wish to tell you that I am not entirely sure where to start," Harriet said. "Things I have no wish for my family to ever know but need to be spoken."

"Do they know you are here today?" Alex asked.

She shook her head.

"Do they know what you get up to? The marching and rallies? The orphans?"

Her hesitation told him she did not want to answer that.

"If we are to deal with whatever is going on in the past or currently, we must have the truth," Gray said.

"My family has no bearing on what we discuss."

"Very well," Gray said. "Please continue with your story."

"What is spoken in this room will go no further," Alex added. Not entirely true; his family would need to know if they were called in to help, which they likely would be.

"First I would like to speak about Frankie," Harriet said, taking a small black book out of her bag.

"I understand Alex told you about your friend making contact with him?" Gray said.

"Spiritually," Alex added. Gray nodded. He understood what his wife and brothers-in-law could do but was not entirely comfortable with it, even though his aunt had had the same abilities.

"This is one of my journals." She handed it to Gray. "I started it the night... ah, the night I found Frankie."

It still hurt her, Alex thought. Deeply. He wanted to know the story as much as he knew Gray now did.

"Before we begin, I want to ask two things of you, Harriet," Gray said.

She nodded.

"Firstly, if you ever have a wish to do what you did a couple nights ago, let Alex or one of us know. That was dangerous."

Well done, Gray.

"I will take no more risks," she said quickly. "That is something I wish to discuss also."

"The risks?" Alex asked.

"No, what happened the night I came to the orphanage."

"We will get to that," Gray said. "Harriet, Alex believes your friend was murdered. Do you?"

Her eyes turned to Alex. "You never said that."

"It's not really something you discuss at a suffragette meeting now, is it?"

"If your friend was murdered and justice has not been done, Harriet, then we must at least look into the matter," Gray added. "Was it investigated thoroughly?"

She shook her head.

"But you believe she was murdered?" Gray asked again.

"I don't know why I believed that, as there was no evidence, but yet I think someone did play a hand in Frankie's death."

"Were you in some way blamed for your friend's death, Harriet?" Gray asked.

Alex stayed quiet. His brother-in-law was good at this; he did it for a living and knew how to get people to talk.

"Yes," she whispered, but he heard it, as the room was quiet. "One story was that I pushed Frankie into the river to drown, so I could have all the things we'd stolen. Another said we argued, and in my anger, I let her drown. Yet another said Frankie fell, and I could not save her." She looked at Gray and then Alex, and her eyes were huge and filled with despair. "I would never have hurt my friend. She was my sister in every way but blood."

Something was nudging at him, but as yet, he didn't know what. Alex thought it was likely Frankie.

"Tell us the rest of your story from the beginning, Harriet, as I have questions, but you may answer them in what you are about to tell us, and then I will read your journal. Very clever of you to keep it, by the way," Gray added.

She nodded.

"My family sent me to attend the Templar Academy for Young Ladies to help me with entering society. I met Frankie the first day, and we became friends. Francesca Morrissey is her name."

Alex watched Harriet as she talked. He knew she would be giving them only the facts; there would be no mention of the life she'd led there, or anything but the detailed account of what happened to her friend.

"How many girls were there?" Alex asked.

"At that time, there were twelve," she said. "Frankie and me, we were different, and as such, became friends."

"Different how?" Alex asked.

Her hands were clenched now, the knuckles turning white.

"Neither Gray nor I wish to upset you, Harriet. But in order for us to understand and help you, we will need to ask questions."

Gray shot him a look but remained silent.

"Of course. I was American, and Frankie's parents had died, and her great-aunt was sponsoring her to attend the Templar Academy, as there was no money left when they died."

"And the other young ladies were all from wealthy English families?" Gray said gently.

"Yes."

"Continue with your story," Gray added.

"Frankie and I were both people who liked the night. We did not want to retire to our beds early like the others. So, we would wait until they slept and slip out of the house. Often, we went to the river that was about a five-minute walk through the trees and simply sat and talked."

He could imagine how hard it was to fit in when everyone was different. He and his siblings had become different and were shunned for it.

"I need to tell you the other part to the story first," Harriet said. Her pretty face was serious as she recounted the horror he was sure she'd endured.

"Two days after we arrived, some of the girls started complaining that their things were going missing. Money, jewelry, and clothes. They blamed Frankie and me, as we were the last to arrive." She looked angry now. "They accused us of going through their things when they were not there. Of course, we denied it, but they did not believe us. Our things were searched, and a necklace found, so we were considered guilty, and Mr. and Mrs. Templar disciplined us."

"What did they do?" Gray asked before Alex could.

"We went without meals and were given the cane across our legs and hands." The words were spoken slowly, hesitantly, as if it hurt to speak them. "Which I understand is normal disciplinary procedure there." Her voice was emotionless, but those lovely eyes were filled with memories of that pain.

Alex swallowed down his own anger. He knew how barbaric some of the discipline meted out to students at Eton was, but it seemed that was not something solely confined to boys' schools. He rose and poured two glasses of brandy from the decanter they kept filled on the side table. He then walked to where Harriet sat and dropped down before her.

"Sip this. It will make you feel better." He held one out to her. She took it with a small attempt at a smile that failed.

"I am quite well, I assure you. This all happened many years ago now."

"Not that many," he muttered, regaining his feet and returning to his place on the edge of the desk. Harriet winced with the second sip as it hit the back of her throat, but she managed to swallow down the cough.

"I've gone over and over that night. Frankie never went to the river without me. Never," she said, her voice stronger now. "But that day she'd found out her mother's necklace had gone missing and was determined to locate it. She told me she was going to search the house the night she died. I thought I'd convinced her not to. Told her she would get in trouble if anyone found her."

Harriet took another sip, and Alex threw the entire contents of his glass into his mouth. Gray raised a brow but did not speak.

"She told me that of course I was right, and she would not

do anything foolish, and I believed her. But that necklace was all she had left, you see. Clearly, she said what she did to appease me and then started searching."

"And you think she was searching for it the night you found her in the river?" Gray asked.

"Yes, but I could prove nothing, and the louder I demanded something be done, the more they turned on me. Mr. and Mrs. Templar said I was simply trying to deflect from the fact I'd been involved in my friend's death and the fact I'd been caught stealing from the other girls. I was sent home in disgrace three days after Frankie died."

"The Nightingales know a thing or two about disgrace," Alex said.

"I tried to get to her. Got in the water, but I couldn't swim, not like Frankie. I couldn't reach her."

He felt her desperation. Knew that she'd done everything possible to reach her friend. That in fact she, too, could have drowned while trying. Alex felt unreasonably angry at the thought of something happening to Harriet and was not at all comfortable with that.

"I'm so very sorry you went through this, Harriet," Gray said. "But it could have been an accident."

"It wasn't." Alex kept his eyes on Harriet as he spoke. "The day Frankie and her lemons filled my head, I also saw a heart-shaped necklace with an angel, plus a pair of hands around a neck."

CHAPTER TWENTY-THREE

"No!" Harriet leapt to her feet, sloshing brandy over her hand. "My dear friend was strangled?"

"I'm sorry." Alex went to her. "I shouldn't have said that. I sometimes forget people can't see what I can." He eased her back into the chair gently. "Take another sip." He lifted the glass to her mouth and watched as she did as he asked.

"There is no need to jump to conclusions." Gray shot Alex a narrow-eyed look. "And I am not sure if we will get anywhere with investigating something that happened so long ago."

"B-but Frankie deserves justice," Harriet said.

"She does," Alex said. "But Gray is right, we will need to go slowly."

"We?" Gray said.

"We," Harriet added, looking determined.

His brother-in-law sighed. "May I keep your book, Harriet?" She nodded. "I would also like you to compile a list of the names of those who were at the Templar Academy with you."

"I can do that. I have an excellent memory. I am the Shaw who remembers most things." She looked determined.

"Leo is our Nightingale with the excellent memory. Are there many of you?" Alex asked.

"I have two siblings, and as your uncle likely knows, my family is wealthy and part of London society," she said after long seconds. "I used the name Short so no one would know me."

"They are part of society," Alex asked, "but not you?"

She shook her head, eyes hooded as she looked at him. "I did not enter society after returning from the Templar Academy."

He wondered if that was by choice, but as she was already uncomfortable, he did not want to make her more so by asking.

"My family is invested in one of your father's consortiums from memory," Alex said. Over the last year, they'd decided to rebuild the Nightingale coffers, and through careful study and investment, he knew they were on track to do that.

"Which one?" Harriet asked.

"The Copal Mine."

She nodded. "Excellent choice. You will do well there."

Alex knew women were the equal of men for intelligence, but often they did not get involved in business dealings, as was the way in their society. Yet, what Harriet had just said told him otherwise.

"Are you involved in your father's business affairs?"

"Of course not," she said quickly. Alex had a feeling there was more to that.

"What else do you wish to discuss, Harriet?" Gray asked.

The glass was still cupped in her hands, and she looked down at the liquid before speaking. "I don't know what any of this means, but coupled with what I learned a few nights ago at the orphanage, I think it is suspicious."

"We had a meeting of the suffragettes at Mrs. Haven's house the day before the rally. Miss Haven's daughter was there, and she had on a necklace that her fiancé had given her. It was the exact replica of the one Frankie had stolen from her. I questioned her about where he got it from, and he overheard me."

"Are you sure it was the same as Frankie's necklace?" Gray asked.

"Yes. The angel on the front had ruby eyes. It was her mother's, and I remember it clearly. I left the house in shock because Frankie once told me her father had it made especially for her late mother."

"So it's unlikely there would be two of the same necklace," Alex said.

"Exactly. He wouldn't tell me where he got it, and said he'd forgotten."

"You didn't believe him?" Alex asked.

"No. I also felt like when he saw me he was surprised, as if he recognized me. I felt the same and asked if we'd met before. He said no. When I got to the street, I looked back, and he was watching me. Later I remembered that he worked at Templar Academy."

"Good Lord," Alex said as Gray scribbled down notes.

"There is more." She sipped the brandy again. "I was walking down a lane—my direction was the lending library. I saw two men talking. One was Tapper, a young man who works at the orphanage, the other was Mr. Sydney, who worked at the Templar Academy. He had helped bring Frankie out of the water and blamed me for her death."

"Did they see you?" Alex asked.

"I don't think so. I went into the closest shop and looked out the window. I bought a book there," she added, frowning.

"You didn't want the book?"

"It matters not." She waved his words away.

"Continue with your story, Harriet." Gray shot Alex a look that he interpreted to mean shut up.

"I ran into Mr. Sydney as I was heading home after hiding in the book shop. He recognized me, and I fled."

Alex thought Harriet should be locked in her room, and the key thrown away.

"There is more," she added. "The night of the meeting and before I met you at the orphanage rescuing Anna…"

Alex studied her pale face; the bruise was not dark but still there. To him Harriet looked vulnerable sitting there in that lovely dress, but he knew different. She was strong and courageous, if too reckless for his liking.

"I went to take tea with some of the other ladies after the meeting at Mrs. Haven's. While we were in the tea shop, I noticed a man looking in the window directly at me. I knew it was the same one I had seen following me before so went outside. I thought it could be Miss Haven's fiancé, but was not certain."

"You were being followed?" Alex bellowed.

"Alex, be quiet."

"Tell me you were not foolish enough to confront that man?" Alex continued, ignoring his brother-in-law.

Gray sighed.

"I realized when I had calmed down that it was a foolish thing to do. I do not need you to comment further," she snapped back. "I followed him into a narrow opening. When I did not see him, I turned to leave. He knocked me down and fled," she said quickly, as if the words tasted foul. "That is how I got this, as my cheek hit the ground."

"I cannot believe you would do something so reckless!" The words exploded out of Alex as he got off the desk to glare at her. "Do you know what could have happened to you?"

"Sit," Gray ordered him. "Now."

He glared at Harriet before returning to his perch on the edge of the desk.

"If I may continue," she said in a tight voice.

"Please do," Gray said, sending him another warning look to keep his mouth closed.

"Nigel, one of the boys who was there at the orphanage, according to Melvin, spends a lot of time snooping and, as yet, has not been caught."

"Excellent, what did he overhear?" Gray added. "Alex said you would have more information about the goings on at Gail Lane. I have started investigating, but anything you can offer will help."

"Nigel told me there were strange goings on and had been for years. He said the children were often used to do things against their will, like steal. He also said once that a child who got too close to what was going on went missing."

"Dear Lord," Gray whispered.

"Also, that Mrs. Secomb from the orphanage is Mr. Templar from the academy's sister, and he believes something is off with the two establishments."

"To do with the thieving?" Gray added while Alex battled to control his anger at her actions and the visions of what could have happened to Harriet. The man could have dragged her into that opening. Could have done any number of things to her she'd never have recovered from.

"Yes. He said they are stealing to order, or so I read between the lines," Harriet said. "When I was at the Templar Academy, there was something Frankie and I thought odd. Children used to appear at the door all the time. I often sat in the window looking down at the drive. They would go to the kitchen door, then leave, often carrying something in a sack.

Frankie used to sneak into the kitchens and take food, as they did not feed us a great deal, and she overheard someone saying that Mr. and Mrs. Templar would be caught one day and sent to hell."

Alex looked at Gray. Something nudged at him, and he let it in. He saw a bookshelf that opened into a room filled with shelves.

"Do you believe the staff were fearful of their employers at the academy, Harriet?" Gray asked.

"Oh yes. Everyone was terrified of them."

Bastards. So many in positions of authority were brutal and ruthless. Feeling that to hold control they must do so using tyranny.

"And now Mr. Sydney and Miss Haven's fiancé have recognized you?" Gray asked.

"I think it's fair to say they have," Alex added in a hard voice. "Either of those men could have followed you and knocked you to the ground when you recklessly—"

"Yes, yes, we get the point, Mr. Nightingale. There is no need to belabor it," she snapped.

There was absolutely no reason to smile, but he felt it tugging at his lips. This woman dragged more emotions out of him than was comfortable, and he just wasn't sure what to do about that.

"You have given me a great deal to think about, Harriet," Gray said. "One last question if I may?"

She nodded.

"Were you interrogated at the time by anyone but those that worked at the academy? Anyone from Scotland Yard or the local magistrate?"

Alex watched her brows draw together as she thought about that. There was color in her cheeks now, likely from the brandy. He wished he could spend a few minutes alone in that lane with the man who had hurt her.

"The local magistrate was called, and he did question me briefly, but Father was with me at the time, so he was not rude as the others had been. I believe I wrote his name in my journal." She gestured to the small notebook.

"I will read this and make some enquiries," Gray said, rising with her.

"But where will you start?" Harriet asked.

"Well, I am a detective and am very good at investigating," Gray said. "You have given me a lot of information, so I will work through that first."

"I think we need to go back to the academy. Surely the answer is there?" Alex said.

"I agree, but we are not rushing into anything. We will proceed with caution," Gray said.

"I have no wish to return to the Templar Academy," Harriet said quickly.

"There will be no reason for you to," Alex said. "We do not want to alert them that we are looking into what goes on there, and having you with us may do that."

"Well, I think for now that is all we need," Gray said. "If there is anything else you remember, Harriet, please let me know," he said. "But I must caution you to have a care, once again. Take no more risks as clearly you have upset someone if they were willing to hurt you."

She gave a nod but didn't speak.

"I will show you out," Alex said. He walked with her to the door and waited as she covered that lovely dress with her long coat. The bonnet was next, which she tied efficiently, and then Harriet donned her gloves. Opening the door, he waved her outside.

"Well good day to you, Mr. Nightingale."

Ignoring her dismissal, Alex walked her down the path to the carriage waiting just beyond the gate. Mungo sat in the driver's seat. Opening the door, Alex waved her inside.

"What are you doing?"

"Mungo will drive you home, Harriet."

"I will take a hackney."

Alex picked her up and put her inside and then followed, nudging her down onto a seat.

"Stop pushing me about, Mr. Nightingale."

"Alex," he said. She clamped her lips into a hard line.

He kissed them again. This time harder, and it was just as enjoyable as the soft brush he'd given her last time. "Address please?" he said, his face now inches from hers.

She gave it to him, her voice gruff, which pleased Alex. Clearly, he was not the only one affected by that kiss.

"Now, Harriet, I need your agreement you will not do anything foolish again."

"I can hardly do that. I have many years to live after all." She wouldn't meet his eyes.

"You know exactly what I am referring to, you little baggage. No more risks going out alone or walking the streets at night. No more rushing off to rescue children. This is not a game, Harriet, but deadly serious, and if your friend was murdered, or anyone else because of what is going on, then they will not hesitate to do the same to you."

Her eyes returned to his.

"Promise me you will show caution, Harriet."

She gave him a tight-mouthed nod.

"Say the words."

"What words?"

Alex did not bother answering her.

"Yes, I will show caution, Mr. Nightingale." She spat out his name.

"Excellent. I will see you again soon. Try not to get into any trouble until then. I would also suggest you do not visit the orphanage, as you cannot be sure no one saw you the night you took Anna."

"They didn't, and those children expect me to go. I will not give you that promise, but I will take someone with me."

He did not press her, even if he wanted to. Alex had no hold over this woman, but the hell of it was, he was starting to want that also.

"Goodbye, Harriet."

"Goodbye."

He stepped out of the carriage.

"Watch her enter the house please, Mungo."

"Aye, I'd already planned to do so. You seem quite concerned for the wee lassie, Alexander."

"No more than anyone."

The Scotsman clicked his tongue and started the horses moving.

"If a'thing's true, that's nae lee," Mungo added as the carriage carrying the angry Miss Shaw rolled away. The woman he now knew had very soft and kissable lips and disturbed him more than any who preceded her.

CHAPTER TWENTY-FOUR

*H*arriet had realized early in her disgrace that she had to fill her life with something. The women's suffrage movement was one, as were the orphans, and another was Mr. and Mrs. Lolly's bookshop, where she was currently.

In the two weeks since she'd visited 11 Crabbett Close, Harriet had shown caution. She'd only gone out during the day and then taken Sadie with her or gone directly to the location and home. She'd sent word to Milly that she would not be able to attend one of the night meetings, but she had marched again, as surely there was safety in numbers.

Today she'd ventured out for the first time alone, as Sadie had a sniffle, but she felt safe enough here and would ask Mr. Lolly to walk with her to get a hackney home.

Mr. Nightingale continued to send word to her about Anna, assuring her she was well, and that, in fact, his family was thinking of keeping her with them. Harriet had been elated over that but wondered what the procedure was. Could a child just leave an orphanage and no one looked for them?

Harriet felt terrible that she had not visited the orphanage for two weeks, but she thought it was best to stay away for a while as Mr. Nightingale had suggested. But she had every intention of returning soon. None of this was the children's fault, and she would not allow them to believe she had abandoned them.

"So if I take three from four, I get one, Miss Harry?"

"Very good, Kevin."

This was one of the things she had refused to give up, as Harriet didn't believe there was danger for her here. She spent two hours on a Tuesday in Lolly's Books. A two-story shop filled with wonderful literature and equally wonderful people, it was one of her favorite places to visit.

The day she'd walked into this shop and met the owners was the day she also met Violet, a young lady attempting to read a book on the top floor of the shop. Harriet had sat and read with her for a while. They'd met again the following week, and with her had been two of her friends. From there it had grown, and the Lollys had been more than happy to accommodate whoever wished to come and learn math or to read.

"I have tea, and Mr. Lolly has baked a fruitcake." Mrs. Lolly appeared at the top of the stairs with a tray, and behind her came her husband doing the same.

Tall and elegant, Mrs. Lolly had red hair in a shade Harriet had never seen before. She thought perhaps it was not her natural coloring, but as she had no wish to ask, she admired it and the woman's bright pink and red dress. Bracelets jangled on her arms, and around her neck was a choker with a large diamond. Harriet couldn't tell if it was real or not.

Mr. Lolly was her exact opposite. He wore beige, gray, or black clothing. His hair was brown and cut ruthlessly short. His moustache was brown, as were his eyes. Where Mrs.

Lolly was a bird of paradise, Mr. Lolly was a large unassuming field mouse. Harriet liked the couple very much.

"Numeration will help you with many things in life," Harriet said to her students, all bent over their slates working out the sums she'd set them.

"I'm finished," another young man, Barry, said. "Can I have cake now?" His smile was eager.

"Let me check you've done it correctly," Harriet said.

"Hello!"

The voice came from the floor below, and Harriet couldn't help it, she stiffened. The fear was still there over what had happened to her, but here she was safe, she reminded herself. And why would anyone intent on hurting her call out a greeting?

"I saw the lights on, Mrs. Lolly. I hope you don't mind us coming inside."

Looking to the stairs, she heard the heavy footfalls and then watched a man and woman appear.

"Well now, what is going on here, and why were we not invited?" the man said with a wide smile on his face. The woman was smiling too. Both had dark hair and green eyes and looked vaguely familiar to Harriet.

"Honestly, Cam, not everyone loves you," the woman said, rolling her eyes.

Clearly they were related, and studying them, she realized why they seemed familiar to her. The man in the bookshop that day she'd visited Crabbett Close had the same look about him.

"Hello," the man said, approaching. "Is that fruitcake?" He sniffed the air like a dog would.

The woman hissed out an aggravated breath. "We just had pies."

"And all pies should be finished with fruitcake, don't you think, Mr. Lolly?"

"Never in doubt, Mr. Sinclair," Mr. Lolly agreed.

Harriet's students were now watching the goings on with interest, their slates forgotten.

"Back to your work now please. You can have tea and cake when you are finished," Harriet said, clapping her hands. "And you have one incorrect, Barry." They grumbled but complied.

"I'm Mrs. Charlton, and this fool is my brother Mr. Sinclair," the woman said, coming forward with her hand held out before her.

Harriet took it. "I am Miss Shaw." The Lollys had only ever known her as Miss Shaw, so she'd kept that name when she started teaching here. Besides, after the confusion with Mr. Hellion, she'd thought it for the best.

"Miss Shaw teaches here on Tuesdays," Mrs. Lolly said, putting cake onto plates. The first slice went to Mr. Sinclair. He sniffed loudly, then sighed.

"Do you really? How wonderful and generous of you," Mrs. Charlton said. "Perhaps we could help while we are here?"

"Shaw?" Mr. Sinclair said after he'd swallowed a large mouthful of cake that would have Harriet choking. "Your accent tells me you could be related to George Shaw?"

Damn, she should have used Miss Short. "He is my father." Harriet found it hard to lie directly to someone's face.

"Is he really?" Mr. Sinclair smiled, and she thought he was a very good-looking man. But her heart did not thud a little harder as it did when Mr. Nightingale was close.

"I met your brother," Harriet said. "In another bookshop actually."

"I have two others," Mrs. Charlton said.

"Was it the old one with gray hair at his temples and a somber demeanor, or the younger one who can be like his older brother but also excessively annoying in that younger child way they have?" Mr. Sinclair said.

"Lord Sinclair," Harriet said.

"Was he attempting to tell you what to do? We get that constantly," Mrs. Charlton asked, and her brother grunted his agreement.

"He and his wife were very kind."

"Well yes, he can be that," Mr. Sinclair said grudgingly.

Barry drew her attention then, so she went to help him. She wasn't used to speaking to those who walked in society, and yet she thought that lately she was getting better at it with exposure.

"Who is learning their letters?" Mr. Sinclair asked, looking at the six students Harriet had tonight. "I'm exceptional at those."

Three hands went up.

"Right, let me see what you're working on," Mr. Sinclair said with the wedge of cake in his hand. "Select a book, Dorrie, and I'll read it after their lessons are finished."

"How do you know they want you to read to them? Besides, Miss Shaw may have a prearranged book to read," Mr. Sinclair's sister said.

"Do you?" He looked at her.

Harriet shook her head. She had a feeling most people fell in with this man's wishes.

"Hello!"

Another male voice had Mr. Sinclair moving to look below.

"What are you doing here, Nightingale?"

Surely it wasn't him? After all there were several Nightingales.

"I could ask you the same, Sinclair. It's late and the shop is closing."

Alexander Nightingale appeared at the top of the stairs,

his eyes finding her immediately before looking at the others in the room.

"I came to escort Miss Shaw home, as she is here alone." The look that followed Alexander Nightingale's words would have felled an oak. Harriet ignored him; she would not engage in any kind of verbal argument with the man while others were present.

How had he known she was here, alone, today?

"You know Miss Shaw?" Mr. Sinclair asked.

"I do."

"Your dark tone suggests you are displeased with her, Nightingale."

"Somewhat. But we will leave it there," Mr. Nightingale said in a tone that had students shooting yet more looks between them.

"And now, if you are quite finished, we will continue with our lessons," Harriet said, glaring at him.

While she spent time with the students, Mr. Nightingale talked with the others. Mrs. Charlton helped Harriet, and Mr. Sinclair asked for the odd word to be spelled or sum to be calculated.

She could feel Alexander Nightingale's eyes on her but did not return the look. They would no doubt have a reckoning but strangely that excited not annoyed her.

When she was done, Mr. Sinclair read his book, which had them all laughing. He used excellent voices and answered any questions about words the students asked him with patience and respect.

After the students had left, the Sinclair siblings, Mr. Nightingale, and the Lollys went downstairs. Harriet slipped into her jacket and picked up her things. Tucking them under her arm, she descended to the lower floor. Mr. Nightingale was nowhere to be seen, which surprised her. After a final goodbye to the Lollys and Mr. Sinclair and his sister, she left the shop wondering what his game was.

"I thought I told you to have a care."

She couldn't stop the squeak of surprise at his words.

"I thought you'd left."

"I'm not sure why you'd think that when clearly I was here because of you."

He wrestled her things from beneath her arm and started walking at her side.

"I can carry those!"

"As can I, now walk. There are crevices where anyone could be hiding ready to leap out and grab you."

"I have been showing caution," she protested.

"Yes, you have until tonight." He kept his long strides small to accommodate her.

"My maid was ill, and how do you know what my actions have been?" She could see him from the corner of her eyes. Impossibly handsome, the man had kissed her... twice now. She'd never been aware of anyone as she was him.

"I have had Percy and another watching you."

She stopped. "I beg your pardon?"

He did the same, his dark eyes locked on hers.

"Wh-what? You have no right," she spluttered. "I can care for myself!"

His hand raised, and then he was cupping the cheek she'd injured. "Really? Because I'm quite sure you injured yourself doing the opposite."

Harriet wasn't entirely sure how she felt in that moment. People didn't watch over her. Maybe the staff, and of course her sisters in the women's suffrage movement, but no one else because she gave them no reason to. But he'd taken it upon himself to have two people watch over her. The small cold knot in her belly began to unravel as heat filled her.

Did this man care about her? Surely not.

"I don't need you to do that."

"And yet I will, as no one else is. Likely because your family have no idea what is going on with you."

He lowered his hand, and she missed his touch instantly. Harriet's body seemed different when he was close. She was aware of him in odd ways that she didn't understand.

"You are far too reckless, Harriet. I understand you like to look after people and champion excellent causes, but now is not the time to do those things without caution."

"I will not miss this, as they rely on me. I have also explained that my maid was ill today."

"Then send word for me, and I will take you if Percy cannot." His expression was serious. This big handsome man would be there for her if she required it, unlike her family who saw her as a burden.

"Has Mr. Fletcher found anything?" Harriet needed to change the subject, or she would start weeping, and that achieved nothing but red eyes.

"The more he delves, the more he is quite sure all is not as it should be. Gray is having to proceed with caution, as he cannot know who is involved."

She looked around them. It would be dark soon, and yes, he was right—there were places here that people could hide.

"And Anna—"

"Is doing exceptionally well and fitting into life in our large, busy household."

"But what of the orphanage? Surely a child cannot just go missing or move in with a family? Are there not forms to fill out and people to be notified?"

"I think we've established that place is run in a shoddy manner, and our guess is the benefactors are unaware of what goes on there and how many children live at the orphanage. Anna is safe, and we will ensure she stays that way."

"You know nothing about her," Harriet felt bound to say.

"Harriet, my family cares nothing for appearance as we once did. My father spent every penny and sold property, and it still did not cover his debts, so he shot himself."

"No! I'm so very sorry, that must have been hell." She touched his hand, and he turned it and took her fingers in his.

"Thank you, but I assure you, we are better off as we are."

"But that kind of thing leaves a stain on your soul that I doubt you would ever erase."

He was silent for long heartbeats, his eyes on hers in the darkening light.

"It was hell."

"And still is in some ways?" She didn't open up to people or discuss their problems, but right then, it felt right.

He exhaled slowly and then nodded. "I don't speak of that time, but yes, like my siblings, I have scars. We are different because of what happened."

"To have lived one life and then be ruthlessly forced from it cannot have been easy," Harriet said.

"No, it was hard... still is, if I'm being honest, which oddly I am around you." He sounded confused.

"Sometimes the time is right."

"Has it ever been right for you?"

Harriet looked away from him briefly. She owed him the truth, as he had given it to her. It was an odd place to bare their souls, and yet she wanted to with him.

"No. I mostly keep things inside me. Until that day in your home, when I spoke to you and Detective Fletcher, I had shared those details from my time at the Templar Academy with no one."

"Then I am glad you were finally able to share that burden, Harriet. It is not good to keep it inside."

They were facing each other now, standing close enough

that she could read every expression that passed across his handsome face.

"As you have?"

"Perhaps. But I think now it is time for us to leave, as you need to get home."

"Mr. Nightingale—"

"Alex."

"Alex, you really don't need to worry about me." As the words left her mouth, she heard a sound. Seconds later he'd turned her.

"Run!"

She did as he asked into a narrow opening between two shops. He didn't stop, just kept moving to the end of the building and then right. They ran behind the buildings, and then he turned again. He kept running, taking left and right turns, and she gripped his fingers as if they were a lifeline.

The breath whooshed in and out of her lungs as she struggled to breathe, but he didn't stop, and she would not be the one to make him. That noise she had heard was a bullet hitting something, Harriet was sure of it, and she was equally sure it had been meant for her.

CHAPTER TWENTY-FIVE

Someone was shooting at them... her. Harriet had been the intended target for that bullet, not he. He could hear the breath rasping in and out of her mouth, but she didn't complain, just let him drag her down lanes and alleys.

He didn't know if they were being followed, had not stopped to listen, but could not take the risk of someone hurting Harriet. He could possibly deal with whoever was chasing them, but he would have her safe, and to do that he needed to find a place for them to hide. This woman was important to him; he knew that now. Knew that the fear he'd felt when he heard that bullet had nearly made his heart stop, because it was aimed at her.

"A-Alex."

"Soon, Harriet." He searched for a place to hide. Alex saw the lean-to. Likely it was to store wood. No one would believe they would choose it to hide in with the front open. Pulling her before him, he nudged her into it. "Get in as far as you can."

He followed and climbed over wood to the rear. There

was a narrow space between the wall and stacked timber. Alex lifted her and sat, then placed her between his legs so they were effectively hidden behind the wood.

"Quiet now," he whispered in her ear as she stiffened and tried to ease forward so she wasn't touching him. He closed the distance between them by placing an arm around her waist and pulling her so her back was pressed to his chest. He held her then with both arms wrapped around her body.

Her breathing was rapid from the run, fear, and likely being seated where she was. Alex listened for any sound. He heard the approach of footsteps, several pairs, and then they passed and slowly receded.

The cold began to seep into their clothes from the dirt floor beneath them. Alex tightened his grip on Harriet. She had a deliciously round bottom, and it was nestled in his lap —a fact his body was very aware of.

The return of footsteps could have been anyone, but he had a feeling it was whoever had fired that shot. The hands Harriet had on his tightened. Alex opened his fingers and trapped hers inside.

"It's all right. I won't let anyone harm you." He whispered the words into her ear. "You smell nice."

She choked out a sound that he thought was possibly a laugh.

She smelled of something soft and sweet, and he fought the urge to bury his nose into her neck. But he did keep his face right there, chin resting on her shoulder, surrounding her and giving her his heat and strength.

Alex was certainly warm. In fact, his body was on fire, but he could hear her clearly.

"I know Frankie told you she was murdered, but why do you believe I played no hand in that?"

He knew his answer was important to her, so only honesty would do.

"That day you came to Crabbett Close I felt your desperation, just as I did that day at the march. You loved Frankie, and you would never harm her. Plus, you are for the most part honest unless someone is trying to stop you doing what you want to."

She was silent for long seconds. "Thank you for believing me, Alex, and also thank you for reconnecting us with those in life that meant so very much. It is a miracle, and never doubt what it means to those you share your gift with."

Her words made him feel like he was choking. No one had spoken that way to him before. Alex felt like right then he could break down and weep.

"You're welcome. Who doesn't believe you?" Alex changed the subject, uncomfortable with her gratitude.

She gave a sad little sigh that nearly broke his heart.

"Most of my family except my youngest sister, Catherine." She felt their disbelief as a deep betrayal.

"I'm sorry they didn't believe you, Harriet."

"I've always been different, but this made it worse."

He pulled her closer, needing her to know he was there for her in that moment, and not just to protect her from men shooting at her.

"Different how?"

"My father, brother, sister, and I rub along for the most part, but our mother is everything that is proper and correct. Society and appearances must be adhered to at all times. My eyes at first made me different, and then I was a bit awkward and not what society would consider accomplished or beautiful—"

"Now that is a lie. You are beautiful and extremely accomplished," he said, outraged on her behalf.

"I did not tell you this for pity, Alex, but thank you. However, I do not need to be like others. I want to continue to live my life exactly as I am."

"Well, it's not like you can be anyone else."

"Haha. What I mean is I like being me for the most part, but my mother doesn't see it that way. She has left me alone since I returned from the academy due to the accusations of my stealing and Frankie's death. All that changed the other day."

He stroked his thumb down her cheek. It was cold to the touch. They would need to get out of here soon.

"What happened the other day?"

"Mother invited Lord Talbot to tea, because she wants a title in our family, and he would make me a perfect husband." Her voice was flat.

Alex felt a lance of anger at the thought of anyone but him touching this woman.

"Bertie is a good man, but not for you."

"You know him?"

"Yes. I was in society, remember?"

"He loves another, but you must not tell anyone that."

"I promise," he said solemnly as relief washed through him. "Now, Harriet, I want you to listen carefully to what I say," he whispered in her ear.

"All right."

"You are a beautiful, intelligent young lady who does not need acceptance from anyone but herself. I understand that your mother sees things differently, and of course she is to be respected, but never change, Harriet."

"Thank you."

"Although perhaps you could be less reckless and tamp down this penchant you have for dashing into danger."

She snuffled again. "I can hardly be blamed for this."

"You should have stayed home, Harriet, and then this would not have happened."

Instead of agreeing or disagreeing, she said, "Alex, when do you think we can leave here?"

"Soon."

He liked hearing his name on her lips. "I think it would be safe to do so now."

Neither of them moved; instead, she turned slightly, and her face was suddenly inches from his.

"Thank you for listening to me, Alex."

He cupped her cheek. "Thank you for listening to me, Harriet."

"I don't understand this."

"Someone is shooting at you, because clearly they see you as a threat, and you have seen too much."

"I understand that," she whispered, her breath brushing his lips, making them tingle. "Not this," she said, touching his upper lip with a finger.

"Ah, this," he said softly, fighting back the shudder at her touch. "I don't understand it either." He then kissed her because there was only so much provocation he could take. The woman he wanted was in his arms, her scent in his nostrils, and he knew what she tasted like.

He devoured her mouth with an urgency he'd never felt before. There, in that small lean-to with the smell of wood and cold ground beneath him, Alex kissed her, pouring his need for her into it.

The small sound she made had his body hardening. Her fingers gripped his lapels, holding him close. His slid inside her jacket, needing to feel the soft curve of her waist. Alex wasn't sure how long they stayed in there with night closing in around them, but in that moment, he was sure he wanted to be nowhere else. He was the first to ease back, pressing his nose to hers.

"For now, we get out of here and get you home to safety. As for the rest, we will discuss it another time, as a wood lean-to is really not the place."

She seemed happy with that as she nodded, clearly not wanting to discuss whatever the hell this was yet either.

Lifting her off him, he went first and climbed out of the lean-to. He then helped her out behind him.

"Don't speak," he whispered, "and stay behind me."

Alex needed to navigate to a busy street and get them a ride to her house. He knew London and had walked much of it, but it was dark, and he was struggling to get his bearings. He inhaled and exhaled, clearing his thoughts. Opening himself to receive anything that would help.

Help is coming.

He wasn't sure who had put it there, but he heard the words in his head.

"I've been looking for you everywhere!"

Alex turned at the voice and watched Cambridge Sinclair and his sister appear. He'd lost his hat, and his hair was standing on end.

"How the hell did you find us?" Alex asked. He tugged Harriet to his side, wrapping an arm around her waist. She didn't resist, which told him she was still unsettled. Hell, he felt the same.

"It's all right now," he said, feeling her tremors.

"My sister and I smelled your scent, Miss Shaw. It was how we were able to locate you when we realized all was not well," Cam said. "We'd just walked out the bookshop and we saw you fleeing."

"You're awfully fast. I could keep up, but Cam is older and—"

"You will not finish that sentence, sister," Cambridge interrupted her. "Care to tell us what is going on, Alex?"

"It's a complex matter, Cam. Did you see anyone following us?"

"I didn't, and we will not push you to explain, but should you need our support, we are here."

"We are grateful."

"Come, our carriage is this way," Cambridge said.

He took Harriet's hand again, and they walked to the carriage. When they reached it, he lifted her inside. As yet, she had not spoken a word in front of Cambridge and Dorrie. He took the seat beside her.

Alex felt the tension inside him slowly ease as they started moving. Harriet was safe for now, but what of tomorrow?

"For pity's sake, Cam, what are you doing?" Dorrie asked after her brother started rummaging to his right.

"I knew these were in here somewhere," Cam said. "My toffee. I got it earlier and hid it from you. Now seems the perfect time to eat it. Miss Shaw has had a shock after all," he added, holding out the toffee pieces for Harriet.

"Oh no—"

"Take one. It will make you feel steadier," Alex said.

She did and then proceeded to nibble on the sweet treat. Alex dragged his eyes from her mouth and took a piece of his own. The hit of sugar was steadying.

"Where shall we drop you, Miss Shaw?" Cambridge said after he'd sucked on his piece, chewed, and swallowed while humming his delight.

She gave the street address but no number. Alex knew where she lived, but clearly, she did not want her family to see her arrive in a fine carriage like this one.

"Number?" Cam asked.

"Just anywhere in that street, thank you." Harriet did not meet his eyes, just took another bite of her toffee.

Cam looked at Alex, but he shrugged. When the carriage stopped, he stepped out first and held out his hand.

"We shall wait here for you, Alex," Dorrie said.

"Come, I will walk you to your door."

She didn't argue and walked silently at his side. They

passed the house Alex knew was hers and went down a lane. She then stopped.

"Thank you, I am safe now." She sounded subdued.

"Harriet, I promise we will get to the bottom of this."

"You could have been killed tonight, Alex, because of me."

"Harriet—"

"I will take no more risks and therefore not put myself or anyone in danger, I promise." She rose up on her toes and kissed his cheek. "Thank you for saving me."

"Harriet, we will find who is doing this, I promise." He felt a desperate need then to keep her there with him. Keep her safe always.

"Goodbye, Alex."

He had to let her go, but he stood watching until she'd disappeared. Only then did he walk back to the waiting carriage.

"That was a smokey business, Alex. You need to have a care," Cam said when he joined him and Dorrie.

"It is not me in danger, Cam, but Harriet."

"I have never met her before, and yet she is George Shaw's daughter. He, his wife, his son, Oscar, and his daughter Catherine walk in society. Why doesn't Harriet Shaw?" Cam asked.

"Something happened in her past is all I can tell you."

"Very well, but I will reiterate that we have many contacts and will happily utilize them on your behalf."

"I'm grateful and will call should we need them."

After they'd dropped him at Crabbett Close, he found his uncle with Leo in the office.

"You look like hell," his brother said.

"And then some. I have something to tell you both, and then we must contact Gray."

He sat there drinking brandy, explaining every detail. His

uncle and brother were understandably upset he and Harriet had been shot at, but Alex could think only of Harriet.

What if he had not been there to protect her? She could, even now, be lying lifeless because someone had taken her from him. He could not allow that to happen.

Harriet Shaw meant something to him, and before he worked out just how important she was, he needed to find out who wanted her dead.

CHAPTER TWENTY-SIX

Harriet poked at the eggs on her plate seven days after being shot and kissed by Alex again. She was slowly losing her mind not leaving the house. She'd done none of the things she normally did and hated letting people down.

A note had arrived for her last night from Alex via Percy. It had not said anything humorous or taken her to task again, merely that investigations were proceeding, and information had come to light. *What information?* It also stated that she was to stay safe and not take undue risks, which was exactly what she was doing, and he would know, as he had someone watching her. He'd also said Anna was in excellent health as he hoped she was.

Yes, she'd been slapped in the face with what her actions had brought about that day at Lolly's. Alex could have been hurt because she'd gone there, and she could not allow that to happen.

When would she see him again? She longed to. How was that possible when they barely knew each other, and yet she felt as if she knew him better than anyone. And his kisses had made her want more. He made her feel alive, and she had not realized until he'd entered her life how much she'd needed that.

"Stop playing with your food, Harriet!"

"Sorry, Mother." She snapped back to attention. It was best to be focused and attentive when in the company of her mother.

"Your father and I ran into Mr. and Mrs. Cargill at a ball, Harriet. Their son Reginald is a lovely young man and will soon be returning to New York."

"Lovely," Harriet said, her mind still on the enigmatic Alex Nightingale.

"He is to call here this afternoon and wishes to take tea with you."

"Why?"

"You will be nice to him," Heloise Shaw plowed on.

"Why are you telling me this and no one else?"

"Because he is a nice man who I'm sure you will grow fond of."

Harriet looked around the table; no one met her eyes. Her father raised his newspaper.

"Which means what precisely?"

"Eat your eggs before they get cold," Heloise Shaw directed.

She wasn't sure she could swallow another bite. What was going on? Why was Bertie no longer being hurled her way, but some man who was returning to America.

"I don't want to eat my eggs. I want to know what is going on. First there was Lord Talbot, and now a man due to return to New York you want me to be nice to," Harriet said with a calm she was not feeling.

They were seated at the table, taking their morning meal as a family. A fire warmed the room from the chill outside, and the food was, as always, plentiful. Harriet's father read the newspaper, as did her brother. She wanted to read the paper but would have to wait for Sadie to slip it to her.

"You will take tea with Reginald, Harriet. That is all we ask," her father said, lowering his paper to glare at her. The wink softened the look.

Harriet loved the gregarious George Shaw, even considering he did not stand up to his wife where she was concerned. He rarely went against her wishes, but he was always ready with a smile or kind word.

"Why must I take tea with him?" she asked again. "Surely you don't wish me to wed a man who is to return to New York?"

"We will discuss this later," her mother said in that tone no one in the family was game to challenge.

"I don't want Harry to leave," Catherine said.

"I'm not going anywhere." Harriet patted her sister's hand. "For years you had no interest in me or my movements, Mother, and now you do. Be honest with me, what is going on?"

"For God's sake, Harry, why is this so hard for you? We let you stay away from society until the stain was erased from your name. It is now time to reenter," Oscar said in that tone that had her wanting to climb over the table and slap his smug face. "You need to grow up."

"Stain?" she said in a hard voice. "There was no stain, as I did nothing wrong."

"Now, Harriet, there is no need to get upset," her father said. "That is quite enough from you, Oscar."

"She is an embarrassment, Father," her brother said. "This suffragette business that I'm sure she is a part of, and the rest of the stuff she gets about doing."

"What?" her mother shrieked. "Tell me that is untrue, Oscar, and you are jesting!" Heloise Shaw locked eyes with her eldest daughter. "No child of mine will behave in such a disgraceful manner, ever!"

The betrayal hit her hard. Yes, her brother clearly had no absolute proof of what she'd been up to, but until now, he'd not cared, and they'd rubbed along together. She'd believed that was because they shared the bonds of loyalty siblings did. Yes, they were as different as night is to day, but she'd never thought he'd speak out against her to their mother, even after he'd told her he suspected what she was up to.

"She is marching with those women," her brother said, glaring at her, "and I'm sure there are other things."

Harriet did not show how much Oscar's words hurt. *No weakness.*

"I forbid it!" her mother yelled. "Never again will you do such a thing. What if our friends or acquaintances found out? We would be a laughingstock." Heloise Shaw looked at her husband. "Did you know?"

Harriet had never discussed what she did with her father, but by the look in his eyes, she could tell he knew. *Percy.* He'd told him.

"I did not know," he lied.

Another betrayal.

"What other things is she doing?" Heloise Shaw demanded. "I insist you tell me at once, Oscar. Or you." She jabbed a finger at Harriet.

She clamped her lips together and dropped her eyes to her plate. They would hear nothing further from her.

"From this day forth, you will not leave this house without someone accompanying you!" her mother roared. "I have left you alone for too long clearly, believing you were living a simple life in your room or the gardens. The lending library and lectures were places you've told me you visited. It seems you have lied to me, Harriet! Oh, the betrayal!"

In that moment, she'd never felt so alone, even

surrounded by people. Her thoughts went to Alex. He understood her, and she felt a desperate need to go to him.

"Raise your eyes and look at me when I speak to you, daughter!"

Something inside Harriet snapped. Suddenly it was all too much. The shame, the loneliness, and the fact that even her family did not love her enough to believe her all came to a head.

"You feel betrayed!" she scoffed. "It is I who feels that at the hands of all of you." She looked from her brother to her mother and father. "I have lived my life the only way I could. Did you really think I would not be lonely and be content shut away upstairs? I am your daughter, and yet you have done nothing but shun and ignore me. Would you have enjoyed that life?"

"It was not like that, Harriet," her father said.

"It was exactly like that. You have cared nothing about what I did or where I went as long as it did not impact you and your social standing—"

"How dare you!" her mother cried.

"How dare I?" Harriet growled. "How dare you turn on me when I needed you most! You believed the word of strangers over your own blood!"

The shock of that impassioned statement showed on each of their faces.

"Why am I no longer an embarrassment to you? The odd-eyed daughter who you've always struggled to understand or want." This time her gaze was on her mother. "The less than perfect child who you believed could steal and have a hand in her best friend's death."

"We did not turn on you, Harriet," her father said when his wife remained mute, her mouth now a perfect tight circle.

"That's a lie, Father, as you very well know."

"Someone needs to rein you in!" Oscar snapped "All this suffragette business and wandering around unchaperoned looking like an old maid. I will not have my future wife and her family embarrassed by you!"

"Future wife?" Harriet asked softly. Oscar dropped his eyes.

She looked to her mother and then her father; none of them met her eyes either.

"You did not even tell me you were engaged, Oscar?" Why that hurt so much, she wasn't sure, but it did. Just another perfidious act that shouldn't make her heart bleed.

"You are our child, and a reflection on us," her mother said. "It is time to stop this nonsense, Harriet. Those women are dangerous, with radical ideas that will help no one. Never again will you meet with them. What is done is done, and we will make the best of it. Mr. Cargill is a good man and will make you a fine husband. He will care little for your reputation."

"I do not want a husband, and I did nothing wrong," Harriet said. "And I support those women and their cause because I believe in them. Believe their voices should be heard," Harriet said.

"I forbid you to see them again!"

"Calm down, Heloise," her father said.

"And you support their words, do you, Father?" She looked at him and saw the sadness but also the resignation. He would do as his wife wanted.

"Of course he supports me. It is how we all feel!" her mother said. "You will go upstairs and change into the dress I have set out for you and prepare yourself to meet Mr. Cargill," she continued as if her husband had not spoken. "And from this day forth, you will leave this house with Catherine and I to pay calls and attend social gatherings as a family only."

She let her eyes move from her mother to her father and then finally Oscar. Harriet realized then exactly what they had planned for her. They wanted her shipped back to New York, so they did not have to deal with her.

The pain slicing through her at yet another betrayal almost bent her in half. But she would not allow them to see that.

"I will never forgive you for this," she said softly, getting out of her seat.

"Don't be dramatic," Oscar said.

"You want to wed me to a stranger and ship me off to New York, so you don't have to deal with me... your own blood," Harriet said. "What is Mr. Cargill bringing to the table, Father? How much money, or is it business connections? I'm sure you are not selling your eldest child cheaply."

"How dare you!" Heloise cried theatrically.

"Harriet, that is enough," her father said.

"It's not nearly enough, but for now, I am leaving. But hear this, if you push me to marry, Mother, I will leave, and you will never see me again." She then walked behind her little sister and placed a kiss on her head before leaving the room.

She locked her door and sat staring at the wall. There were no more tears inside her, just hollowness now. Even the pain had gone; she was numb.

A tap on the door had Catherine telling her to let her in.

"I'm sorry, Harry," her sister said when she'd let her in and relocked the door.

"It's not your fault. Will you tell me who Oscar is to wed?"

Catherine sat beside her on the bed.

"Oscar fell in love with Miss Evangeline Caruthers. She is the daughter to Lord Caruthers, and he is an earl."

"And?" Harriet prompted.

Catherine took Harriet's hands in hers and squeezed.

"And they want to meet all his family. They are absolute sticklers for propriety according to Mother, which is saying something considering how she is. Her and Oscar put their heads together and decided that it is time to bring you up to snuff."

"But I don't want to be brought up to snuff."

"I know, and I told them that," her sister said softly. "I'm so very sorry, Harry. You have shocked Mother and Father, and when you left, they looked worried."

"I don't care how they feel."

"Oscar looked guilty."

"Good, I hope he does. How dare he tell Mother what I've been doing."

"He wants this match and fears when they find out about you it will put the family off, which is entirely foolish. Anyone who knows you, knows how wonderful you are, Harry."

She grabbed Catherine and hugged her close. "Thank you for always believing in me." Her little sister just hugged her back. "Why did you believe me when I came home from the academy, Cat?" Her mother hated nicknames, but she and Catherine had always used them.

"Because you would never lie to us. In fact, I can't remember a time you've ever misled me, Harry. I asked you the day after you returned if you had anything to do with Frankie's death, and you looked me in the eye and said no."

"Thank you. It means a great deal hearing that."

"I'm so sorry, Harry. But know that I believe you and am here for you. I'm not terribly brave like you and will never stand up to Mother, however."

"She is not easy to stand up to, but I love you, little sister."

"I love you too."

Another knock sounded on her door, and Cat went to answer it. Oscar stood there.

"Go away," Harriet said. "Now."

"Look, Harry, I just need you to—" Harriet leapt off the bed and slammed the door in his face.

Cat snorted, and Harriet found herself giggling, and seconds later they'd collapsed on the floor together. Oscar hammered on her door twice more, but they ignored him. There was absolutely nothing to laugh about but still they did.

CHAPTER TWENTY-SEVEN

The Templar Academy was a twenty-minute carriage ride from the center of London. Ellen had decided after she'd got all the information about Harriet out of her husband, she needed to come also.

"I still can't work out how you managed to get Gray to agree," Alex said to her.

She and Gray were seated across from him.

"Well, we are going there to look at it as a future place to send our daughter," Ellen said.

"You don't have a daughter."

"It is not the truth for pity's sake, Alex," Ellen snapped. "But a cover, and a very good one too."

"You don't look old enough to have a child that would attend such a place," Alex said, continuing to needle his sister for no other reason than he could.

"Thank you," she preened.

"On second thought," Alex added.

"Children," Gray said. "That will do."

"So what's the plan?" Alex asked.

"The plan is for me to go and ask questions and you to

stay quiet and simply observe," Gray said.

"That doesn't sound like fun," both Nightingale siblings said at once.

"Besides, you know we are helpful, as Ellen will get a vision, and I can hopefully find some spirit in there that wants to talk," Alex added. "Aunt Tilda is also here with us, so she will help no doubt."

Gray actually looked around him.

"I can see her shadow, Gray. Now you are part of our family, she is a constant visitor when you are around. Who wears her necklace?"

"Me," Ellen said, smiling.

"She's pleased."

"It's unsettling is what all this is," Gray said.

"But you are doing so well." Ellen patted his hand. "You barely flinch now when I mention something that may happen."

"Thank you, my sweet." Gray gave her a tight smile. "I understand Ellen's reason is a solid one for being here, Alex, but not how I explain why you are. I can hardly mention you are here to chat with any spirits of the dead for those we meet."

"Of course not," Alex said. "I'm the concerned uncle who has all the money and will be paying for my dear, sweet niece to attend the Templar Academy."

Gray just stared at him for long seconds before saying, "Nightingales," then shaking his head. "There is no debating or talking rationally to any of you."

Ellen smiled at Alex, and that Nightingale sibling look of understanding passed between them.

He looked out the window as Mungo turned into a driveway with a sign that stated, "Templar Academy for Young Ladies."

Harriet had attended this place. The woman who occupied far too many of his thoughts, awake or asleep.

He'd not seen her since the night they'd hidden in that wood lean-to and avoided whoever had shot at her. The night he'd shared a part of himself, as she'd shared a part of her. He wanted to see her again. She was like a thorn in his side that he couldn't remove, as it was jammed in tight. The worry was constant too. Was she being careful? Had she left the house? Who wanted her dead?

Percy and the man he had watching her kept a close eye on her and, so far, had reported that if she left the house, it was during the day and accompanied. Frustratingly, they were no closer with finding answers to questions.

Gray had told him to have a care, as now whoever was after Harriet knew what he looked like too, but Alex didn't hide from anyone. In fact, he wanted them to come after him, so he'd deal with at least one of the men who wanted her dead.

"I feel like someone is blocking my every line of questioning on this case," Gray said. "It is exceedingly odd. I've made enquiries to the trustees of the Gail Lane orphanage for an interview, and they have constantly put me off. When I started asking questions about this place, the same thing happened."

"Which is odd?"

"Very. Someone usually talks," Gray said. "But I did ask Ramsey to speak to Miss Henshaw, who he knows. Apparently she is madly in love with him. He asked her about her time at the academy. She said it was ghastly, and her favorite necklace was stolen. She said the Templars are bullies, but still society send their children here believing the strictness is what is needed to mold young ladies for society."

"Aren't you glad none of us walk among those fools anymore," Ellen said.

"Extremely."

"We need to speak to someone who was there when Harriet and Frankie were," Alex said.

"Lady Carmichael," Ellen said. "She was Miss Tautly before she wed and attended the Templar Academy and would be Harriet's age."

"You are just guessing," Alex scoffed.

"No, unlike you, I am observant. And if my memory serves, which it usually does, she was rather enamored with you before she wed that fool Carmichael."

He remembered her as a happy, pleasant enough sort.

"I didn't know she was enamored with me, as so many were," he said to annoy Ellen.

She rolled her eyes. "Perhaps you could call and see her."

"Perhaps." But who he really wanted to see was Harriet.

Was she all right? Was her perfidious family treating her well? He hated that they had not been there for her when Frankie died. He would have been.

"Alex?"

"Ellen," he said with his eyes on the approaching building.

"Do you care for Harriet?"

His eyes turned so quickly he was sure they would be displaced, and he would forever be staring at the inside of his head.

"What?"

"Harriet. You know, sweet yet serious young lady who we have to thank for the wonderful Anna now being part of our family," Ellen said. "Short, and doesn't appear to have a great deal of humor—"

"She does," he protested. "You just have to know her."

"Which you do." His sister's look was smug.

Alex's eyes went to Gray, who was watching him. He would not add any weight to his wife's hypothesis, but he had seen how Alex was with Harriet that night when she'd told her story.

"Shut up, Ellen" was all he came up with. Her smirk told him she thought she was right, which she was, but he wasn't telling her that.

"We will continue this discussion later," his sister added.

"No, we won't."

The long tree-lined drive opened up to give them their first view of the academy. The building was brick and four stories that, from the front, looked like a large rectangle. He saw plenty of windows, and the entrance was made up of wide steps leading up to a black wooden front door.

Stepping out of the carriage behind Ellen, he saw ruthlessly weeded gardens in rows. He let his eyes roam before returning to the building. *Which room had Harriet slept in?*

"Everything is pristine and just so," Ellen said.

In the distance Alex saw two outbuildings, and beyond that, he guessed, was the river where Harriet had found her friend Frankie. What must she have felt that night. The terror and pain of finding her friend drowned and not being able to save her. He could almost feel her desperation.

"Is Frankie here?"

He shook his head. Her presence had not been as strong lately, but he knew she was around.

The sound of singing came from somewhere, and then a group of young ladies appeared. Five to be exact. They stopped when they saw Alex, Ellen, and Gray.

"Good day," Ellen said.

The girls bobbed curtsies and ran up the stairs giggling.

"I've never understood the need for the constant giggling some young ladies do," Gray said.

"It is certainly a mystery," Alex agreed.

They walked up the steps and through the door the girls had left open. The interior was as immaculate as the exterior. Paneled walls ran to halfway up, and then deep blue paper with gold diamonds the rest of the way.

"Good day to you."

The woman approaching wore a pale gray dress that stopped just under her chin and black boots. Her hair was scraped back into a bun so tight Alex was sure she was squinting.

"I am Mr. Fletcher. I believe you are expecting me? This is my wife, Mrs. Fletcher, and her brother Mr. Night," Gray added.

Gray was using his name in case anyone recognized him but was not advertising the fact he was a detective. Alex, however, was using a different one, as Nightingale was not common.

"Your academy is charming," Alex said. "I'm sure my niece will be quite happy to be schooled in such a place."

The woman nodded her head as if she was royalty.

"I am Mrs. Templar. Please come this way. We will discuss what we can offer her at the Templar Academy for Young Ladies and then tour our facilities if you should wish it. My husband will be with us soon."

"Wonderful," Ellen said, falling in beside the woman as Alex and Gray followed.

"How many girls do you have here at a time, Mrs. Templar?" Ellen asked.

While they chatted, Alex looked around him. The place was not unwelcoming but not welcoming precisely either. Those girls had seemed happy enough, he supposed. Had Harriet found any happiness in these walls or been miserable the entire time?

"I left my notebook in the carriage," Alex said before they walked into the room. "If you'll excuse me while I retrieve it. I like to take notes, you see, before we make a decision, and I would not like to forget anything, as dearest Alexia is so important to me."

Gray sent daggers his way as he retraced his steps. He

found Mungo standing beside the carriage.

"That was fast," the Scotsman said.

"Go to the stables, or wherever the horses are, and look around, Mungo. Find out anything you can."

"I cannot believe that wee lassie was treated so poorly here."

"Why do you believe she is telling the truth?" Alex asked.

"She would not have been there that night saving wee Anna if she was a rotten one. Plus, you like her, and while you annoy me, you're a good judge of character."

"Good God, did you just compliment me?"

"No, it was the truth," Mungo said before climbing back up on the driver's seat. Alex thought about that as he watched the carriage roll away in the direction of the outbuildings.

The thing about the Nightingale household was there were no secrets. If you did not want anyone who lived there to know something, the words never left your mouth, or someone would find out. Mungo was a member of their household; he was family. Therefore, he knew everything that went on.

Walking around the side of the building, he followed the path to the rear and found gardens and neatly trimmed lawns. It was a nice setting, and he could see the girls spending time out here on summer days. But then appearances, as Alex knew, were deceptive. Take him. He looked normal but, in fact, was far from it.

"Thank you for reconnecting us with those in life that meant so very much. It is a miracle, and never doubt what it means to those you share your gift with." Harriet had said those words to him when they were hiding. Each one spoken in her solemn little voice, and he'd heard the sincerity. No one had ever thanked him before.

Harriet. Alex sighed. "What am I going to do about you?"

CHAPTER TWENTY-EIGHT

What was it about her that got to him? Her fierce determination? The kindness? The glimpse of the lost girl he'd seen. He needed to focus, and thinking of Harriet Shaw was not doing that. The sweet little American who had more secrets than him.

Alex heard voices and moved toward them. If someone saw him out here, he'd say he was having a look around the property with an eye for his niece coming. After all he did dote on her.

"They want us to do all the things and pay pittance," a man groused from up ahead.

The door was open to what Alex presumed were the kitchens and staff entrance. Something nudged at him, and he let whoever was trying to talk to him into his head.

"She refused me, Mr. Maris." A woman's voice drifted to him through the opening. "I've been here for years and asked for nothing. Now my sister needs me while she grieves, and they won't even give me two days to be with her. They're shocking nipfarthings, and what with all the shoddy goings on that happen around here, you'd think they'd want to keep their staff loyal."

"We've turned a blind eye, Mrs. Maris. It's my wish we could find new positions, but at our age it's not likely."

Alex poked his head in the door at those words, knowing when he was in the presence of disgruntled staff and hoping they were in the mood to talk about their nipfarthing employers. "Hello."

Two people were taking tea at a scarred wooden table. Both didn't look happy to see him but rose to acknowledge him with a bow and curtsy.

"Are they shortbread biscuits?" He pointed to the table. "My driver is Scottish. They're his favorite," Alex lied. In fact, he had no idea what Mungo's favorite of anything was, as he never offered that information—*any* information—about himself.

"It's my recipe," the woman said, softening slightly. The man still looked ready to toss him out.

"May I ask you a question, sir?" Alex moved closer. The man nodded, looking wary now. "Do you believe in spirits communicating with us from the dead?"

The woman snorted. "Him, he's my husband and don't even believe in coincidence. Me"—she tapped her chest—"I believe in the past trying to communicate with us. I've a sister who can do that. Talks to my late ma all the time, she does."

"Well now that's a shame," Alex said. "Because a man named Barry... no, Barney, I think, is wanting me to tell you that he passed without pain, and thanks you for easing his passing by reading to him."

All color drained from the man's face, and he swayed slightly. Alex nudged him back down into his seat. You were never quite sure how someone was going to take what he told them.

"Barney?" he whispered.

"You take a mouthful of your tea, Mr. Maris," the woman said. "You sit too, sir, and take a biscuit. Would you like tea?" All hostility was now gone as she bustled about sorting Mr. Maris and plating up his biscuit.

"Barney is here with you," Alex said. He then took a large bite of the biscuit and let the buttery sweetness fill his mouth. "He wanted to let you know that it was his time, and he's showing me boots. Were they special to him?" Alex was piecing together the visions and words filling his head.

"I polish them every night," Mr. Maris whispered, pointing to his feet.

"That he does." Mrs. Maris nodded.

Alex smiled. "He's grateful."

"I put a drop of brandy in your tea," the woman said as Alex hummed his enjoyment after taking a sip. "It's a cold day, and it'll warm you. I'm Mrs. Maris," she added.

"I'm Mr. Nightingale, and I can't stay for long, as my sister and her husband are looking at the Templar Academy for my niece, and I decided to accompany them."

Mr. Maris had regained some color in his cheeks now, and it was him who spoke. "You'll pardon me for saying, and I'd be grateful if it got no further than the three of us, sir."

Alex nodded solemnly. "No word of what is spoken in here will pass my lips."

"Anyone my brother is comfortable with is good enough for me to trust," Mr. Maris continued. "He passed two years ago now, and I miss him every day."

"He was a good man and thought highly of you, Mr. Maris," Alex said.

Mrs. Maris handed her husband the handkerchief she'd pulled from a pocket in her skirts, and he dabbed his eyes. And this, Alex thought, was why he did what he did. To make a man like this have some peace for the loss of his much-loved brother. It made the craziness have meaning.

"This place is not somewhere I would send blood of mine," Mr. Maris said. He then shot a look over his shoulder to the door that presumably led upstairs. "There are odd goings on, and the Templars are a mean-spirited, tight-fisted couple. Cruel, too, to the ones they see as beneath them."

"Really? What sort of odd goings on, just out of curiosity? I mean it's a girls' school. I can't imagine what type of thing you allude to."

This time it was Mrs. Maris who looked at the door. "They've been doing bad things for years. Now I need my job, so I won't say more than that. But I'd not let my dog stay here—if I had one, that is," she added.

Mr. Maris nodded.

Alex needed to hurry before someone came looking for him, but he also wanted information. "I did hear a rumor about this place once, about a death here, but of course that was society gossip, I'm sure." Alex waved the words away. "My sister certainly thinks highly of the Templar Academy and is happy to send our beloved Alexia here."

The Marises looked at each other, and something passed between them.

"We shouldn't say," Mrs. Maris said.

"Of course, and I'd not want to push you." Alex ate another mouthful of very good shortbread, giving the appearance of a man not in a hurry, which he was. Another memory filtered into his head.

"Who is the woman who wore the lavender scarf?" He looked between them, and this time it was Mrs. Maris who looked shocked.

"It was your Aunt Ruth, Mrs. Maris," her husband said.

"I'm seeing a lot of laughter. Was she someone who enjoyed a lark?" Alex asked.

Mrs. Maris grabbed the handkerchief she'd given her husband as she nodded.

"She's showing me a knitted blanket."

She gasped and then dabbed at her eyes. "Sh-she used to throw it over her head and chase us around the house."

"She's showing me the memory," Alex said.

Mrs. Maris clutched her hands to her bosom.

"Shaw." Alex clicked his fingers. "I remember the name now. The woman was Miss Shaw. There was a scandal connected to her and the Templar Academy."

Mr. Maris took his wife's hand and squeezed the fingers. "I'm not rightly sure we should be discussing this with you, sir."

"Oh my," Mrs. Maris whispered. "He's one of them, Mr. Maris. A Notorious Nightingale. You remember our Rebecca's Tommy's great-uncle lives on their street?"

"Great-uncle?" Alex asked. "And yes, I am a Notorious Nightingale." If it got him information about Harriet's time here, he would use the name they'd been given by the residents of Crabbett Close.

"Mr. Douglas."

Alex smiled. "I know him well. Wonderful man."

"You found his granddaughter when she'd gone missing," Mr. Maris said.

It always amazed Alex how far the residents of Crabbett Close's connections reached. There was always someone who knew someone, somewhere. In that moment he was extremely grateful for that.

"Yes, we did find her," Alex added.

The Marises looked at the door again. "Harriet, Miss Shaw, was a good girl," Mrs. Maris whispered. "Sweet to us, but very serious minded, unlike that friend of hers, poor sweet Frankie." Mrs. Maris made the sign of a cross on her chest.

"I vaguely recall someone telling me there was a death and accusations but little else," Alex said, leading the Marises to tell him more. "I believe it was Miss Tautly."

The breath hissed from Mrs. Maris's mouth. "She was a poisonous one, that girl. Horrid to both Harriet and Frankie. Blamed them for stealing her necklace while all the time it was them who runs the place."

He filed that piece of information away as he finished off his shortbread.

"Those two girls were different, so the Templars treated them that way, and the other students did too. They were wrong to blame Harriet. What happened was a tragedy. I never believed Miss Shaw had a hand in her friend's death or that she was capable of stealing. It's that other business, you mark my words."

Alex wanted to ask more details about the other business but knew he'd already pressed them enough for information. They were staff who had been here a long time, and he had no wish to endanger their positions.

"Tragedy indeed. And now I must get back, but first I must thank you for the delightful chat and wonderful shortbread."

"You'll take some with you," Mrs. Maris said, getting to her feet. "As a thanks for what you told us. Mr. Maris will be a great deal happier now he knows about his brother."

"Aye, it's a wonderful gift you've given me, Mr. Nightingale," Mr. Maris said.

"Good day to you both." Alex left through the door he'd just entered with a few wrapped shortbreads now tucked into his pockets. Thoughts churning, he wandered back to the entrance and entered the Templar Academy once more.

Harriet was treated terribly here, and that made him even more determined to find out what was going on. He wanted justice for the girl who had lost her friend and then been blamed for her death. The girl who lived a lonely life because her family would not allow her to enter society.

She'd thanked him for believing her, but her own family should have done that before him. He'd have something to say to them too when he met them. He now felt it was inevitable he would.

CHAPTER TWENTY-NINE

Making his way back to the room he'd left, he tapped on the door and reentered.

"There you are, brother. Where did you get to?" Ellen gave him a hard look. She was pale, which suggested to him that she'd had a vision.

"I wandered over the property a bit. I wanted to ensure my precious niece would have room to walk with her book should she wish it. You know how much she loves to read."

Gray gave him a hard look he could not interpret.

"I must commend you on the gardens." He turned his eyes to the woman. With her was now a man, presumably her husband, Mr. Templar. "It is a lovely place, and any young lady would be happy here, I'm sure."

They both nodded, pleased with his words. Where Mrs. Templar was neat, severe in the cut of her clothes and hair style, her husband was a big bull of a man. His necktie was crooked, and his jacket had a smudge of dirt down one lapel. His hair was cropped ruthlessly short. The word thug screamed in Alex's head, and he knew this man had been one of the people responsible for hurting Harriet in her time here.

"Alex, this is Mr. Templar," Ellen said.

"Good day to you." Alex forced himself to smile and acknowledge the bow Templar gave him.

"The Templars have been telling us all the things the residents who attend the academy will get when they come here. It seems our darling daughter will be cared for as well as she is with us," Ellen added.

Not bloody likely. No way was a niece of his, even one who didn't exist, coming here. His eyes went to the bookcase, and he remembered the vision he'd had. This was the room.

"Do you mind if I study your titles? I'm something of a collector, you see. I have paid large sums of money for books that I like."

Mr. Templar puffed out his chest. "Of course. We have some fine examples of literature here. We keep them for the girls. It's important all our students leave with an educated mind."

"You are to be commended," Alex said, nearly choking on the words as he wandered closer. He could feel the eyes of Ellen and Gray on him, wondering what he was about.

Talk resumed about what his phantom niece would get here while he studied the titles, not taking any in. Pulling out a couple of books, he pretended to study them as he searched for levers and anything that would alert him to the fact this was indeed a door.

"Did you find anything that interested you, sir?" Mr. Templar joined him. Something in his demeanor told Alex he was growing nervous over his inspection of the books.

"There is one that caught my eye. I was just working my way down to it." Dropping to his haunches, he pulled out a book and settled his hand on the shelf, letting his fingers stretch right and left as he had with the others. His middle finger brushed something. He rose with the book in his hand.

"You wish to buy the *Elite Woman's Housekeeping Manual?*" Mr. Templar said.

"For my sister, you understand," Alex said, studying the book. "Alas, however, it is not a first edition. I only purchase those," he said in a snooty voice.

"Well, I think we have all the information we could need," Gray said. "If we could have that tour of your facilities now, we would be most grateful."

Alex handed the book to Mr. Templar. "Thank you for allowing me to look over your collection, sir. Good day to you."

Alex hated to think of her here. Harriet was not meant to be in a place like this; she needed to be with people who understood her.

People like him.

They were shown where the girls slept, and the dining hall and other areas that the Templars thought they needed to see. There was apparently a large waiting list, and Ellen assured the Templars they would be contacting them soon to have their fictitious daughter enrolled.

Alex loathed the place and could not put his finger on exactly why, other than he hated what had happened to Harriet here. It was clean, and the rooms comfortable with plenty of light. But there was a darkness that unsettled him.

They left the Templars and made their way back to the carriage.

"Here, I got this for you because unlike you, I'm a nice person." Alex handed Mungo one of the biscuits from his pocket. "I'll hear what you learned later," he added in a softer voice. The Scotsman grunted.

Alex drew in a large breath and exhaled it slowly as they

rolled away from the academy. The tension he'd felt since entering that place drained away.

"No child of my blood will ever attend there," he said. "Never."

"Agreed," Gray and Ellen said together.

"Now tell us where you really went and who you spoke to," Gray asked. "And why you needed to inspect that bookshelf because I, for one, know you do not have an extensive book collection or a wish for one."

He told them everything he'd discussed with the Marises, and the vision he'd had of the bookshelf.

"Only you would get shortbread while ferreting out information," Ellen said, eating hers in large bites.

"The point is that the Marises said there were some bad things going on at the Templar Academy. They also did not believe Harriet capable of harming her friend, or of stealing."

"You're angry," Ellen said, lowering the last bite of her biscuit.

"Of course I'm bloody angry! Someone in there hurt Harriet through no fault of her own. Plus, she was treated terribly because she was American. Then she was sent home with the shame hanging over head that she may in some way be responsible for the death of her friend and the thieving that was going on in the Templar Academy. She loved Frankie like a sister."

Ellen and Gray were both staring at him intently now.

"You really do like her," Ellen said softly.

"It's nothing to do with liking her. It's to do with how she was treated." Knowing Harriet had been in that place and suffered made him unreasonable.

"No, you like her," Ellen said, emphasizing the word like.

"Saying it louder does not make it any truer," Alex snapped. "Now tell me what you found out," he said, dismissing her words. He wasn't about to talk about Harriet.

"Stop annoying your brother, my love," Gray said. "As for what we found out, only that the Templars are horrendous snobs who threw about titled names like birdseed."

"I asked about a rumor I'd heard at a society event—"

"Which was a lie, my sweet, as you don't walk in society," Gray added.

"I said I'd heard there was a tragic event," Ellen continued, undaunted by her husband's strict moral code, "and the Templars did not look happy about my question. They rallied and said there was a bad experience with two very foolish young ladies that ended in tragedy. Mr. Templar added that the truth to what happened would never be known, but that it was the fault entirely of one of the girls."

"Bastard," Alex hissed. "Now tell me about your vision, Ellen."

"You had a vision in there?" Gray shot her a look. "You didn't say anything."

"I was hardly going to say, 'Gray, I feel a bit queasy due to the fact I've had a vision where Mr. Templar was disciplining a young girl.' His wife was in the room too, and Mr. Templar was using a cane on her."

"Dear Christ," Gray hissed. "I'm sorry, love. I didn't realize."

"Not your fault, and I was fine, as you were close," Ellen said, allowing her husband to grip her fingers. "The thing is, Alex. I can't be sure, but I think that vision was of Harriet."

He wanted to roar but instead looked out the window at the city of London as it rolled by while he attempted to control his rage. People were scurrying about in the cold weather, and he saw nothing, only the red mist of anger.

"Alex, do you still believe Harriet completely? Believe she is innocent, and her friend Frankie murdered?" Gray asked. "Or could it have been an accident?"

"It was no accident, Gray." He looked at his brother-in-law. "Frankie was murdered. I saw the hands around her neck."

Gray nodded. "Right then, we need to find a solid link between the Gail Lane orphanage and the Templar Academy."

"Isn't that your job?" Alex snapped.

"Which I am trying to do," Gray replied calmly.

"There are several links," Alex said. "The two boys Melvin and Nigel who told Harriet about the matron being related to Templar. Harriet saw a man from Templar and the orphanage together. Then there is Miss Haven's fiancé and Frankie's necklace."

"Yes, Alex, but we don't have anyone who can testify. The word of two young orphans and a woman with Harriet's reputation are not enough to convict the Templars or anyone from the orphanage. Especially as, on the surface, they appear to be good people."

"Harriet's reputation is not her fault!"

"I know that too."

"I'm walking home," Alex muttered, banging a fist on the roof of the carriage.

"I don't think that is a good idea in your current mood. You don't have anyone with you to extract you from trouble if you should find some," Ellen said.

"I rarely need extracting from anything," Alex said. "You have no need to worry. I am a big boy and can handle myself." Kissing his sister's cheek, he stepped from the carriage once it had stopped.

"Where are you going alone?" Mungo demanded, his brows a straight line as he glared down at Alex.

"Walking home. I need to think. Did you find out anything in the Templar Academy stables?" Alex asked him.

"Only that the owners are penny-pinchers and don't have enough staff."

Alex nodded and then raised his hand in farewell.

"Don't get into trouble," Mungo said.

"As if I would do that," Alex replied.

The carriage rolled away, and he dug his hands into his pockets and walked. They had to find the information they needed; only then would Harriet be safe.

The scent of lemons filled his head again.

"What do you want, Frankie?" Harriet slid into his head, and he felt her desperation. Walking faster, he cursed himself for getting out of the carriage. Now he'd have to run home. Once there he'd send a note to Harriet asking if she was all right.

Something told him she wasn't.

CHAPTER THIRTY

Harriet took tea with Mr. Cargill in her mother's favorite parlor because Heloise Shaw said she would refuse to allow Catherine to attend her friend's birthday party tomorrow if she didn't. She knew her mother was ruthless when her mind was set on something, but it had shocked her that she'd punish her youngest daughter to ensure Harriet cooperated.

"Harriet loves music and is an excellent piano player."

At least that wasn't a lie. She was a proficient piano player and did love music.

"How wonderful. I never learned, but I do like to sing," Mr. Cargill said.

He was a great deal older than she'd thought he'd be. In fact, she was quite sure he had twenty years on her. Tall, thin, with thick brown hair and a nice smile, the man was pleasant enough and chatted about books and his love of music, prompting her to offer her opinions on each.

"Harriet loves to read also," her mother said, smiling at her benevolently as if she had not lied to get her into this room. As if their earlier argument was forgotten, and her eldest daughter did not loathe her for what she had done and continued to do.

She might always love her mother, but she did not like her very much and knew she never again would.

The hour dragged into the next, and Oscar joined them to chat with Mr. Cargill. Harriet refused to acknowledge him unless he spoke directly to her, and then she answered in as few words as possible.

Mr. Cargill likely thought she was shy. What she was, was hurting and furious.

When finally their guest rose, Harriet knew only relief.

"I would like to take you driving while I am here in London, Miss Shaw. I will hire a carriage. Perhaps two days from now?" Mr. Cargill took both her hands in his and looked deep into her eyes.

Harriet knew then that he would offer for her, and she would be forced to accept. Her family would make it impossible for her not to.

"Of course, she would love that," her mother said before she could speak.

They waved him goodbye, and then Harriet started for the stairs.

"Well, he is a lovely man," Heloise Shaw said.

"Harry?" Oscar followed her. "What did you think of Mr. Cargill."

She didn't speak, simply walked away and didn't look back.

In her room, she shut and locked the door, then paced. Today she would normally be at the orphanage and wanted desperately to go there now. The children needed her as right then she felt a need to be with them.

She had to speak with her parents and make them see reason. They could not force her to wed Mr. Cargill. Harriet had to tell them exactly how she felt, as her entire future was at stake.

She inhaled and exhaled several times. Then stalking back to the door, she unlocked it and left her room. Making her way down the stairs, Harriet prepared her speech. They were her parents. Surely, they would want what was best for her, and she was the one who knew what that was.

"Cuthbert, are my parents both still here?" she said when she found him polishing the glass of a painting on the first floor.

"They are both in Mr. Shaw's study, I believe, Miss Harry."

"Thank you." Harriet hurried in the direction of her father's favorite room. The sound of raised voices had her stopping when she arrived at the door. She heard her name and leaned in to listen.

"She will wed Cargill and leave, George. She is never going to change, and the stain on her reputation will hinder the chance of a good match for Catherine, as it will always be there. Someone will always know what she has done. Oscar's fiancée has already started asking questions about his older sister who she has yet to meet. If she is not here, we can say she is married to her childhood sweetheart and living in New York."

"Harriet is our daughter, Heloise. We cannot simply force her to wed Cargill, then banish her from England."

Ice was slowly filling her veins as she listened to her mother discussing her fate as if her opinion mattered for nothing. At least her father was protesting.

"It is the only way. She has family in New York, and they will care nothing for her reputation there. It is the right thing to do. Harriet is unruly, disrespectful, and an embarrassment. I will not be challenged on this, George. Mr. Cargill was enamored with her and will wed her in a quick ceremony before he leaves London. My mind is made up."

She'd not thought they could hurt her anymore. She was wrong.

"If you believe it is the right thing to do, Heloise, then I will ensure it happens. But I will miss her."

"Yes, yes, we love her, but she can no longer live in this household," her mother said. "It is the right thing to do, George. But I fear this will not be easy to achieve. In fact, I believe if she hears our plans—"

"I think it likely she is aware by now of your plans, Heloise."

"Then I believe she must be watched constantly. No leaving the house at all and have a staff member watch her. We cannot allow her to ruin everything we have planned. We were fooled into thinking she was living a quiet life when she was marching with those women!" Her mother spat out the word.

"An alliance with Cargill will be good for business," her father said, dashing Harriet's last hope that he would not see her wed and forced to live in New York.

"And soon we will have nobility in the family through Oscar's marriage. Now drink your tea, George, and then we will set things in motion. If need be, I will lock Harriet in her room to achieve what we want."

Harriet did not stay to listen to her father's response but walked quietly back to her room.

Her mother would not hesitate to put her plans in motion, and while Harriet may protest and refuse, Heloise Shaw would find a way to make her wishes happen.

She did not want to wed Mr. Cargill and return to New York. Her life was here. She'd created it and intended to live it.

"I have to leave now," Harriet whispered.

Without giving herself time to think about what she was to do, she rose and went to the cupboard. Taking out her largest bag, she packed it with clothes. Harriet then took another that she put the four books she treasured most in. It would break her heart leaving the rest, but that could not be helped. Gathering any other possessions that she could not bear to leave behind, she placed them in the bag and then left both by the door.

Sitting at her desk, Harriet took out her writing things. After penning two notes, she left them where they would be found.

Lastly, she opened the drawer beside her bed. Harriet took out a small box. It was inlaid with pearls and small paste gems. Oscar and Catherine had given it to her one year for her birthday. Inside she found a black velvet pouch. There was enough money in here to live off for many months. After that she would find a position or do what she must to survive.

It broke her heart she could not say goodbye to Catherine, but there was no time to do so in case her parents saw her.

She fastened her heavy velvet cloak and tied on her bonnet. Tucking her gloves in her pockets, she was ready. After a last look around her room, Harriet opened her door and left.

She hurried down the stairs with her bags, hoping to encounter no one. Reaching the bottom floor, Harriet slipped into the small parlor with a window that faced the gardens. Her father's office looked out to the house beside theirs, so her parents would not see her leaving.

Harriet wanted to avoid the kitchens, as the staff would be there, and she had no wish for them to be questioned over her disappearance. Raising a window, she threw her bags into the gardens, finding a perverse pleasure in flattening several of her mother's treasured petunias.

Climbing out, she raised the hood of the cloak. Picking up her bags, she then walked around the house to the rear. Taking the gate, she slipped past the stables undetected and out onto the street.

Harriet then walked, not even noticing where she went or the people she passed.

Her family were going to discard her like yesterday's unwanted washing water. She meant nothing to them. They could not love her if they were willing to do such a thing.

She could not allow the panic to set in. Right now, Harriet had to find lodgings for the night; tomorrow she would work out her next steps.

One thing she did know was that she could not return to her family. Would not be a pawn in whatever game her mother played. She was strong and intelligent; she could survive without them.

She carried her bags with biting cold slicing through her but felt nothing but numbness. After she had secured lodgings for the night, she would pay a last visit to the orphanage. They needed the knitted garments Miss Alvin and the other ladies had made. It was colder each day, and the children were in dire need of them.

Alex had told her not to return, but she would not linger, only stay to drop them off, as one thing had become clear. She would need to leave London, or her parents would find her, which was funny really, as leaving London for New York was the reason she'd left her family.

But it's different, Harriet thought. I would have been married to Mr. Cargill, a man I don't know. Plus, New York was not a carriage ride away from her family.

The thought of leaving tugged at her heart. The

suffragettes, the orphans, her students, and, of course, Alex. It was almost unbearable to think of not seeing them again.

"Miss Short?"

Coming toward her were Mrs. Greedy and Miss Alvin. Both wrapped in layers of clothing, holding the other's arm as they strolled as if the day was warm and sunny, not frigid.

"Good day to you," Harriet said, hoping none of the desperation she felt showed on her face.

Mrs. Greedy moved closer and studied her. "What's amiss with you, Harriet?"

"Why nothing at all. Now if you'll excuse me, I must—"

"Why are you carrying those large bags?" Miss Alvin cut her off.

"I, ah, I have to take them to the orphanage."

"Do you now? Well I have a bag of knitting. We'll just go to Crabbett Close, which is not a ten-minute walk from where we're stood, and collect it."

"Actually, I have that wrong. These bags are clothing I wish to donate to those in need," Harriet said quickly. "Silly me, I quite forgot." Her voice was high-pitched now and bordering on hysterical.

"But today is the day you go to the orphanage?" Mrs. Greedy asked.

"It is, yes. I was going to drop these bags on the way. I need to see the children today." She was determined in this, as it could be the last time if she chose to leave London. She would see them and explain that she might not be able to return for some time, if ever.

"My day is complete," a deep male voice said. "Three beautiful women stand before me."

Old Miss Alvin's face seemed to disappear in on itself as she smiled. Harriet thought about simply fleeing as she looked at Bramstone Nightingale. She was fleeing her family, so why not these people?

"Miss Shaw, are you well?" he asked her.

The fact that she saw Alex in the face before her had tears stinging her eyes. Everything she'd done in the last... actually, Harriet had no idea how long ago she'd left her house, but it was taking its toll.

"Who is Miss Shaw?" Miss Alvin asked.

"I am," Harriet said. "I lied to you about my name." She would lie no more. That, at least, was done with. "I'm sorry."

"You're a good girl, so the reason would have been a pure one," Mrs. Greedy said, patting Harriet's cheek with a gloved hand.

"Let me take those bags for you. They appear heavy," Mr. Nightingale said.

"No! I need to go. Really, and thank you." She wasn't sure what she was thanking them for, but she did anyway. "Are you returning to Crabbett Close, Miss Alvin? I will call there shortly and pick up the knitting before taking it to the orphanage."

"I am returning there now. Would you like to come with us?" Miss Alvin asked.

"Soon," Harriet said. She needed to find lodgings.

"Miss Shaw, is there anything we can help you with?" Mr. Nightingale said, moving closer to Harriet. "Clearly you are upset."

"What? No, I am not and quite well. Please excuse me, I must go. I shall see you soon, Miss Alvin. Good day."

"Let me—"

Harriet ran then. Crossing the street, she kept running until her aching sides forced her to stop. Leaning against a building she caught her breath. Bramstone Nightingale will now think she is mad.

She saw the sign then. *Lodgings available.* Gripping the handles of her bags, she hurried to the door. Stepping inside a small front entrance. A woman was seated behind a desk.

"Can I help you?" She rose as Harriet approached.

"I would like a room please."

"I'll expect payment up front."

For all she'd believed herself practical and independent, she wasn't when faced with doing something like this. What she was, was naïve. Other than staying at the Templar Academy with Frankie and the other girls, she'd never been away from her family or, if she was honest, independent. Shelter, food, and clothing had always been provided, and staff had been there to meet her needs. It was terrifying to feel so completely alone.

Handing over what seemed a large sum of money, she followed the woman to her room. The place wasn't what she'd call clean. The walls were dirty, and rugs frayed, and the lady leading the way up the stairs had a grubby air about her too, but Harriet could not afford to be picky. She needed a room, a place where she would be safe, at least for tonight.

Dear Lord, she would be sleeping here alone. Be brave, Harriet.

Following the woman who had said her name was Mrs. Smith through the door she'd just opened, she found it had a chair, bed, and washbowl, but nothing else. Harriet wondered if the bedding was clean.

"The door will be locked by ten p.m. Be sure you're inside before that, and no gentleman callers."

"Thank you." Harriet knew that didn't apply to her but made no mention of that fact.

The woman left, and she looked around the small, dismal space and had a momentary twinge of doubt over what she'd done. But the memory of her parents discussing her future so callously reminded her she'd made the right decision no matter how terrifying.

She sat on the bed and took out her writing things; then she wrote a list. If she was organized, she would feel better.

1. Find a location to travel to.

AN IMPERFECT GENTLEMAN

2. Write a list of accomplishments and references.

Harriet would need to write her own, as she did not have any. But she was proficient in many things, so surely there was a need for someone like her? Could she be a governess? Perhaps a companion?

3. Find the stagecoach timetable.
4. Say goodbye.

She looked at the last notation and thought of Alex. Harriet felt ill at the prospect of never seeing him again. Milly, too, had become her friend.

Feeling nauseous over what she must do, she put away her things. Harriet would collect the knitting and visit the orphanage tomorrow, she decided. No one would tell her otherwise, so she could be at Gail Lane early and stay as long as she liked.

"I can do this."

Leaving the building, she struck out for Crabbett Close; she would get something to eat on the return journey and take it to her room. She would then lock the door and climb into her bed and pray for the oblivion of sleep eventually, because when she woke, the fear and uncertainty would return.

CHAPTER THIRTY-ONE

Alex sprinted to the office library when he arrived home. Sitting at the desk, he penned a note to Harriet. Once that was done, he searched for Mungo, who would see it safely delivered into Percy's hands. He was not on the lower level, so he headed upstairs. Alex did not locate him there either.

Where was that bloody Scottish behemoth?

Making his way back downstairs, he found Anna sitting on the bottom step studying the portraits of his grandparents above her.

"Hello." He sat beside her. Alex could take a few minutes with the little girl. After all she was now part of his family.

Her appearance was vastly different from the pale, injured child they'd brought here that night. She wore a dress of pale blue muslin with a bow of deep blue ribbon in her hair.

"Those are our grandparents. He was an austere fellow, our grandfather," Alex said.

Anna did not talk much; she was usually quiet and watching when they were all together. His younger siblings said she chatted with them but was wary around adults, which was understandable considering the life she'd led, and no doubt the punishment she'd received at their hands.

"Was he nice?" Her eyes were still on the paintings.

"Yes, if a little gruff. But he did tell wonderful stories."

"I don't have family." The words were solemn and made his chest ache.

Alex might curse his family at times, but he would never be without them.

"Yes, you do. You now have us."

She turned to look at him then. Her blue eyes were serious. "Why do you want me?"

A simple question and yet anything but. Alex knew his answer was important to her. They'd discussed her coming to live with them. Everyone had to agree and had wholeheartedly.

"Because we were missing something in our lives, Anna. There was a small space in here"—he tapped his heart—"that needed filling, and you have done that."

Her eyes continued to study him, face expressionless.

"Do you want to stay with us, Anna?" Alex wasn't sure if anyone had asked her that.

She nodded.

"Excellent." He was used to children who talked constantly, but not this one. He doubted anyone had listened to her before she'd come here.

"Thank you, Alex." The words were whispered, but he heard them.

"For what?" It was the first time she'd spoken his name.

"For wanting me."

Christ. He wanted to pull her onto his lap and hug her hard like he'd used to do with Matilda, Theo, and Freddy. But Anna did not like to be touched.

"Wanting you in our lives was easy, sweetheart. We want you to be happy here with us. Do you think you can be?"

She nodded. "Yes, I know I can."

He realized then who she reminded him of when she spoke. Harriet had the same steady, serious way about her. The same vulnerability that tugged at his heart.

"I don't want to go back there, Alex. I will miss my friends and am sad I didn't get a chance to say goodbye."

"I had planned to visit the orphanage soon. Do you want me to say goodbye to them for you?"

Her blue eyes widened, and then she was nodding. "Especially Melvin, but why would you want to go there?"

They'd not questioned her about what she knew, because she'd been too ill and fragile, but perhaps she knew something that would be helpful to the investigation.

"We think something is not right there, Anna."

"I know where they hide things," she whispered.

"What things?"

She looked around her as if someone would be there and stop her from speaking.

"No one will ever hurt you again," Alex vowed. "Remember you are one of us now, Anna. A Nightingale."

"Anna Nightingale," she whispered. "I never had a last name."

"Well now you do," Alex said, his voice tight with emotion.

"In the orphanage, there's a room. It's upstairs in Matron's office. One day Nigel and me heard Mr. Sydney who was visiting from the academy roaring for Matron to come quick. She did, fair flew past us down the stairs. Them are sharing a bed, you see, and she'd do anything for him."

He knew this, as Nigel had told him, but let her talk.

"Nigel told me this was our chance to see her room. We ran up to her office. He stood outside, and I went in. There's a bookshelf in there, and that day it wasn't locked, just pushed closed."

The room he'd seen wasn't at the Templar academy; it was at the orphanage, Alex realized.

"What was in the room, Anna?"

"There was a large wooden box open, and it was full of sparkling jewelry. Rings, necklaces, and the like. A shelf was full of money—piled high, it was. Books too and paintings. I couldn't take it all in before Nigel whistled to me that it was time to leave."

People were fools if they didn't realize that children saw more than they should.

"Thank you, that information is very helpful, Anna."

"Mr. Tookie found it too one day. I saw him leaving there. Him and Matron had a right awful argument. He never came back."

Dear God, what was going on in that place?

"You need to stop them, Alex. Matron and them others are bad people. They tell them fancy women who come and visit and check the place is run well that we're looked after, but it ain't true. Matron threatened us to behave and not speak bad about the orphanage, but it is a bad place."

"But not a place you'll ever return to," he said, running a hand over her head. That she did not pull away was a small win for Alex. "We will do what we can to ensure your friends are looked after, Anna, and the information you've just given me will help with that."

"Miss Harry cared for us. She was always bringing us things to eat and warm clothes."

"She is a very kind lady," Alex said.

She nodded. Her smile was small, but to him felt like the sun coming out on a bleak day.

"And I promise to visit there soon and tell your friends you are well and say goodbye on your behalf."

Anna climbed to her feet and moved to stand before him. She then leaned in and placed a soft kiss on his cheek.

"Thank you."

"You are most welcome, and never ever doubt we want you in our family, Anna. Think of me as your big brother, so if you want anything, you come and see me."

She nodded again and then ran up the stairs. Alex rubbed his chest to ease the burning ache his time with her had created.

The front door opened, and Alex watched his uncle walk in, bringing a blast of cold air with him.

"Alex, why are you sitting on the stairs?"

"I was just having a chat with Anna. She's gone upstairs now."

Uncle Bram looked worried. "Is she all right?"

"Very much so, and she thanked me for wanting her."

His uncle closed his eyes briefly. "God. Did she really?"

"She's well, Uncle, and happy to be here with us. We are saving her like you saved us."

"Which your aunt and I will forever be grateful for."

"We know," Alex said, and he did because the day he entered Uncle Bram and Aunt Ivy's life was the day he knew true love.

"Anna was worried about her friends at the orphanage and not saying goodbye to them, so I promised to do that soon on her behalf." Alex rose as his uncle removed his outer clothing.

"It will take time for her to trust us, but it is beginning."

"Yes, we are not an easy family, but I think in time Anna will fit in. She told me some things about the orphanage that I must pass on to Gray at once," Alex said. He then filled his uncle in on what she had said.

"Yes, get this information to Gray, but before you leave, I wanted to mention that I just saw Harriet, Alex. Something is not right with her. She ran away from me when I asked if she needed my assistance."

"What? Why would she do that?" His heart started thudding hard inside his chest at the prospect of something not being right with her.

"She was alone, carrying two large bags. She seemed scared to me and upset."

"She was alone, when clearly her life is in danger?" Alex demanded.

"I asked her what was wrong. She said nothing and then ran away before I could stop her. Mrs. Greedy said, according to Harriet, the bags she carried were donations for charity, and that she was dropping them off and then coming to Crabbett Close to collect the knitting for the orphans. I looked for her, but she had disappeared."

"I'll find her," Alex said, shoving his arm into the sleeve of his overcoat.

"Would you like me to do the buttons up from behind?" Uncle Bram asked.

Looking down, he realized he'd put the coat on back to front. "I will find out what is going on with Harriet and then yell at her for taking yet more foolish risks with her safety," he added, righting the overcoat.

"Do not yell at her, Alex. The woman I just saw was suffering in some way, I'm sure of it."

"Really?" He stopped on the doorstep and looked back at Uncle Bram. "Why do you believe that?"

"Because she wore the same look you and your siblings had when I found you in London."

Christ. He didn't speak again. In seconds he was down the steps and out onto the street. Striding toward the Alvin house, he felt cold air on his head and realized he'd left the house without his gloves and hat.

Knocking on the door of 22 Crabbett Close a minute later, he waited impatiently for someone to answer it.

"Good day to you, Mr. Alvin."

"It's a good day to you, Mr. Nightingale. We've another guest keeping us company as we speak. Come in and take tea with her."

"I would not want to bother you—"

"The soul's joy lies in doing," Mr. Alvin interrupted Alex. "Now come along. I'm sure Miss Alvin and Miss Short, who is now Miss Shaw, would like to see you. Although if I'm honest," the man whispered loudly, "Miss Shaw has been trying to leave from the moment she got here, but Miss Alvin is not letting her."

"Excellent. Lead on, Mr. Alvin."

Careful where he stepped, Alex followed the old man down the hallway lined with the Alvins' possessions. Reaching the parlor he'd sat in for many hours drinking tea and eating treacle cake while debating poetry, he found Harriet. If he had one word for what she looked like, it would be desperate. It came off her in waves, and he knew that Frankie had been right. Something was very wrong with Harriet.

"Hello," he said. Her eyes shot to his and away just as quick.

"Goodness, Mr. Alvin, another visitor," Miss Alvin said. "We'll need to refill the teapot."

He'd not taken his eyes from her, and she'd not looked his way again. His uncle had been right; Harriet Shaw was suffering. Alex was moving in seconds after the Alvins had left the room. He dropped into a crouch before her, reaching for her hands, which were clutched around a large bundle.

"What's wrong."

"Nothing is wrong." She was at least looking at his necktie now.

"Frankie thinks differently."

She tugged her hand from his grip, but it did not reach her mouth before a sob escaped.

"Tell me," he demanded, lowering the bundle to the floor. Before he could speak again, she was in his arms. Hers wrapped around his neck and held him tight. "Harriet, I am here," he whispered into her hair.

She didn't weep, but he felt her tremors and simply held her against him, running a hand down her slender spine until she calmed. Only then did he ease back to look at her.

"What is going on, Harriet? My uncle told me he saw you and you were upset, which I can see with my own eyes."

"I-I have left my family, Alex, and will not be returning."

He hadn't expected that.

CHAPTER THIRTY-TWO

"What did they do to you?"

His big hands were on her arms now, and for the first time that day, she felt safe. Felt the desperate fear and sadness inside her ease, simply because this man was with her.

"They want to wed me to a man from New York, and then I would have been forced to leave England."

"You are not leaving England." His words were a low growl.

"I ran away so that did not happen."

"When my uncle saw you with two large bags you had just left your house, hadn't you?"

She nodded.

"You should have come to me, Harriet."

"I am not your problem, Alex."

He grabbed her chin, raising it to meet his eyes. "You are my problem." He kissed her quickly. Seconds later, he had regained his feet in time for the door to open.

What did he mean, *"You are my problem?"*

AN IMPERFECT GENTLEMAN

"Harriet!" Ellen Fletcher walked into the room. "How fortuitous you are here. You can be on our team."

The day at best could be termed horrendous, but it seemed she'd lost the ability to think with any clarity. Harriet was sure she hadn't heard Alex's sister correctly.

"I beg your pardon?"

"Hello, Harriet. Wonderful to see you again." Bramstone Nightingale was next in the door, and suddenly the overfull room seemed to have shrunk even more.

"Miss Harry!" Anna slipped by him and ran to her side.

"Oh, Anna, look at you." Harriet rose to greet the girl. "Y-you are h-happy?"

The child had never instigated touching, but she did something then that nearly brought Harriet to her knees. She wrapped her arms around her waist and hugged her.

"Why is Miss Harry weeping?" a child's voice said.

"Weeping!" a younger voice parroted.

"She is happy," Bramstone said.

"Thank you for saving me that night, Miss Harry," Anna said, looking up at her now.

"You are so very welcome, Anna." Harriet cupped her cheek and then kissed her forehead. "Be happy."

"I am."

"Right then," Ellen sniffed loudly after these words. "Everyone out, as we have a race to win. Wrap up warm. The night air is bracing at best."

"That was quick. I just left you," Alex said to his uncle.

"Yes, Mr. Greedy knocked on the front door. I'm surprised you did not see them setting the games up. But perhaps you were preoccupied," his uncle said.

Harriet still had no notion as to what they were discussing.

"Right then, everyone out!" Ellen Fletcher said.

Harriet then watched everyone leave the room but Anna.

"Will you come with me, Miss Harry?"

"Where are you going, Anna?"

"To the Crabbett Close games. Matilda, Freddy, and Theo have told me about them."

Curious and happy to have a diversion from her thoughts, Harriet picked up the bundle of knitting and then allowed Anna to tug her from the room and to the door. She found Alex standing with his uncle and Detective Fletcher, all wore serious expressions.

Alex wore a thick scarf, overcoat but no hat. He looked large and vital, and so very handsome it made her want to weep again.

"It's all right, Harriet." He took the bundle from her, and lowered it to the floor on top of a pile of books. "We will return for your things later. Everything is going to be all right I promise you. Now put on your cloak." He took it off the peg and held it out for her. "Where are your bonnet and gloves?"

She found the latter in her pocket and realized she'd not worn a bonnet. He pulled up her hood.

"I should return to my lodgings."

"And where might they be?" His eyes narrowed.

"I found a small place not far from here."

"Absolutely not," he said.

She was very aware of the people listening. Some lined the hallway; others stood outside the open door.

"I will not discuss this with you." Mortified, she allowed Anna to tug her out the door.

"Oh, we will be discussing it." Alex's voice followed her.

"My creed is love and you are its only tenet," Mr. Alvin said as he walked by her.

"Did he just quote Keats to you, Harriet?" Lord Seddon said from the gate, where he stood looking at the party walking to join him.

"As to that, my lord, I am not entirely sure, as I don't spend a great deal of time reading poetry."

"Leo," he said, "and I wouldn't say that too loud around here were I you. It could be considered blasphemy. Especially by Alex."

"Did I just hear you say you did not like poetry, Harriet Shaw?" Alex demanded.

"You did," she said, feeling safer surrounded by these people even if it was only for a short time.

"Come on, Anna," Theo urged the girl on. "We need to get in a good team, and dragging your feet will not achieve that." The boy stood at the gate beside his oldest brother glaring.

"I am not dragging my feet; I was waiting for Miss Harry."

"Alex will bring her," Theo said.

Harriet had experienced more emotion today than she had in many years, and watching Anna happily walk away with the youngest Nightingales made the tears she'd thought she could no longer shed sting her eyes.

A large hand on her back nudged her forward.

"Alex, my day has been a trying one. I'm quite sure I am not good company," Harriet said.

"I know it has been trying, my sweet Harriet. However, this will be fun, and as you do not have to go home to your family, but are staying in a lodging house, which we will discuss soon, you have time to have some fun."

"I don't think I am capable of that," she said honestly. "My life is a mess."

"I know, but as I am something of an expert on messy lives, we shall set it to rights, but for now come with me."

This time it was him who took her hand, and soon they were walking with the others to the small grassed area in the middle of the close.

"I'm feeling grumpish!" Matilda yelled.

Alex sighed and released her hand. In fact, all the

Nightingale siblings sighed. They then started flapping their arms like a bird.

"Is grumpish the word of the week?" she asked Ivy Nightingale, who was holding her daughter now.

"Yes, Matilda chose it."

Harriet looked at the usually elegant, well-spoken, intelligent people who shared a bond of love making fools of themselves and thought being raised in such a family would be a wonderful thing.

Her thoughts went to hers. They would likely know by now she was gone and read her notes. Would anyone come looking for her? She thought they would, but they would not find her. Harriet would make sure of that. She would not let her family know where she was until any thought of marrying her to Mr. Cargill was a distant dream on her mother's part.

"Come along, Harriet, don't tarry," Alex said, doubling back to get her after his bird flapping performance.

"You do a very good bird impression, sir."

He smiled, the corner of his mouth lifting as they walked. "I have many hidden talents, Miss Shaw."

"I don't know what madness this is, or if I should even be here, Alex."

"For now and tonight, Harriet, stop thinking and just enjoy. I promise things will work out. You are safe here with us."

"I know," she said softly. "Thank you."

His answer was to squeeze her hand.

"Percy may come looking for me here," she said.

"He may, but we shall deal with that if it arises. Now prepare yourself, my dear Miss Shaw. You will never be the same once you have experienced the Crabbett Close games."

Darkness was steadily falling as they walked onto the

grass, and it was then Harriet saw that many other people were gathered there.

"What do these games actually entail, Alex," Harriet said, feeling a dose of apprehension suddenly.

"My advice is to not resist, Harriet."

"But what is it I am not resisting, Detective Fletcher?"

"Gray, and it is best to show you. You would not believe any explanation I attempted," he said. "It took me time to adjust, but I have for the most part. My sensible soul still rebels when the Crabbett Close games take place. If I may offer a second piece of advice?"

Harriet nodded.

"Don't eat anything slimy or pickled. Leave that to those that love them."

Her apprehension doubled.

"There is Nancy!" Matilda shrieked. "Come along, Anna. She will have a bowl of sugarplums."

"Do you like sugarplums, Harriet?" Alex asked.

"I've never tried them."

He gasped.

"Not everyone is ruled by food, Alex," his uncle said.

They were now on the edge of the gathering of people, clearly waiting for something; she had no idea what. In fact, she wondered now if the entire day was a dream or nightmare, and she'd soon wake up in her bed.

"Good day to you all!" A man dressed in constable's clothes appeared. He had a spectacular moustache, blue tailcoat with armlets, white gloves, and top hat.

"What's so bleeding grand about it?" Mungo said. Harriet wasn't sure when he'd appeared. With him was a lady she had never met.

"That's Bud, our housekeeper," Alex whispered in her ear. "Constable Plummy is in love with her."

"Does she reciprocate his feelings?" Harriet asked the

question rather than the other fifteen forming in her head like, *what is going on? Will I be made to eat pickled food? Why am I here when my life has imploded?*

"No, but he is not deterred."

"Detective Fletcher!" Constable Plummy boomed. "We are honored here in Crabbett Close to have you take part in our games."

"I have taken place in every game for the last year, Plummy."

"Miss Bud," the constable then bellowed. "How beauteous you look this evening!"

Miss Bud looked like she wanted to hit him hard with the nearest heavy object.

"Now, Mrs. Greedy will select the teams, as her memory is better than her husband's," Alex said to Harriet.

"Teams?" His answer was to squeeze her fingers, which told her absolutely nothing.

She really should not let him hold her hand with so many people watching, and yet Harriet did not seem able to let his fingers go.

"I just hope Mavis Johns has gout or something like that," Leo muttered. "The woman always wins."

Harriet liked a plan. Direction and routine were important to her; they'd helped her through Frankie's death when little else had. Today she no longer had that, and it terrified her.

"It will be all right," Alex said as if sensing her thoughts. Could he do that?

"Are you reading my mind?"

"No, I can't do that, but it is not hard to work out what you are thinking, Harriet. For now, put your thoughts to one side, and have some fun."

She felt the almost uncontrollable need to laugh but feared it would come out maniacal and she'd never stop.

AN IMPERFECT GENTLEMAN

"Are there any new people here?" a loud voice boomed.

"Mr. Greedy has the loudest voice in the street."

Rising to her toes, Harriet found a grizzled old man with a cane. It was he who was talking, and beside him was Mrs. Greedy.

"His voice is surprisingly loud for his appearance."

"This street has plenty of people like that," Alex said cryptically. She waited for him to elaborate, but he stayed silent.

"We have a guest, Mr. Greedy!" Bramstone Nightingale called. "Miss Shaw is here today."

"Hello, Harriet!" Mrs. Greedy called, looking over the heads before her.

"Good evening, Mrs. Greedy," Harriet called back because her life had descended into chaos, so she might as well continue on that path.

"Welcome!" people greeted her, which made her want to weep again for no other reason than these people had accepted her presence without question, when her own family didn't even like her.

"Mungo, Bud, Lord Seddon, and young Marvin Douglas who is visiting with his uncle and aunty," Mr. Greedy called.

"What is he doing?"

"Organizing teams," Lord Seddon said from her other side. "And I'm most happy with my team."

"Matilda who will be paired with Anna, as it's her first time. Mrs. Varney and Bramstone."

"The winning team," Bramstone said to the little girls who had returned eating sugarplums that Harriet thought looked very nice. She watched Anna smile shyly up at the big man. He simply placed a hand on her head gently and patted.

Harriet pressed her free hand to her mouth.

"What?" Alex asked.

"Today has brought about many emotions," she managed to get out.

Alex released her hand and instead wrapped it around her waist and pulled her into his side.

"I don't think you should do that," Harriet hissed.

"Too bad."

More names were read, and Harriet heard hers; she was in Alex's team with Theo and another she did not know.

She looked around those closest to them, and no one seemed overly upset that she was being held by Alex. Ellen gave her a lovely smile, which she took as approval.

Surely not? These people didn't know her, so therefore how could they accept her? And yet that was exactly what she felt standing here surrounded by strangers. Acceptance.

"Take your places!" Mr. Greedy boomed.

"Go with Ellen, Harriet. I shall reach you shortly." Alex kissed her cheek. "Sister, tell her what she must do."

"Of course." Ellen took her hand and towed her in the direction they'd just walked. "Now, Harriet, this is a relay. Have you ever participated in one of those?"

"We once had to write our sums, and when we finished, the person next to us did them until we all finished."

"Not quite the same, but the basic idea is right. On the street are trestle tables set up. On them is food and drink. Participants must drink, eat, and perform the tasks at each. The first to finish wins."

"You're serious?" Harriet asked her, wondering if this was some kind of elaborate hoax. It wasn't like the Nightingales were normal after all.

"Deadly. We take this seriously, Harriet, so put your best foot forward."

"I shall try," Harriet said when in her head the word run was echoing loudly.

Ellen led her to a table outside the Alvin house, which she was sure had not been there before. On it was an array of dishes and glasses.

"You'll be on your mark!" the loud voice of Mr. Greedy boomed. "You'll get set. Go!" A loud clap had a flurry of activity down the road. She saw several people running toward her. One was Alex, and his eyes were on her. She felt that tingle in her belly she got when he was near.

"Usually, the men start, as they tend to hold their alcohol better than us due to their size. Mavis Johns is the exception, as she can outdrink them all," Ellen said.

"She is certainly a strong woman," Harriet said, watching the chaos unfold as they jostled for position and wondering what madness she had strayed into. Alex elbowed his brother, and Mungo attempted to leg trip Bramstone Nightingale.

"Alex likes you," Ellen said softly so no one standing close could hear. "I've never seen him with another like he is with you. Alex is always just Alex. Happy, and never serious. Around you I've seen another side."

That should not make her as happy as it did, considering her circumstances.

"Don't break his heart, Harriet," Ellen said, her words serious now. "He's more fragile than he lets people see."

"I would never hurt him." But she had a feeling he could hurt her.

CHAPTER THIRTY-THREE

"Excellent," Ellen said, smiling now. "Prepare yourself. They have arrived."

She watched Alex reach her. His smile was wide as he took the mug Mr. Alvin passed him.

"Pixie, hand out the rest of the drinks," Mr. Alvin then said.

"Her name is Pixie?" Harriet whispered to Ellen.

"Mr. Alvin only ever calls her that at these occasions."

Bramstone threw back the contents of his mug, as did Mungo. Mavis Johns was already on her way to the next table having swallowed hers on the run.

"I thought we had to stop?" Alex asked.

"You tell her that," Miss Alvin, also now known as Pixie, said.

"True," Alex said, holding out his mug for Harriet. "Take a sip. It's bracing in this cold."

She took it and a mouthful, then gagged.

"It's a bit whiffy," Alex said, laughing.

"What is that?" she rasped.

"The Alvins' cousin's recipe. Gin, treacle, and the secret ingredient of mutton fat."

Harriet gagged as Alex raised the plate he was handed and swallowed the contents.

"What was that?"

"Pickled whelks." He licked his lips. "Yum."

She gagged again. The alcohol seared its way down her body to land in her empty belly. She'd not eaten much today.

"Right, let's go, as Theo is fiercely competitive and will be furious if we do not pick up the pace." Alex took her hand in his, and soon they were running with the others down the street. Harriet simply held on.

The next tables were manned by the Varneys. Tabitha appeared to be displaying a vast amount of chest again considering the freezing conditions.

"Now, Harriet, we separate the things that need eating and drinking. There are tasks now too, and Theo can do those."

"Because I can't drink," the boy said. "Which is unfair as I am seventeen and a half."

"Even at your advanced age, Theo, you are not drinking what is in that mug!" Bramstone Nightingale called from his position down the table.

Harriet stared at the food. The kippers made her stomach rebel. However, the cake looked tasty. As she reached for it, Theo beat her. *Damn.*

"Give her the drink. It will warm her up," Mungo said.

"Lord Seddon, you look very handsome this evening." Tabitha Varney batted her eyelashes at him.

"Not now, Miss Varney, he has to concentrate," Matilda snapped; she had a wide-eyed Anna with her.

"Drink for pity's sake, Miss Harry," Theo ordered. "I refuse to lose to my three sisters."

WENDY VELLA

Harriet watched Anna shoot him a look because Theo had counted her as a sister.

"Do not cry," Alex whispered. "Drink instead."

She took the mug Tabitha handed her and sniffed. The smell was not as pungent. She didn't gag this time as the fire traveled down her throat; in fact, it warmed her. Beside her Gray gagged, which made Harriet proud she hadn't.

"I've said it before, but it bears repeating. You'd think a man from Scotland Yard would be able to hold his liquor," Alex said.

"He'll be pickled by the end." Ellen smiled at her husband.

Harriet thought she'd like to smile at Alex like that. She felt suddenly a great deal happier than she had been only twenty minutes ago.

Alex once again took her hand, and they were running down the street with Theo now. The houses had lamps or candles outside, as darkness was falling. People were cheering their support to the participants. She stumbled, and Alex caught her.

"All right?"

"Yes, I feel mush… much better, thank you."

"Excellent."

They reached the next table in a remarkably short time. Mavis Johns was there, stationary this time, as she chatted with a man.

This time they collected a young boy wearing a wool hat pulled to his eyebrows, who was now on their team.

"This is Brian," Alex said. "Mr. And Mrs. Greedy's grandson."

"Evening." He nodded to her.

"What do you want, Harriet?" Alex asked.

She studied the table and missed out on the cake again as Brian took it.

"Jellied eel," Theo said, grabbing it. "I love them."

"No, really?" Harriet shuddered as she watched him eat it.

"There are two drinks, Harriet, which one do you want?"

"You'll like it, Miss Shaw," a man said.

"Mr. Douglas," Alex whispered in her ear.

"Thank you, Mr. Douglas," she said slowly, as her head felt a bit light now. Taking the mug he handed her, she drank. The consistency was thick, and she tasted molasses as it stuck to the sides of her mouth.

"I love the molasses-laced whisky," Mungo said, throwing it back like it was water.

Harriet took another mouthful and managed to swallow it.

"You'll sing us a Scottish ballad. Mr. Mungo will lead," Mr. Douglas said.

"Do they all know Scottish ballads?" Harriet asked anyone listening.

"Indeed we do," a spritely looking lady said from beside her. "Mr. Mungo has been teaching us for years."

The Scotsman started singing in a deep, melodious voice that would have angels weeping, seconds later Theo and Alex joined in, and then the others. It was lovely. Harriet stared in wonder as suddenly everyone but her seemed to be singing. Even if she knew the song, she would not be partaking. Her voice sent animals running.

"Join in, Miss Shaw." Alex nudged her, his tone teasing.

"I don't think I want to." She went for honesty. "I sing like a rusty hinge."

"I doubt anyone as sweet as you sings like a rusty hinge."

His eyes held hers for long moments, and she realized he meant what he said. He really did think she was sweet. When you'd thought yourself odd and in no way attractive all your life, it was almost too hard to believe.

"I love your eyes," he added before continuing to sing.

Harriet sipped her drink, forgetting it was potent and thick. Alex thought her sweet, and he liked her eyes. Harriet thought his words might be the best part of a truly horrendous day. That and Anna's hug.

"Right, onto the next," Theo said.

"There's another table?" She wasn't sure how she felt about that. Harriet was a bit lightheaded if she was honest.

"Two actually."

"Dear Lord," Harriet whispered.

"You are eating the food at the next table," Alex said, taking her hand.

When they ran, this time it was with the girls giggling and Theo annoying them. People still sang; a few staggered.

"Oh, look, it's Chester," Harriet said as the large dog appeared, loping at the side of his people.

"He is not forced to compete," Gray said. Harriet couldn't be entirely sure but thought his words sounded a bit slurred.

"He's a dog, Gray," Theo said.

By the last table, Harriet had eaten a large wedge of delicious treacle cake, which made her feel a great deal steadier. Her eyes felt squinty, but she still had control of her limbs.

"Right then," Alex said, sounding remarkably steady. "Who wants what?"

Theo picked up the mug. Leo, as she now thought of him —it was amazing how a few nips of alcohol made you see people differently—took it from his little brother. He then handed him a large biscuit. Theo grumbled and then broke it in half and handed it to Harriet.

"I have drunk before you know."

"Very likely, and yet you are not," Alex said.

"What is that?" she asked after thanking the still muttering Theo. The plate she was looking at seemed to be wobbling.

"Aspic jelly," the lady behind the table said.

Harriet squinted to focus on her.

"Meat jelly," Alex whispered in her ear.

"No, thank you," she said, stuffing the biscuit into her mouth. It was lemon and seemed to melt; her taste buds sighed.

"At least we're not last," Theo said with his mouth full.

"Gray was tripped by Leo and is now crawling down the street," Alex said.

She looked for the detective and saw that Mr. Alvin was helping him up.

"He is a detective with Scotland Yard, do you think that's wise of your brother?" Harriet asked.

"He can't arrest family, it's law," Ellen said, seeming unconcerned about her husband's current state.

Alex held out the mug, and she sniffed.

"That's Mr. Peeky's famous spiced rum, take a sip," he said.

She did and almost sighed as it slid down smoothly. "Oh, that's lovely."

"Isn't it though," he said, throwing back the entire contents of the mug.

"We beat Fred, Matilda, and Anna," Theo said. "Not Mavis Johns though. No one beats her."

"It's over?" Harriet asked, looking at the happy people around her. Some were weaving where they stood; others standing and chatting. Two women were dancing what appeared to be a jig. No, she looked closer and saw one was Mungo, and he was dancing with Bud.

"How are you feeling now?" Alex asked her.

"Much better thank you, and now I should go."

"My nephew told me you are staying in lodgings, Harriet, is this true?" Bramstone said, coming to stand before her with his wife. In his arms was the now sleeping Charlotte. They looked a wonderful picture to her.

Harriet wasn't sure she'd have children, but if she could ever experience the love these three obviously shared, she thought she'd like to try. Her eyes went to Alex, and he was looking at her.

What did she feel for this man?

"I am, yes," she answered Bramstone's question. "And I'm s-sorry I ran away from you today."

"That's all right. You are safe now. I would be happier if you stayed with us. We have the room."

"Oh no, I couldn't."

"Excellent, that's settled then. Now we shall collect your things and return shortly," Alex said.

His fingers wrapped around her wrist, and they started walking.

"Alex, I am quite able to stay in the lodgings I have secured," she protested. "Really, they are adequate. Tomorrow I will—"

"No."

They walked along Crabbett Close, acknowledging the people still lingering around the tables eating and drinking now the race had finished.

"Yes, and don't you want to stay and enjoy the festivities? I assure you I can make my way alone."

He turned her to face him as they reached the Alvins' front door. His hands settled on her shoulders.

"I care about you, Harriet, very much. No woman I care about is staying in a lodging house alone. And especially not a woman who ran away from her family, whom she has lived with her entire life."

"I lived at the academy too," she pointed out.

"With people to look after you," he added.

She watched him walk to the front door and open it. He then returned with her bundle of knitting.

"We shall deliver this tomorrow. Right now, let us collect your things."

She should protest, but then all she could think about was what he'd just said. He cared very much about her. Harriet knew then, without a doubt, that she also cared about him. In fact, she loved him.

CHAPTER THIRTY-FOUR

"You are not staying here."

Harriet and Alex stood outside the lodging house looking at the building.

"I will not allow it. Anyone could walk in and accost you."

"My door has a key that locks." Harriet waved it before his face.

"I don't care." He looked large and angry on her behalf, standing there with her bundle of knitting in his arms.

It was dark now, the kind that you couldn't see a hand in front of you if it weren't for the streetlamps. The moon was tucked behind clouds.

"Let's go. The sooner we get inside, the sooner we can leave," Alex said, waving her forward.

"I need to check Mrs. Smith is not downstairs, as she said no gentleman callers," Harriet said.

"It doesn't matter if she sees me, as you are not staying here," Alex said.

"I cannot live at your house," she hissed. "Now be quiet." She opened the door and looked inside. The lamplight showed her the entrance was empty. She waved for Alex to follow her.

They hurried up the stairs—well, she did. He simply walked with very heavy feet. Reaching her room, she unlocked it and entered, dragging him in behind her. She then locked the door again.

"Why, Miss Shaw," he drawled as she hurried to light the candle. "Imagine you being improper enough to bring a man into your room."

"Very amusing. Now put that bundle there."

"You are not staying here, so pack your things," he said after dropping the knitting on the only chair in the small room. "This place is grubby and horrid. Have you even checked the bedding?"

She had; it looked clean, but appearances she knew could be deceptive.

"Alex, you need to understand that my parents will be looking for me now. Percy will call upon you, I'm sure. I will not have you involved in this."

The lovely floating feeling she'd felt had now well and truly gone. The Crabbett Close games were over, and reality had returned.

"I won't have you hurt, don't you see." She tried to explain how she felt. "No one has thought of me as you do. No one has seen anything in me to inspire—"

"Harriet, stop." He moved to stand before her. So close that his boots brushed hers. One large warm hand cupped her cheek.

"You're always warm when I feel like I've been cold for so long." Perhaps she was still a trifle foxed if she was speaking this way.

"Shh now and listen to me." He kissed her softly. "I care nothing about what your parents think of me or my family, as they would not care either. We are more than capable of protecting you and withstanding anything your parents, or anyone, throw at us."

"No, Alex, you don't understand. My father is a very wealthy man, and my mother ruthless and determined. If she sees that I can in any way bring shame down upon the family, she will move heaven and earth to make sure that does not happen."

He didn't speak, just looked at her for long seconds. His thumbs stroked circles over her cloak. Harriet told herself she couldn't feel his touch, but her body said differently.

"Harriet, I care about you."

"I, ah, I care about you too, Alex."

His smile was slow and reached his eyes.

"I like your smile," she blurted. She had the ridiculous urge to climb to her toes and kiss him. Let him hold her again. In that moment he was simply a man she wanted. A man who could briefly make her forget the hell that was her life.

"I like yours too." He leaned closer, his breath brushing her lips now. "Very much."

"I don't smile," she whispered.

"Which makes them all the more special." He kissed her softly.

"Alex," she sighed.

"Harriet." He kissed her again. "I've never felt about a woman like I do with you."

"Really?" She looked at him, and his eyes told her he spoke the truth.

"Really."

"No one has said anything like that to me before."

"I should hope not."

She snorted. "What I mean is, I was never sure that I would inspire that kind of... ah, that kind of—"

"Desire, emotion, affection?" he prompted.

"You are very comfortable with words, and I am not," she said.

They were still close; their noses nearly touched.

"Well then how incredibly honored am I to be the first to tell you how I feel. And just to be clear, Harriet, I do desire you, just as I respect and admire you for the strong woman you are. You are intelligent, beautiful, and someone I would like to spend a great deal more time with. Plus, I love your eyes."

It seemed almost unbelievable that a man such as he—handsome, popular, and confident—felt as he did about her, plain Harriet Shaw.

"Alex?"

"Harriet," he said the words against her lips and then kissed her slowly. It was long heartbeats later before she could form a coherent thought once more. She could always think rationally but not when he was close.

"When I was at the Templar Academy, some of the girls talked about what happens between a man and a woman, extensively. It sounded awful. However, this is not that."

He reared back as if she'd struck him. "What?" Shock was the only word for how he now looked.

"I have never seized any moments, Alex, and that's possibly because none have been presented to me, but still, I don't want to die—"

"You're not dying!"

"I'm saying this wrong."

"I don't think you should say it." He looked panicked now.

"I would like for you to—"

"Do not finish that sentence, Harriet." He backed away from her.

"You don't know what I was going to say." She followed.

"You are a lady. I am a gentleman. There will be none of

that unless we are wed… which I'm definitely leaning toward us doing by the way."

That stopped her. "What?"

The breath hissed from his throat. "Ignore my words. You have me all over the place. It is not time to discuss that."

She blinked. He was unsettled; it was quite the revelation, as he was never anything but assured and confident. Had he just mentioned that he was leaning toward them one day marrying? The elation that surged to life inside her had her smiling.

"You're smiling," he gritted out.

"Alex, why are you backing away from me when you have just told me you care for me?"

Harriet felt different with the knowledge that Alex experienced strong emotions for her. It empowered her that she could inspire feelings in him. That she—plain, disgraced, and odd-eyed Harriet—could possibly be loved by this wonderful man.

"We need to go." He sounded desperate.

She moved closer when he reached the door and had no more room to retreat. Rising to her toes, she then pressed her body to his and kissed him. Harriet was not experienced with such things, but the shudder that ran through him told her he liked her touch.

"Harriet." Her name sounded like a plea. "I would not keep that up were I you."

She continued to kiss him, finding courage in the belief that he thought her beautiful and intelligent. That he thought her worthy of his care.

His body was rigid, pressed to hers. Muscles tense, and then suddenly his arms came around her on another moan, and he was kissing her back.

"I want you," he whispered. "Very much."

"I want you too. I am responsible for my own decisions, Alex, and right now I choose to be with you."

He pulled back far enough to look at her. "My little suffragette. One day of running away from home and the Crabbett Close games, and suddenly you're empowered."

Harriet grabbed a handful of his hair and tugged. Their lips met and clung.

Where one kiss finished, another started. Her cloak fell to the floor, and then his hands were on her body. One stroked up and down her spine while the other was under her hair, touching the sensitive skin of her neck.

"If we are being honest," he said between kisses, "I love you, Harriet."

"Alex, do you really?" she whispered against his lips.

"Yes. I didn't plan on loving you, but you slipped into my heart and never left."

"I've never felt this way before, Alex."

"Excellent. Whatever this madness is, we are in it together, and for now that is enough."

"Yes, it is enough."

His overcoat followed her cloak and then his jacket. She felt his fingers on the buttons of her dress.

"Let me touch you, my sweet."

Heat invaded her body, and the cold places inside her were warmed when Alex touched her. When his lovely mouth was pressed to hers. The feel of his fingers on the skin he'd exposed with each button he opened made her shudder.

"Harriet." He sighed her name against her lips. "You have a luscious mouth, and a body I wish to worship, but we will not be doing that tonight, here in this grubby place. Some, but not all."

He picked her up and carried her to the bed, lowering her to her feet before it. Alex then pushed her dress from her shoulders.

"I want the final act between us to take place in our marriage bed, Harriet."

She managed to nod as his eyes ran over her body through the chemise.

"But there is much we can do before that."

"Really?"

"Really." He ran a finger around the bodice of her chemise, leaving a trail of fire wherever he touched. Picking up the necklace her late grandfather had given her, he studied it.

"It is the New York coat of arms. My grandfather had it made for me." Her words came out in a nervous rush.

"Like you, it is beautiful." He kissed her as his other hand moved to her thigh; Alex then raised the hem of her chemise, his fingers sliding beneath.

"Oh my," Harriet whispered as she felt his touch with no barriers between them.

"Oh my, more?" he asked, his voice a rasp now.

"More."

She had a tie at the front of her chemise. He tugged it open, exposing her breasts.

"Beautiful," Alex whispered, and then he lowered his head and licked her. One long, hot swipe of his tongue over one curve, and this time it was her who moaned. "I'm sorry your day was hell, and your family doesn't understand you, Harriet. But I do, and always will."

Closing her eyes on those lovely words, she simply felt what this wonderful man was doing to her body.

His hands slid up, taking her chemise with them, and soon she was naked. Harriet felt no fear. This was Alex, the man who cared for her.

"Beautiful is too simple a term for what you are, Harriet." Picking her up again, he lowered her to the bed. Toeing off his boots, he joined her in his shirt and trousers.

He then proceeded to kiss her while his hands mapped her body, and Harriet was beyond any thought but what he created inside her. The tension rose with every lick of his tongue and touch of his fingers.

"Feel, Harriet," he whispered into her ear.

When he moved again, this time to take her nipple into his mouth, she cried out, arching off the bed. His hand was between her thighs, urging her to open for him.

"I will never hurt you." The words were a vow.

"I know."

When he touched the sensitive place between her thighs, she shuddered. His mouth took her nipple again and pulled it deeper. The tension inside her rose higher.

"Alex?"

"Soon, Harriet. Just feel."

His finger touched the hard bud and then slid deep inside her. The feelings were indescribable. Every thrust made her moan.

"That's it, my sweet girl, let go for me." He stroked his tongue over her nipple as his fingers moved, and suddenly, she did as he said, and sensation after sensation crashed through Harriet.

"Oh my," she managed to whisper when reality returned. "I never knew... Alex?" She looked up at him. "You didn't find your release. The girls, they told me—"

"Shh, it is enough for now that you did, my sweet."

He climbed off the bed and found her chemise. He then urged her to sit and threw it over her head.

"What are you doing?" Harriet asked as he picked her up and pulled back the bedcovers before depositing her beneath.

"I'm too tired to leave now." He climbed in beside her and pulled her back to his front. "Sleep now, Harriet, and know that I am here with you. Tomorrow we will deal with whatever you face together. Remember you are mine, as I am yours."

"I don't know how to express what is inside me, Alex."

"You already have, Harriet. Now go to sleep."

She felt the hardness of his arousal, and that he had wanted her to find pleasure alone, when it could have been both of them, was humbling. She drifted in that place between sleep and wake and thought how wonderful it was that the first time she slept with a man it was with the one she loved.

HARRIET WOKE to the cold and realized that Alex was no longer with her. Fingers of light filtered in through the cracks in the curtains, telling her it was morning. Climbing out of bed, she found a note he had written with her supplies.

GOOD MORNING, *my love, did you know you snore? However, you are very cute when you sleep. I left because I did not want Mrs. Smith to find us, as I know that following rules is very important to you.*

As the sun is now rising, I know you will be safe until I return, which I will do so at 10:00 a.m. Please be ready, as you are not staying another night in this place.

Yours always, Alex

"HE LOVES ME." She hugged the letter to her chest and did a little dance around the room as she searched for her pocket watch. Locating it in her bag, she saw the time was 8:30 a.m. Harriet could wash, dress, and then, with her things, take a hackney to the orphanage to drop off the knitting to the children. She need stay only a few minutes, and then she could surprise Alex by arriving at Crabbett Lane. She would pick up apricotines on the way.

Calculating the timing, she thought it would take fifteen minutes to get to the orphanage. Ten minutes there to speak to the children and tell them that her circumstances had changed, but she would return to regular visits as soon as she could. Then she would go to Alex.

Yesterday she'd known despair. Today she knew what elation and hope felt like. Knew how it felt to be loved.

Hurrying to wash and dress, she collected her things and went downstairs.

"I will not need the room for any more nights. Thank you, Mrs. Smith." Handing over the keys, she left. Her luck was in; even at the early hour, a hackney was passing. Climbing in, she was soon on her way to the orphanage.

The journey was spent remembering last night, and the bliss of what she and Alex had shared. Sleeping with him had been a revelation too. Would they do that every night when they were wed?

He'd said he wanted to marry her... *hadn't he?*

"No, I will not allow doubts to creep in."

When the hackney stopped, she climbed out and paid the driver, asking him to wait while she dropped off the knitting.

Hurrying in through the front doors, she made for the stairs. It was earlier than usual, and no one about, but the children would be here, as most were earlier risers, or so they'd told her.

Reaching the second floor, she heard voices and went to tell Matron she was dropping off supplies. Stepping into the doorway, she found four people inside. The shock of who they were held her immobile for seconds, and then when she turned to flee, a hand grabbed her.

"Well now, Miss Shaw, it seems we meet again."

"Let me go, Mr. Templar!"

A hand covered her mouth. "I don't think so because you have caused all of us a great deal of trouble. People are asking questions about the orphanage and the Templar Academy, and that is due to your meddling. You and those Nightingales and that detective. We know you saw your dead friend's necklace, and Billy was a fool to give it to his girl. We should have sold it."

"I wished we'd drowned you that night too," Mrs. Templar said as Harriet was dragged into the room and the door slammed.

"We have to leave England because of you." Matron leaned in to spit the words into her face.

"And you're going to ensure we leave with lots of money, Miss Shaw," Mr. Sydney said.

Harriet tried to fight with everything she had. Alex wanted her, and she wanted a future with him. These people would not take that from her, she vowed. She would find a way to escape; she had to.

CHAPTER THIRTY-FIVE

Alex had slipped into the house and up to his room without being seen, as it was still early. He'd slept the night with Harriet. An entire night holding her, and upon waking, he'd vowed he would be doing that for the rest of their lives together.

He loved her. The thought almost made him lightheaded. He'd believed himself incapable of love, and then Harriet Shaw had marched into his life. Shy, determined, serious, and so bloody sweet she made his chest ache. He loved her and all the facets of her personality. He couldn't seem to stop smiling.

She'd responded to him last night as he touched and kissed her luscious body. He could not wait for them to be together in every sense of the word. Yes, he'd been so aroused it was painful, but he'd meant it when he said he wanted to consummate their union in their marriage bed.

He washed and then lay on his bed. Falling into a deep sleep in seconds, he dreamed of her.

Alex woke covered in blood and with panic tightening his

chest. Looking down at his body, he saw no red. Why then had he dreamed—

"Harriet!" He leapt out of bed and pulled on his clothes. Grabbing his knife in its sheath, he was soon out the door and running down the stairs. Looking at the clock, he saw it was now midday. He'd slept through the time he was to pick her up. Was she still at her lodgings? Surely, she was not foolish enough to leave?

"Why are you running down the stairs muttering to yourself?" Leo appeared at the bottom. "What room is Harriet in?"

"She's at the lodgings," Alex said. "I need to get to her."

Leo frowned. "I thought she was staying here?"

"Long story, which I do not have time to tell you. What?" Alex demanded when his brother frowned.

"It's strange, but I have an urge to find something."

"What something?"

"I don't know. A necklace I think." He touched his neck. "It has some kind of small disc on it, gold, but I can't work out what's engraved on it."

The doors opened, and Ellen ran in; one look at her face told Alex she was worried about something.

"What's wrong?" he asked as she hurried toward him. Gray entered behind her.

"I had a vision, and it involved Harriet. She was in a room with lots of books, and her hands were tied." She threw herself at him, hugging him hard. "Tell me she is here."

"She's at the lodging house." *Please be there.* "I woke feeling I was covered in blood with panic gripping me," Alex said. "I need to get to Harriet."

"What's going on?" Uncle Bram appeared.

"It's Harriet. She's in trouble," Alex said, running for the door with his siblings on his heels.

"Mungo is bringing the carriage, as I was just about to go to the lawyer's!" Uncle Bram yelled. "Arm yourselves!"

Minutes later they were sprinting out the door. *She had to be all right.* He'd left her sleeping. Surely, they were wrong, and she was safe, but even as he thought it, he knew she was in danger. Their instincts were never wrong.

"Change of plans, we need to find Harriet," Uncle Bram called to Mungo.

Alex gave him the location of the lodging house, and in seconds, they were moving.

"She was well when I left her," Alex said.

"When was that?" Uncle Bram demanded.

"A few hours ago, and before you ask, no I did not take advantage of her. We just fell asleep talking," he lied.

"Your aunt and I used to do that, and I'm going to add that Harriet is perfect for you, and you have our blessing."

"Where is she?" he whispered.

"We will find her, brother." Leo held out a hand, and Alex gripped it briefly. "This necklace I am seeing, it has a symbol on it."

"What kind of symbol?" Alex said, feeling the fear in his veins turn to ice.

"I see an eagle and women—"

"Harriet wears that symbol. It is the coat of arms of New York, where she was born." He saw it again nestled between her lovely breasts as he had last night.

"I love her."

"We know," Ellen said.

"First we check the lodging house she stayed at," Uncle Bram said.

The tension in the carriage was thick as Mungo pulled them to a halt. Alex was out the door in seconds and running into the lodge.

"Is Miss Shaw here?"

The woman looked shocked at his demand.

"N-no she left early. Eight thirty, and she said she would not need the lodgings for another night."

"Did she say where she was going?"

She shook her head. Alex ran back out the door and into the carriage again.

"She's gone, left early, and my guess is she was coming to me."

"Where is she then?" Ellen demanded.

"Would she go home? Do you think a member of her family located her, and she returned there?" Gray asked.

"I don't see how they would have found her so soon," Alex said as the panic clawed at his throat. His love for Harriet nearly choked him in that moment.

"The orphanage," Gray said. "Would she have gone there?"

Ellen had seen her bound in a room with books. Could that be at the orphanage or Templar Academy?

"I told her not to go there alone, but...." His words fell away. Harriet had the knitting to drop off to the children. He'd told her he'd take her, but would she have gone there and then was coming to him?

Danger. Harriet. Hurry. The words filtered through his head.

"We need to split up and search for her," Gray said. "We can cover more ground that way."

"I feel her desperation," Alex said. "She needs me."

"Then we will find her," Uncle Bram said.

"You know where her family lives, Alex. Go there with Leo and Bram. Ellen and I will go to the orphanage, as they know me, and we'll see if we can locate her there," Gray said. "Take the carriage, and you will have Leo's title to impress her mother, who I gather is something of a snob. We will meet in an hour somewhere halfway between the two places."

"Hamster tea shop," Leo said. "It is about halfway."

"How can you think of food?" Alex glared at him. Leo wisely remained silent.

"You will not yell at or threaten them," Uncle Bram said as they walked up to the front door of the large, impressive residence of the Shaw family a short while later. A house that yesterday Harriet had felt she needed to flee.

"Alex!" Leo snapped. "Stop it."

"What?"

"You look like you want to kill someone," his brother hissed.

He wasn't wrong. *Where was she?* Please be inside, he prayed. But he knew she wasn't deep in the pit of his belly.

Uncle Bram knocked on the front door, and it only took a minute before it was opened. The epitome of an English butler stood before them, and when he spoke, it simply reinforced Alex's first impression, although on closer inspection, there was a wide-eyed, panicky look in his eyes.

"The necklace is not here," Leo said suddenly.

"Good day. I am Mr. Nightingale. These are my nephews, Lord Seddon and Mr. Alexander Nightingale. We wish to speak with Miss Harriet Shaw please."

The butler's eyes flickered to the left and then back to them.

"Miss Shaw is from home."

"Then we wish to speak to her parents if you please," Uncle Bram said in a cool voice.

"They are not receiving visitors at this time."

"They'll receive me," Alex said, pushing past the butler and into the house.

"Alex," his uncle sighed but followed.

"Take me to the Shaws now, or I will find them," Alex said to the butler. "The safety of their daughter is at stake."

"Follow me," the butler said. "We, the staff, fear for Miss Harry," he added quietly.

"I will find her."

"Please do," the man said.

"I told you there will be no blood let or threatening," Uncle Bram said.

"They deserve it," Alex snapped. "They are mean to Harriet."

"What did they do?" Both Leo and Uncle Bram looked at Alex.

"I knew something was not right with her but had no idea her family was one of the causes," Leo said. "What did they do?"

"So many things. They believed what happened at the academy was Harriet's fault and never allowed her to step into society because of the scandal that she played no hand in. Her mother is also embarrassed by her eyes."

"What is wrong with her eyes?" Uncle Bram demanded. "Ivy said they make her original, and I tend to agree. They are perfect for Harriet."

"Yes, they are. She left yesterday because her family wishes her to wed a man from New York and leave England. They said she's an embarrassment to the Shaw name."

"By God, did they indeed!" Uncle Bram was now angry, and by the tightening of Leo's mouth, he was not far behind. "We'll just see about that."

The butler opened a door and announced them. Leo stepped into the room first, with his family on his heels. He found the Shaws in an uproar.

Her father was standing before the window while his wife —a woman Alex had vowed always to dislike intensely even if she was to be his mother-in-law—was seated in a chair weeping. A younger man stared into the flames of a fire that was lit in the fireplace. A young lady, Catherine—Harriet had said she was the only Shaw who loved her unconditionally—sat beside her mother weeping also.

All turned to stare at them when they entered.

"Who are you, and why are you here?" George Shaw demanded.

"We have reason to believe your daughter is missing and not because she chose to," Alex said, glaring at her family. "I know that yesterday she packed her bags and left here because, and these are her words, you were forcing her to wed a man and leave England, due to the fact she is an embarrassment to your family!" His words had risen as he'd spoken; anger made them sound like the crack of a whip. "Which she is not. Harriet is kind, gentle, and sweet, and you made her feel like a pariah! How bloody dare you treat your own blood in such a way." His eyes were on Mrs. Shaw.

"What do you know about my sister's whereabouts?" Oscar Shaw demanded.

"I know she stayed last night in a lodging house and was not there this morning when I went to collect her."

"Alex," his uncle said. "Stay calm."

He felt Leo move closer, no doubt getting ready to grab him if he lunged at a Shaw.

"How do you know Harriet?" Mrs. Shaw demanded.

"We met at the lending library," he lied. "She is a friend. It was me she turned to when you all treated her abysmally. Let her believe she was not worthy of being a Shaw. That you did not love her."

"I love her," a small voice said.

"I know you do, Miss Shaw." Alex found a tight smile for Harriet's younger sister. "She told me you were the only one who cared for her."

"W-we did what we must," Mrs. Shaw said.

"Treating your daughter like she was not worthy of your love is what you felt you must do?" Alex snarled.

"Mr. Shaw, have you had word from your daughter?" Leo demanded before Alex could launch into yet more insults. "Time is of the essence if she is missing or in danger, as we now believe."

Harriet's father threw his wife a look.

"No, George."

"Yes, Heloise. What we did was wrong, and I should have been stronger and not allowed you to follow the path you took. My daughter is in trouble because I was weak and did not stand up to you." He then walked to them and held out a note. Alex took it, and his uncle and brother read it with him.

Mr. Shaw,

We have your eldest daughter. If you want her back, then do as we say.

The sum of money they wanted was large, but he knew Shaw could get it. They were to deliver it by five p.m. tomorrow night to a location that would be sent to them tomorrow.

Do as we say, or the next time you see your daughter, she will be dead.

"No," Alex whispered.

"No," Leo said. "That is not happening."

"Do you have anyone who'd want to extort money from you, Mr. Shaw?" Leo asked.

"No. I thought about that, but I can think of no one who would harm Harriet."

"It is to do with the investigation," Alex said. "We know that."

"What investigation?" Heloise Shaw demanded.

"That, in fact, Frankie was murdered, as your daughter

suspected," Alex said. "We believe there is a large thieving network being run between the Gail Lane orphanage and the Templar Academy, and people have lost their lives because of it."

"Dear Lord," Oscar Shaw said.

"Your daughter got that injury to her cheek when someone threatened her because she got too close to what could be happening. She was thrown to the ground and has been followed ever since. Her life has been in danger, Shaw."

"Why did she not come to me?" her father said, ashen-faced.

"Because in her eyes, you saw her as a burden. Someone to be seen and not heard," Alex snapped. "Shame on you all," he added, meeting their eyes. "Except you, of course, Catherine, and I look forward to furthering your acquaintance when I have your sister back. Let's go now." Alex walked out of the room. "We need to find Harriet."

"I will come with you," Oscar Shaw said. "She is my sister."

"So now you wish to play the role of brother. One wonders what took you so long." Alex did not wait for a reply but simply headed back to the carriage.

"I can offer no excuse, sir," Oscar Shaw said in a tight voice.

"The Shaws have received a ransom note for Harriet, Mungo." Before Alex could add anything further, he saw the Knights Templar symbol in his head.

"What?" Leo grabbed his arm. "You've gone pale, Alex. Breathe for pity's sake."

"She's at the Templar Academy," Alex wheezed. Turning to find George Shaw on the doorstep of the house, Alex yelled, "Send word to the Hamster tea shop to Mr. and Mrs. Fletcher to head to the Academy at once! Now, Shaw, there is not a moment to lose."

"I will see it done," the man said. "Bring my daughter home, Mr. Nightingale."

"When I find her, if she chooses to come here, then I will bring her. If not, then you will need to come to her. I am also going to marry her."

CHAPTER THIRTY-SIX

*H*arriet had fought, but Matron, Mr. and Mrs. Templar, and Mr. Sydney were too strong for her, and soon she'd been bound and gagged. A sack was dropped over her head, and she was carried from the orphanage and into a carriage.

Alex was going to be furious with her when he found her, because he'd told her not to go to the orphanage alone. She had, thinking it was safe.

You are a foolish girl, Harriet Shaw.

She did not doubt he would find her; she just had to stay alive until then. There was no way these people were taking him away from her too. They'd killed Frankie, but they would not stop her finding happiness. Alex loved her, and she, him, and they would live their lives together. Harriet would fight with everything she had to ensure that was their future.

Find me, Alex.

At least she was sitting on a carriage seat and not lying on the floor, as that would have made her nauseous. She couldn't see anything and breathing was not easy inside the sack, but Harriet was alive, and that was a start.

"The ransom note has been delivered. Shaw has money. He'll pay." She thought that voice belonged to Mr. Sydney.

Harriet wasn't entirely sure her father would pay it, or if her mother would let him. After all Harriet's death meant she was no longer a problem to their family. *Could Heloise Shaw be that ruthless? Would her father allow that to happen?*

She brought Alex's face into her head again. He loved her; she had to hold on to that. He would find her.

"The magistrate called yesterday. Seems Scotland Yard is growing suspicious," Mr. Templar said.

"They've been sniffing around the orphanage since the night of the fight," Mr. Sydney added.

"It's time. We've made enough, and with what Shaw gives us, we can start fresh somewhere far from here," Mrs. Templar said.

"We'll pack and be ready to go when we get the ransom money," Mr. Templar added.

"And what of the others who work for us?" Matron asked.

"I care nothing for them, only us. We'll take four with us to help, but no more. After we've cleaned up the loose ends, we'll leave." Mr. Templar's words were deep and had an ominous ring to them.

That they were speaking openly about what they were doing worried Harriet, because it suggested they didn't care what she overheard, which told her they would not be letting her live, even after the ransom was delivered. If it was delivered.

By the time the carriage halted, her hands and feet were numb, and the gag had cut the corners of her mouth. Harriet focused on the pain and let the anger build. She was strong. Alex thought her worthy of his love, and she would ensure that faith was not misplaced.

No one was taking her from him. Not now. They would wed and live a happy life together like Gray and Ellen.

"Stop in the stables," she heard Mr. Templar say what seemed like hours later but was possibly only one. "We'll put her there while we get everything ready for our departure tomorrow after we receive the money."

She was dragged out like a sack of flour and thrown on what she thought was a pile of hay.

"Should we see if she's all right?" Mrs. Templar asked.

"She's caused us trouble. It's all due to her that we're having to leave now. I don't care if she's all right—in fact, I hope she's in pain," Mr. Templar snapped.

Harriet heard footsteps recede, and then someone was grabbing a handful of her hair and pulling her upright. "It's Mr. Sydney, Miss Shaw. I killed your friend because she was snooping around and found stuff she shouldn't. So, you can go to your grave knowing that at least." He dropped her head, laughing.

She heard footsteps leaving and the rasp of a bolt locking the door, and then she was alone, as she'd spent much of her life in the last few years.

...

"The necklace is here," Leo said.

"Harriet is here too," Alex added as they pulled to a halt before the Templar Academy driveway. "I can feel her, plus the lemons are nearly choking me."

"What lemons?" Oscar Shaw said.

Alex hadn't spoken to the man, but Uncle Bram and Leo had. Instead, he'd sat in the corner looking out the window, focusing on Harriet. Telling her to be strong and he was coming. He let images of last night fill his head. Of her laughter and delight at his declaration of love.

How could she believe she was unlovable when the opposite was true. He'd never loved like he did his Harriet.

"We'll walk in. You stay with the carriage," Alex said, glaring at Oscar Shaw.

"I want to come," he said, looking like his sister in that moment.

"Have you shot and killed anyone?" Alex demanded. Oscar paled. "I didn't think so. The man driving this carriage has and is one of the best men I know. You"—Alex pointed at him—"I don't know, and the few things I've heard about you are not flattering. You stay here."

They all got out, and Oscar went to hold the horses.

"Walk them up and down the road," Mungo said. "Don't let them get cold."

"If anyone stops and asks what you're doing, say your driver has gone to get something to fix the wheel," Leo added.

"Let's go," Uncle Bram said.

That it was daylight did not help, as the trees lining the drive didn't offer good coverage. Reaching the end, Alex looked to the outbuildings.

"I think she's in one of those," he said, pointing.

"You love her. Your intuition will be strong when teamed with your abilities," Mungo said. "It's about bloody time you stopped thinking about yourself and focused on someone else," he added.

"I'm taking you to task for that comment when I have Harriet back," Alex said.

They had to run past the building, and he hoped none of the students or staff were looking out the windows. Reaching the stables, he stopped, raising a hand, as he heard voices inside.

"We're leaving as soon as the money is paid. Prepare all the carriages and carts. We'll need plenty to load everything," someone was saying from inside the stables.

"Who's going? Just four of us and them."

"Plenty to go round then."

"Let's have a drink, and after we'll see to the carriage. I'll be glad to get away from those bloody sniveling orphans. I hope we go somewhere warm."

He heard footsteps growing distant.

Alex started forward and slipped in through the small opening between the doors. A carriage stood with four horses attached. If he had to guess, it had just arrived.

Moving behind it, he opened a door and looked inside; it was empty. He pointed to the right of the row of stables and then left, tapping his chest and acknowledging the large Scotsman.

Leo and his uncle headed right.

They looked in stalls, but all were empty. Reaching the last, he found it bolted from the outside. The tension inside him had risen; Harriet was close.

"Easy now." A large hand settled on his shoulder.

He waved to his brother and uncle and pointed to the door. They joined him.

"Stand watch, Uncle," Alex whispered. He then slid the bolt and eased the door open. The interior of the stable was dark, and only a sack lay in the rear on a pile of hay. "There is nothing here," he said softly.

"That sack just moved," Leo said.

Alex ran, reaching it in seconds. The grunting coming from inside told him that whoever was in there was human. *Harriet.*

He managed to get the knot untied and then opened it. Two mismatched eyes stared up at him. He pulled her out with Leo and Mungo's help.

"I have you now," he whispered as his brother freed her legs and hands. Alex untied the cloth around her throat. "Harriet, my love, I have you."

She clung to him, her heart thudding against his chest, burying her face in his neck.

"They're coming," Uncle Bram whispered from the doorway.

"Stay here, Harriet."

"Don't leave me." She clung to him.

"Never." He squeezed her tight, then pulled her arms from his neck. "I'll be back soon. Stay here and be quiet."

She was dirty, hair loose and pale; blood had dried around her lips, and he was killing someone for that. But she was alive, and he'd never leave her again. Placing a kiss on her lips, he rose and crept out of the stable.

The men were with the horses. Leo moved around the carriage, and Alex stood at the back of the other man. Uncle Bram stood ready if he was needed.

"Which one of you is responsible for putting the woman I love in a sack?"

"No!" The man spun and charged Alex. He heard Leo's gun go off but focused on the angry man running at him. He had no time to pull out his sticks, but he could inflict pain without them.

Lashing out with his foot as the man reached him, he caught him in the thigh, and sent him stumbling back, but he did not fall and ran at Alex again. He struck out with a fist, and it glanced off Alex's jaw. He then threw a punch of his own in the man's belly, winding him. Alex followed it with a knee to his nose, and he dropped to the floor.

Leo dragged his man to where the other lay and lowered him to his knees. Blood poured from his nose.

"Tie them up and throw them in the stable."

Harriet was in front of him before he could stop her. She then drew back her fist and punched the man in the nose again. He moaned and fell backward to the floor.

"That was for Frankie!"

"That had to hurt considering I'd already broken his nose," Leo drawled.

"Nice punch, my love. Remind me not to annoy you."

"Mr. Sydney told me he killed Frankie, but I want all of them to pay for her death, Alex." Her mouth was bleeding, eyes bloodshot, and hair a wild mass of curls. She had never looked more beautiful.

"Let's see that done then," Uncle Bram said, grabbing one of the men's feet, and Mungo took the other. They then dragged them to the stables. Tossing them both inside, they then bound and gagged them.

"I recognize that other man. He is Miss Haven's fiancé," Harriet said.

"The man who knocked you down?" Alex snarled, and Harriet nodded.

"And he is subdued, so there is no need to seek more revenge there, brother," Leo said.

"Our carriage is out at the gate. Will you go there, Harriet, and await us?" Alex asked making himself leave the two bound men in the stable, when in fact he wanted hurt them further for the pain they had inflicted on Harriet.

"No." Her lips were in a hard line.

"Very well." If anyone had a right to see this through to its conclusion, it was her. "But you must stay behind us."

"I will try," she said.

He laughed and then took her hand, leading her from the stables.

"The Templars, and Matron are inside there." She pointed to the main building. "They are planning to leave tomorrow after my father pays the ransom."

"Is that right?" Leo looked mean, as did Uncle Bram. "We might have something to say about that."

"Let's go in through the servant's entrance," Alex said. "I made friends with Mr. and Mrs. Maris."

"They were kind to Frankie and me," Harriet said.

They walked in through the kitchens and found only Mrs. Maris. She looked at them with wide eyes; Alex held a finger to his lips.

"There is trouble afoot, Mrs. Maris. Unfortunately, the game is up, and we are here to speak with your employers," Alex said softly.

"Miss Shaw," the older woman said. "What happened to you?"

"Mr. and Mrs. Templar kidnapped me."

"No! Those two are no-good people."

"Do you know where they are now, Mrs. Maris?" Alex asked.

"Well, I just had Mr. Maris take up tea, as a Mr. and Mrs. Fletcher have arrived without an appointment to take another look about the place."

Leo smiled. "Excellent."

They left Mrs. Maris and made their way upstairs. Reaching the room he'd visited when last here, Alex raised three fingers; he then counted down and entered.

"Gray, how wonderful to see you," Alex said. "You remember Harriet?"

"Of course I do." Gray rose, pulling out his gun. "Welcome back, Harriet. I'm pleased to see you are well."

Mrs. Templar squawked like a chicken, and her husband ran at Gray. Ellen, who had been seated in front of her husband, stuck out her foot, and the man fell.

After that it was all rather easy. Mungo located the orphanage matron, and then they rounded up all those involved and locked them in the stable.

Mr. Maris, who informed them he was handy with a rifle, stood guard outside until Gray could organize their transportation to jail.

"It's over, Harriet," Alex said as he led her down the long

driveway back to the carriage. "I need to tell you that Oscar is with the carriage."

"What? Why is he here?"

"I went to your parents' house. They showed me the ransom note, and then I had a vision of where to find you. Frankie put it there, I believe. Oscar said he wanted to come, as you are his sister."

She snorted. "I doubt he cares. He'll have another motive."

Alex didn't add anything, as in her eyes, she was likely right after what she'd suffered at the hands of her family. Her brother saw her, and the relief in his face was real.

"Don't hold on to the anger, my sweet. It festers. Believe me, I know. Until you came into my life, I hadn't realized how much I needed to forgive my father for, to move forward," Alex said.

Mungo took the horses, and Oscar approached his sister slowly.

"Can you ever forgive me... us, Harriet? I can offer no excuse for my behavior. I'm sorry." Oscar had his head lowered.

"It will take time, but you are my brother, and clearly I am to be saddled with you for many years yet, so it seems I must."

His head shot up, hope on his face.

"But never be the fool my mother made you again, Oscar."

"I promise I won't." He took a step closer, and then the siblings were hugging, and while Alex wasn't ready to forgive Oscar yet, it seemed his love was.

His love. Alex was fairly sure he'd call her that every day from now on. She released her brother and turned to him.

"Let's go home, Alex. I'm ready to start our life now."

"So am I, my sweet. So am I."

CHAPTER THIRTY-SEVEN

*A*lex had not seen Harriet for two days, and he was not happy about that. Two months had passed since she'd been taken by those fiendish people, who were now rotting in Newgate prison.

"You are meant to smile on your wedding day," Oscar, his future brother-in-law, who he now quite liked, said.

"I am smiling on the inside," Alex replied.

It was his wedding day, and tonight Harriet would sleep in his arms, and this time, never leave them.

"I still can't believe Mother relented enough to hold the wedding here," Oscar said.

Heloise Shaw, who'd now decided she was quite happy for her daughter to marry into a family that had a lord, even a disgraced one, had a grand wedding planned for them. Both Alex and Harriet had refused. After days of arguments, they had finally won, but only because her daughter had told her they would elope if she didn't allow them to have a simple ceremony at Crabbett Close like Ellen and Gray. Heloise had relented but only because Oscar's future wedding would be grand in every way when it took place next year.

"She is sitting in the front row, stony-faced but putting on a show when anyone looks her way," Leo said. "Plus, there are a couple of lords, a duke, and a marquis here to ease her agony. You'll pardon my rudeness, Oscar."

"Think nothing of it. We, her family, are very aware of our mother's personality flaws."

The sun shone after a dismal start to the day. The pews, located from somewhere by Mr. Greedy, who said never you mind when Alex had asked where they came from, were full. He had an image of a congregation of worshippers seated on the floor of a church somewhere.

A carpet was rolled down the center aisle, and flowers were tied to pews with big white bows.

Crabbett Close residents were seated to the left with the Nightingale friends and family. To the right sat the bride's family. Unlike with Gray and Ellen's wedding, where the residents supported both sides, that was most definitely not the case.

"I overheard Miss Alvin saying Mrs. Shaw is a right gabster, but she will not cut a wheedle with her," Leo added.

"Which means what?" Alex kept searching for Harriet, and so far, he had no luck in finding her.

"She's an old windbag who has a lot of self-important stuff to say but none of it is likely true."

"Perfectly accurate," Alex whispered back so Oscar didn't hear.

Uncle Bram and Aunt Ivy sat with Mungo and Bud in the front pew. His cousin Stephen also was there. Behind them was the entire Sinclair and Raven family, again, who had insisted on an invitation when they heard another wedding was taking place here. They'd been last to leave when Gray married Ellen.

"Is that the carpet from Ramsey's front entrance again?" Alex asked, his eyes still searching for Harriet.

"It is," Leo said.

"You look quite fine, Lord Seddon!" Tabatha Varney was standing as she called out the words to Leo. Her dress was a bright orange that almost hurt the eyes when you looked directly at it. On her head was an entire bouquet of flowers.

"Who can we marry that woman off to?" Leo asked.

"You," Alex said. "Or him."

Leo and Oscar looked at Ramsey as he strolled down the aisle as if nothing greater than spending the day seated with friends in the sun overindulging was before him... which it was.

"That could work actually," Leo said.

Ramsey arrived at the front and nudged Mungo along so he could take the seat beside him. The Scotsman scowled; Ramsey smiled.

"And here comes your love," Leo whispered. "Be happy, brother."

"I am," Alex said, locating Harriet. She wore lemon, and he could not take his eyes off her. It fell in a long sweep of satin, and on her head was a simple gold band with small diamonds.

His love. He'd never thought his chest would feel so full. He loved his family, but this was different. She was his as he was hers. Harriet Shaw, for only a short while longer, was the keeper of his soul.

She'd changed. There was laughter in her now, and she spoke freely. Her mother no longer intimidated her, as Alex would not allow that. In short, Harriet was happy.

"No one looking at those four would think they were as much trouble as they are," Theo, who stood beside Leo, said.

Fred, Matilda, and Anna wore pink matching dresses and looked sweet. Lottie was once again hurling petals from her basket at people. Behind them came Catherine, Harriet's sister, and Ellen.

"For the love of God, man, breathe. It would not do for the groom to pass out before the wedding," Ramsey called to him.

It whooshed out of his mouth as Harriet started walking toward Alex down Ramsey's carpet runner on her father's arm. He sucked in another breath.

"You grooms are all alike," Leo muttered. "Pathetic."

Ignoring his brother, he smiled as Harriet reached him.

"Hello, my love."

"Hello, Alex. We are getting married," she whispered, and he could hear the excitement.

"That we are."

They would move into the house he and Leo were to live in, and Leo would stay with Uncle Bram and Aunt Ivy until another was found.

They spoke their vows, both with voices that shook at times. And then he took her hands and looked deep into her lovely eyes and thought, finally, she was his.

"I love you." He leaned down to kiss her softly.

"And I, you."

After the service, they moved out to the street, where tables were set up and a trestle held a banquet of food to feed twice as many people as were here.

"It was a lovely service," Cambridge Sinclair said, "but now the good part begins." Clapping his hands, he wandered off with his wife to find a seat.

"If I may have your attention." Bram rose, tapping his glass when everyone was seated.

Harriet and Alex sat together, her hand on his thigh, his around her shoulders.

His wife.

He kissed her soft cheek. "You smell nice."

Her smile was small but just for him.

"I am incredibly proud of the man Alex has become. He is strong, and resilient, but more importantly, he has loyalty and a huge capacity to love. We will miss him in our household, but through his marriage to sweet Harriet, we have gained another to love," Uncle Bram continued. "We wish them every happiness."

Harriet sniffed into the handkerchief he'd just handed her.

"Never forget your aunt and I love you both very much," Uncle Bram added. "I would ask you all to stand with me and celebrate the newly married couple."

"To Alex and Harriet, we wish you every happiness!" everyone yelled.

They then ate and danced in the streets.

"I think it is the oddness that draws us to Crabbett Close and, of course, the Nightingales," Alex heard Captain Sinclair say as he danced by with Harriet. *His wife.*

"I have something I want to tell you. It's your wedding present," Alex whispered in her ear.

"I don't need more gifts, Alex. I now have everything in my life I could want." Harriet looked up at him.

"As do I, but this will add to our future happiness, I assure you. Mr. and Mrs. Maris are coming to work for us."

"No!" Her smile would light the darkest day. "But that is wonderful." She hugged him hard.

"The second part of your present is that Leo and I got a group of people together to finance the orphanage. It will now be run by us, so you can have a hand in how the children live."

She burst into noisy tears.

"You have made her cry already. God's blood, brother, it is but two hours since you wed the woman," Leo said.

"They are happy tears, I assure you, brother."

Her arms went around his neck, and right there in the street she kissed him.

"I love you so much, Mr. Nightingale. I'm so pleased that Frankie made you find me."

"Oh, my love, so am I. And now I have one last gift." He pulled a slim black case out of his inside pocket. He then opened it.

"Alex," Harriet whispered awed. "How did you get Frankie's necklace b-back?"

"I asked Miss Haven, and as she has recently found out her ex-fiancé is a fiend, she was more than happy to part with it," Alex said.

He took the necklace from the case and put it on his wife. Taking out a second handkerchief he then blotted her tears.

"And now, my sweet wife. We celebrate."

They spent the night dancing with friends and family, and Alex could say, never in his life had he felt so complete. He had everything he needed now, right here in his arms.

...

Thank you for reading AN IMPERFECT GENTLEMAN. I hope you enjoyed Alex and Harriet's story.

Book #3 in the Notorious Nightingales series THE FALLEN VISCOUNT will be available in July, read on for the blurb!

Could she be the one to save him?

Leopold Nightingale was a man who could find things no one else could. He'd denied this gift until the night a bracelet slid into his head, especially as it was on the arm of the woman he'd once loved.

Lady Hyacinth Armstrong was destined to be his wife, but when society turned on his family, he did the only thing he could, Leo walked away from her. When years later he finds her in dire need of his help, he's shocked to find her a widow. His second surprise comes as she's no longer the sweet natured lady she once was. But one thing was soon startlingly clear to him, the woman intrigued him far more now than she used too.

Could he see the woman behind the façade this time?

When Lord Seddon saves Cyn from two thugs, her shock at seeing him again soon turns to anger over his disappearance. She'd once loved him desperately. Now she wants to slap him… hard, especially when he tells her his actions were completely justified.

Marriage had given her two children and a life to live as she wished, but there are those who would see her stopped for the path she had chosen. Cyn will do what she must to keep her charges safe, but never again would she give her heart away to someone who cast it aside so easily. Even if it's the only man she's ever loved.

ABOUT THE AUTHOR

Wendy Vella is a USA Today and Amazon bestselling author of historical romances filled with romance, intrigue, unconventional heroines, and dashing heroes.

An incurable romantic, Wendy found writing romance a natural fit. Born and raised in a rural area in the North Island of New Zealand, she shares her life with one adorable husband, two delightful adult children and their partners, four delicious grandchildren, and her pup Tilly.

Wendy also writes contemporary romances under the name Lani Blake.

You can also follow her here:
    Website: wendyvella.com
    Facebook: authorwendyvella
    Instagram: wendy.vella_author
    BookBub: bookbub.com/profile/wendy-vella
    Readers Group:
    facebook.com/groups/wendyvellareaders

Printed in Great Britain
by Amazon